# Hold That Knowledge

# Hold That Knowledge

STORIES ABOUT

## *Love*

FROM THE
FLANNERY O'CONNOR AWARD
FOR SHORT FICTION

EDITED BY
ETHAN LAUGHMAN

THE UNIVERSITY OF GEORGIA PRESS
ATHENS

Published in part with the generous
support of Mrs. Lorraine Williams

© 2019 by the University of Georgia Press
Athens, Georgia 30602
www.ugapress.org
All rights reserved
Designed by Kaelin Chappell Broaddus
Set in 9/13.5 Walbaum 12pt

Most University of Georgia Press titles are
available from popular e-book vendors.

Printed digitally

Library of Congress Control Number: 2019933146
ISBN: 9780820355283 (pbk: alk. paper)
ISBN 9780820355290 (ebook)

# CONTENTS

## ACKNOWLEDGMENTS

The stories in this collection are from the following award-winning collections published by the University of Georgia Press:

Sandra Thompson, *Close-Ups* (1984), © 1984 by Sandra Thompson

Daniel Curley, *Living with Snakes* (1985) © 1985 by Daniel Curley; "The First Baseman" originally appeared in the *Cimarron Review*

Tony Ardizzone, *The Evening News* (1986), © 1986 by Tony Ardizzone; "My Mother's Stories" first appeared in the *Black Warrior Review*

Gail Galloway Adams, *The Purchase of Order* (1988), © 1988 by Gail Galloway Adams; "Inside Dope" first appeared in the *North American Review* and was selected for inclusion in *Editor's Choice*

Debra Monroe, *The Source of Trouble* (1990), © 1990 by Debra Monroe

Dennis Hathaway, *The Consequences of Desire* (1992), © 1992 by Dennis Hathaway

Christopher McIlroy, *All My Relations* (1994), © 1994 by Christopher McIlroy; "Simplifying" first appeared in *TriQuarterly* (fall 1989)

Wendy Brenner, *Large Animals in Everyday Life* (1996), ©
1996 by Wendy Brenner; "A Little Something" first appeared
in the *New England Review*

Hester Kaplan, *The Edge of Marriage* (1999), © 1999 by
Hester Kaplan; "Live Life King-Sized" first appeared in
*Press*

Bill Roorbach, *Big Bend* (2001), © 2001 by Bill Roorbach;
"Big Bend" first appeared in the *Atlantic Monthly*

Anne Panning, *Super America* (2007), © 2007 by Anne
Panning; "Tidal Wave Wedding" first appeared in *Five
Points*

Margot Singer, *The Pale of Settlement* (2007), © 2007 by
Margot Singer; "The Pale of Settlement" first appeared in
the *North American Review*

Linda LeGarde Grover, *The Dance Boots* (2010), © 2010 by
Linda LeGarde Grover

Siamak Vossoughi, *Better Than War* (2015), © 2015 by the
University of Georgia Press

A thank you also goes to the University of Georgia Main Library
staff for technical support in preparing the stories for publication.

# INTRODUCTION

The Flannery O'Connor Award for Short Fiction was established in 1981 by Paul Zimmer, then the director of the University of Georgia Press, and press acquisitions editor Charles East. East would serve as the first series editor, judging the competition and selecting two collections to publish each year. The inaugural volumes in the series, *Evening Out* by David Walton and *From the Bottom Up* by Leigh Allison Wilson, appeared in 1983 to critical acclaim. Nancy Zafris (herself a Flannery O'Connor Award–winner for the 1990 collection *The People I Know*) was the second series editor, serving in the role from 2008 to 2015. Zafris was succeeded by Lee K. Abbott in 2016, and the press has just announced that Roxane Gay will be the next to assume the role, choosing award winners beginning in 2019. Competition for the award has since become an important proving ground for writers, and the press has published seventy-four volumes to date, helping to showcase talent and sustain interest in the short story form. These volumes together feature approximately eight hundred stories by authors who are based in all regions of the country and even internationally. It has been my pleasure to have read each and every one.

The idea of undertaking a project that could honor the diversity of the series' stories but also present them in a unified way had been hanging around the press for a few years. What occurred to us first, and what remained the most appealing approach, was to pull the hundreds of stories out of their current packages—volumes of collected stories by individual authors—and regroup them by common themes or subjects. After finishing my editorial internship at the press, I was brought on to the project and began to sort the stories into specific thematic categories. What followed was a deep dive into the award and its history and a gratifying acquaintance with the many authors whose works constitute the award's legacy.

Anthologies are not new to the series. A tenth-anniversary collection, published in 1993, showcased one story from each of the volumes published in the award's first decade. A similar collection appeared in 1998, the fifteenth year of the series. In 2013, the year of the series' thirtieth anniversary, the press published two volumes modeled after the tenth- and fifteenth-anniversary volumes. These anthologies together included one story from each of the fifty-five collections published up to that point. One of the 2013 volumes represented the series' early years, under the editorship of Charles East. The other showcased the editorship of Nancy Zafris. In a nod to the times, both thirtieth-anniversary anthologies appeared in e-book form only.

The present project is wholly different in both concept and scale. The press plans to republish more than five hundred stories in more than forty volumes, each focusing on a specific theme—from love to food to homecoming and homesickness. Each volume will aim to collect exemplary treatments of its theme, but with enough variety to give an overview of what the series is about. The stories inside paint a colorful picture that includes the varied perspectives multiple authors can have on a single theme.

Each volume, no matter its focus, includes the work of authors whose stories celebrate the variety of short fiction styles and subjects to be found across the history of the award. Just as Flannery O'Connor is more than just a southern writer, the University of Georgia Press, by any number of measures, has been more than a regional publisher for some time. As the first series editor, Charles East, happily reported in his anthology of the O'Connor Award stories, the award "managed to escape [the] pitfall" of becoming a regional stereotype. When Paul Zimmer established the award he named it after Flannery O'Connor as the writer who best embodied the possibilities of the short-story form. In addition, O'Connor, with her connections to the South and readership across the globe, spoke to the ambitions of the press at a time when it was poised to ramp up both the number and scope of its annual title output. The O'Connor name has always been a help in keeping the series a place where writers strive to be published and where readers and critics look for quality short fiction.

The award has indeed become an internationally recognized institution. The seventy-four (and counting) Flannery O'Connor Award authors come from all parts of the United States and abroad. They have lived in Arizona, Arkansas, California, Colorado, Georgia, Indiana, Maryland, Massachusetts, Texas, Utah, Washington, Canada, Iran, England, and elsewhere. Some have written novels. Most have published stories in a variety of literary quarterlies and popular magazines. They have been awarded numerous fellowships and prizes. They are world-travelers, lecturers, poets, columnists, editors, and screenwriters.

There are risks in the thematic approach we are taking with these anthologies, and we hope that readers will not take our editorial approach as an attempt to draw a circle around certain aspects of a story or in any way close off possibilities for interpretation. Great stories don't have to resolve anything, be set any particular time nor place, or be written in any one way. Great stories don't have to *be* anything. Still, when a story resonates with enough readers in a certain way, it is safe to say that it has spoken to us meaningfully about, for instance, love, death, and certain concerns, issues, pleasures, or life events.

We at the press had our own ideas about how the stories might be gathered, but we were careful to get author input on the process. The process of categorizing their work was not easy for any of them. Some truly agonized. Having their input was invaluable; having their trust was humbling. The goal of this project is to faithfully represent these stories despite the fact that they have been pulled from their original collections and are now bedmates with stories from a range of authors taken from diverse contexts. Also, just because a single story is included in a particular volume does not mean that that volume is the only place that story could have comfortably been placed. For example, "Sawtelle," from Dennis Hathaway's *The Consequences of Desire*, tells the story of a subcontractor in duress when he finds out his partner is the victim of an extramarital affair. We have included it in the volume of stories about love, but it could have been included in those on work, friends, and immigration without seeming out of place.

The selection process for this volume was perhaps more complicated than for any other, in part because of the sheer number of stories in the series that portray characters who are in love and who work through issues and problems related to love. In fact, few thematic categories had as many candidates, and the series offered an incredibly rich and varied range of stories that could be chosen. Authors in the series dramatize love's power to bind as well as to liberate, how love can either inspire and or arrest change, and how it can affect the old as well as the young. For this volume, we chose stories that offered an original perspective and that also, when grouped together, could make some claim to a comprehensive view of the subject. In light of this aim and the number of powerful treatments, we tried to assemble a richly varied constellation of stories, rather than simply the most compelling the series had to offer. Taken as a whole, the stories in this volume challenge the reader to think of love not just as an inspiring force for change or as a comforting refuge, but also as source of frustration in how it reveals limitations and can prevent change from occurring at all.

Siamak Vossoughi's "You Don't Leave," from the collection *Better Than War*, centers on the story of a young man making a journey to see a woman who—although he has no concrete romantic relationship with her—inspires his devotion nonetheless. Vossoughi's protagonist gives voice to an emotion felt by many: "He laughed to himself inwardly—he still hung on her words, hoping for a slight change in the phrasing: *There are some murals I want to show you.* He would drive up *every* Saturday for a sentence like that." The young man knows that the object of his affections deserves his patience, making it all the more endearing to the reader to know that he is perfectly content to wait, ensnared by love as he seems to be. A similar mutual trust and respect colors Daniel Curley's "The First Baseman," in which a baseball fan finds himself fawning over a local softball player. Over the course of a month spent buying her beers and engaging in superficial conversations—strange for a man who "was never one for small talk"—he timidly pursues the relationship, constantly checking his actions against how she will perceive them and terrified of seeming too domineering lest she turn away. Curley and Vossoughi present us with men who love strongly, despite personal limitations that prevent them from fulfilling their desires.

Wendy Brenner's "A Little Something" shows love's ability to inspire us to rise above such limitations and fundamentally change. The story is a character study of Joe, a charismatic Jack Nicholson look-alike who gives Helene the confidence to reach for what she wants. Here as elsewhere in the volume, love can open our eyes to new possibilities and change our perspectives. Gail Galloway Adams's "Inside Dope," a story of neighbors and community as much as of love between a couple, centers on the character of Bisher, whose personality similarly transforms the heart of the narrator, despite some less-than-honorable actions later in the narrative.

This collection's next two stories dramatize the transforming influence of new love in characters of advanced age. Christopher McIlroy's "Simplifying" is the story of emphysema-stricken Julia who, late in life, opens herself to a blossoming, reinvigorating love. The urgency of Julia's sickness and the ephemeral nature of the relationship provide the narrative's tension. In Bill Roorbach's "Big Bend," a young man shares with the aging Dennis and the rest of their sundry work crew an anecdote from the later life of the Greek tragedian Sophocles, seventy years old at the time. When asked, "At your age, Sophocles, what of love?" Sophocles replies, "I feel I have been released by a mad and furious beast!" At this point in the narrative Dennis believes himself free of the madness of love, but love's alluring torment will compel our protagonist to pursue a newfound relationship, despite resistance on his part.

Love of neighbors and community permeates the remaining stories. Debra Monroe's "The Widower's Psalm" takes place in a small town populated by people with a shared history. Whether this small-town closeness is a good or a bad thing is debatable, but the couple is inextricably bound to their community. Anne Panning's "Tidal Wave Wedding" shows how a community can love those within and without. The climax celebrates not only a newlywed couple's love for one another but the community's love as well, as people from varying walks of life come together to help them. Dennis Hathaway's "Sawtelle" follows Charles as he decides where and how he will choose to show love in all of its forms: at work, among friends, toward other members of the community, and to his family. Hester Kaplan's "Live Life King-Sized" centers on Blaze, a bullhorn of a man who must rely on the goodwill of others in order to find peace.

The next three stories in the volume explore familial love. In Tony Ardizzone's "My Mother's Stories," the narrator recol-

lects stories told him by his mother about her miraculous birth
and recovery, her lifetime of ailments and futile "treatments,"
and the devoted protection of her children. The mother apparently spent much of her life caring for her children, upholding
her faith, promoting their welfare, and caring for her husband in
their Chicago house. Though the stories seem almost too good
to be true, Ardizzone ultimately frames her as a loving mother
putting her family first no matter the cost. The final two stories
portray the struggles of marginalized groups who fight to pre-
serve their heritage. Linda LeGarde Grover's "Maggie and Louis,
1914" recounts the first meeting of Louis and Maggie, the even-
tual diarchy of a Native American family whose history is elabo-
rated in the collection the story is taken from, *The Dance Boots*.
Maggie and Louis have little in common at their first meeting,
but their shared heritage and language allow them to establish a
bond that will last generations. Margot Singer's "The Pale of Settlement" is an immensely satisfying conclusion to this volume
for several reasons. Like "Maggie and Louis, 1914," "The Pale of
Settlement" portrays the genesis of a lasting, enduring love story
that spans generations and whose subsequent chapters are related in the collection from which the story is taken (*The Pale of
Settlement*). Despite some questions about the trustworthiness
of the narrative, mythologizing the romance of our matriarchs
and patriarchs may do us some good. "Settlement" fantastically
ends the collection, showing how love informs and transforms
how we think of generations, culture, war, environment, memory, necessity, and community.

In *Creating Flannery O'Connor*, Daniel Moran writes that
O'Connor first mentioned her infatuation with peacocks in her
essay "Living with a Peacock" (later republished as "King of the
Birds"). Since the essay's appearance, O'Connor has been linked

with imagery derived from the bird's distinctive feathers and silhouette by a proliferation of critics and admirers, and one can now hardly find an O'Connor publication that does not depict or refer to her "favorite fowl" and its association with immortality and layers of symbolic and personal meaning. As Moran notes, "Combining elements of her life on a farm, her religious themes, personal eccentricities, and outsider status, the peacock has proved the perfect icon for O'Connor's readers, critics, and biographers, a form of reputation-shorthand that has only grown more ubiquitous over time."

We are pleased to offer these anthologies as another way of continuing Flannery O'Connor's legacy. Since its conception, thirty-seven years' worth of enthralling, imaginative, and thought-provoking fiction has been published under the name of the Flannery O'Connor Award. The award is just one way that we hope to continue the conversation about O'Connor and her legacy while also circulating and sharing recent authors' work among readers throughout the world.

It is perhaps unprecedented for such a long-standing short fiction award series to republish its works in the manner we are going about it. The idea for the project may be unconventional, but it draws on an established institution—the horn-of-plenty that constitutes the Flannery O'Connor Award series backlist—that is still going strong at the threshold of its fortieth year. I am in equal parts intimidated and honored to present you with what I consider to be these exemplars of the Flannery O'Connor Award. Each story speaks to the theme uniquely. Some of these stories were chosen for their experimental nature, others for their unique take on the theme, and still others for exhibiting matchlessness in voice, character, place, time, plot, relevance, humor, timelessness, perspective, or any of the thousand other metrics by which one may measure a piece of literature.

But enough from me. Let the stories speak for themselves.

ETHAN LAUGHMAN

# Hold That
# Knowledge

# You Don't Leave

SIAMAK VOSSOUGHI

From *Better Than War* (2015)

They figured he had a girl up in Bellingham, and Armon didn't
know how to tell them that Caroline Cooper was a girl but that
it wasn't that sort of thing. He had certainly hoped it would be
that sort of thing for a long time, all through college, but in their
third year she had told him about something that he couldn't
tell them about. It was her father, and she had been a little girl.
When she had told him, he had gone home and looked in the
mirror and cried. He had asked her later if she had told many
other people, and she had said she'd told a few of her friends but
that he was the only man she had told. He had asked her why,
and she'd laughed and said, "Men leave. You don't leave."

He'd left in the morning and drove the one-and-a-half-hour
drive up the highway, and he thought, It's just one day. It was
easier not to dream of her now that she was in another city, and
seeing her would knock him back a ways, but he could get over
it. Along the way he saw many beautiful things that he thought
he would tell her about, and then he thought maybe he would
and maybe he wouldn't.

She lived in a little house across the street from a park. The
smell of the place sent him back to her old apartment and to
nights they laughed together and a few nights she had cried.

When he saw her, her whole face turned warm and open, like there was nothing she wouldn't trust him with. I wonder what her face looks like when she opens the door to the men who leave, he thought.

It was nice, though, being here. He told her about a few of the things he had seen along the way. She listened so effortlessly that he found himself hoping that those men have at least had some things to say.

They walked from her house through a trail that ran into town. It had been difficult for her to come to Bellingham for graduate school because it had been where her father had gone after he'd left. He'd had a store and gotten to know a lot of people. She said she had a fear that she would meet someone who knew him and thought he was a good man.

"It's crazy, I know," she said.

"It's not so crazy."

"Well, it's not as if we have the same last name anymore, so there's no reason that someone would make that connection. Unless they thought I looked like him, but I don't think I look like him."

"It's not crazy because what he did was crazy."

She smiled. "Yes," she said.

They walked past a reservoir where they could look out and see an old cannery.

"It's funny," Armon said. "You look at an old factory, and if it was still in use, I might not think about it very much. But as soon as it's abandoned, I wonder about it a lot."

"I think you would still like it if it was in use."

"You're right, but I would think about it differently."

"How?"

"I don't know. It's easy to like old, abandoned things."

"They have stories."

"Right. Things in use have stories, but it's harder to see them."

This was probably something that the men who left didn't do.

They didn't go around making declarations about factories in use and abandoned ones. They probably knew how to talk in a way that moved naturally to whispering in her ear and putting their arm around her in the grass. Talking of factories wasn't the thing.

They walked through the park where the trail ended.

"It's nice to see you," she said.

"Nice to be seen." It was a joke he didn't mean, just an effort to keep his heart up. She smiled at the joke and the effort both.

"I appreciate you driving all the way up."

"I like driving," he said. "And of course it's nice to see you too," he added. He didn't need to say it. The benefit of the doubt was something he had already won, and he was sad to realize it. Steady and dependable. But what did he have to show for it? No girl in Bellingham and no girl back in Seattle either.

If you wanted to, if you were into that sort of thing, you could walk into any of the bars in his neighborhood and join a table where a group of young men were sitting together and fall into a conversation about how girls did not like young men who were nice. Even if they were right, he was still glad that he had met Caroline Cooper. He was still glad that he had known her the way he had and that he had seen the part of her that she had shown him. She had opened up a world to him. It was a place of feeling. A person could hold their love and hold their hate, and if they were sure of them, they could let them come out the way they would, and they didn't have to rush them. He felt like he had all the time in the world with her because a day was so full.

And then there was the way she listened. She made herself comfortable when he spoke. She could be walking alongside him, and she would still give him the feeling that she was leaning back in an easy chair when he began to tell her his feelings about canneries. That was what made a woman to him. And yet there was something in her womanliness that he couldn't meet.

Once he found that thing . . . , he thought. But it seemed like it was too late with her.

The one thing he wouldn't do, the one thing he felt proud to have not done so far, he wouldn't ask her: What did those men do? What did they do before they left?

And the truth was, he didn't want to know. If what they did meant that she laughed at the thought of telling them about her father, he didn't want to know.

He almost felt like he had skipped girls and gone straight to women, only he didn't know what to do once he got there. In college there was a kind of girl that he told himself he ought to forget about Caroline Cooper with and go after instead. A denim skirt and low-cut sneakers. Maybe she had books that she lived and died over and maybe she didn't. And one or two times he had found her. But he would look for the tragedy, either personal or philosophical or both, and if it wasn't there, he felt like the girl was only telling half the story.

"Let's go up to the square," she said. "There are some murals there I think you'd like to see."

He laughed to himself inwardly—he still hung on her words, hoping for a slight change in the phrasing: *There are some murals I want to show you.* He would drive up *every* Saturday for a sentence like that.

They walked up to the square, and he thought of how much he would have to say about the people of the town if they were going to end the night together. He would love them, first of all, and they would know it by looking at him. He would let them all in, and it wouldn't matter that it was his first time walking through their town.

She was right. The murals were beautiful. One of a whale gave him a peaceful feeling. It was nice to think of something that big swimming thoughtfully under the water's surface. There was more to the world than what he could see.

"I like the whale the best," she said.

"It's nice," he said.

"I'm glad that I live close to the water at least," she said. "I don't think I could live somewhere where I couldn't look at the ocean."

"Yes," he said. "I like the ocean the way it is here."

"How do you mean?"

"It doesn't have to make a big deal about itself. It just shows up on your way to town."

She laughed.

"The whole town is like that," she said. "It makes it a good place to study, I suppose. Not as much to do as in Seattle. You must be having fun there, though."

He shrugged. "There are a few places I go to." He did not want to show her that her absence was often the main feature of those places, especially as it got nearer to the end of the night. Somewhere between the truth and her trust in him, that was where he was aiming. But he knew too how perceptive she was.

"Let's look for a place to have lunch," he said.

They went to a place that had fish sandwiches and sat outside and watched the people go by. They sat together, and maybe some of the people going by thought they were a young man and a young woman together, and maybe some of them didn't, but either way it didn't matter too much.

The thing that he respected about Caroline Cooper was that she had given him a chance in college—not to be one of those men but to walk away after she'd told him she did not feel the same way. It was only after he'd stuck around that she'd told him.

They walked around town after lunch and stopped in a few shops. They talked things over with some kids running a lemonade stand back in her neighborhood.

They sat on the steps outside back at her house, drinking coffee. Maybe it's for the best, he thought. It would be too fine. It would be too fine to have the day go by as easily as this and have the night go by so easily too. Where would be the tragedy in that?

They watched the kids playing in the park across the street. It wasn't the first time he had watched kids playing with her and thought about her as a little girl. He knew a little bit about how to do it. She didn't want him to ignore it, and she didn't want him to fall apart over it. She just wanted him to know it and to hold that knowledge.

But even so he felt a thought coming up in him. She was beautiful, and the dusk was falling, and it would be a very wonderful thing to stay, and he felt the thought coming up: If you hadn't told me about your father, I would've left too. Not as quickly as those other men and not under the same circumstances, but I would've left. I'm a man too.

Something wouldn't let him say it. Suppose he did—what would the world look like on his way home? Nothing. It would look like nothing. As long as he held it inside him, the world had a chance.

"I like it here," she said. "I feel like I am getting stronger, like I am getting healthier."

"That's great," he said.

If he hadn't been lost in his own thoughts, Armon might have heard that inside her words she was saying that she was beginning to see a time when the man who stayed the night and the man she told her heart to would be the same man. But he didn't, and a little while after that, he stood up and embraced her and told her that it had been very good to see her, which it had been, and he began to set out for home, and for about the first third of the drive he went back and forth between wondering if he was the saddest man on the road or the most foolish, until he couldn't do that anymore, and he decided for about the next third that he was actually the one most in awe of the setting sun, until an unspeakable happiness came over him in the last third, driving in the darkness, something that carried him all the way to the bar around the corner without going home, where the fellows were sitting just where he thought they would be, where they saw him come in with an aliveness that made them not even know how to ask him about it, too amazed that he had made it all the way up to Bellingham to see a girl and still made it back in time to have a beer with them.

# My Mother's Stories

TONY ARDIZZONE

From *The Evening News* (1986)

They were going to throw her away when she was a baby. The doctors said she was too tiny, too frail, that she wouldn't live. They performed the baptism right there in the sink between their pots of boiling water and their rows of shining instruments, chose who would be her godparents, used water straight from the tap. Her father, however, wouldn't hear one word of it. He didn't listen to their *she'll only die anyway* and *please give her to us* and *maybe we can experiment*. No, the child's father stood silently in the corner of the room, the back of one hand wiping his mouth and thick mustache, his blue eyes fixed on the black mud which caked his pants and boots.

*Nein*, he said, finally. *Nein*, die anyvay.

With this, my mother smiles. She enjoys imitating the man's thick accent. She enjoys the sounds, the images, the memory. Her brown eyes look past me into the past. She draws a quick breath, then continues.

You can well imagine the rest. How the farmer took his wife and poor sickly child back to his farm. How the child was nursed, coddled, fed cow's milk, straight from the tops of the buckets—the rich, frothy cream. How the child lived. If she hadn't, I wouldn't be here now in the corner of this room, my eyes fixed on her, my mother and her stories. For now the sounds and pictures are *my* sounds and pictures. Her memory, my memory.

I stand here, remembering. The family moved. To Chicago, the city by the Great Lake, the city of jobs, money, opportunity. Away from northwestern Ohio's flat fields. The child grew. She is a young girl now, enrolled in school, Saint Teresa's, virgin. Chicago's Near North Side. The 1930s. And she is out walking with her girlfriend, a dark Sicilian. Spring, late afternoon. My mother wears a small pink bow in her brown hair.

Then from across the black pavement of the school playground comes a lilting stream of foreign sound, language melodic, of the kind sung solemnly at High Mass. The Sicilian girl turns quickly, smiling. The voice is her older brother's, and he too is smiling as he stands inside the playground fence. My mother turns but does not smile. She is modest. Has been properly, strictly raised. Is the last of seven children and, therefore, the object of many scolding eyes and tongues. Her name is Mary.

Perhaps our Mary, being young, is somewhat frightened. The boy behind the high fence is older than she, is in high school, is finely muscled, dark, deeply tanned. Around his neck hang golden things glistening on a thin chain. He wears a sleeveless shirt—his undershirt. Mary doesn't know whether to stay with her young friend or to continue walking. She stays, but she looks away from the boy's dark eyes and gazes instead at the worn belt around his thin waist.

That was my parents' first meeting. His name is Tony, as is mine. This is not a story she tells willingly, for she sees nothing special in it. All of the embellishments are mine. I've had to drag the story out of her, nag her from room to room. Ma? Ask your father, she tells me. I ask my father. He looks up from his newspaper, then starts to smile. He's in a playful mood. He laughs, then says: I met your mother in Heaven.

She, in the hallway, overhears. Bull, she says, looking again past me. He didn't even know I was alive. My father laughs behind his newspaper. I was Eva's friend, she says, and we were walking home from school—I watch him, listening as he lowers the paper to look at her. She tells the story.

She knows how to tell a pretty good story, I think. She's a natural. She knows how to use her voice, when to pause, how to pace, what expressions to mask her face with. Her hand slices out the high fence. She's not in the same room with you when she really gets at it; her stories take her elsewhere, somewhere back. She's there again, back on a 1937 North Side sidestreet. My father and I are only witnesses.

Picture her, then. A young girl, frightened, though of course for no good reason—my father wouldn't have harmed her. I'll vouch for him. I'm his first son. But she didn't know that as the afternoon light turned low and golden from between distant buildings. Later she'd think him strange and rather arrogant, flexing his tanned muscles before her inside the fence, like a bull before a heifer. And for years (wasted ones, I think) she didn't give him a second thought, or so she claims—the years that she dated boys who were closer to her kind. These are her words.

Imagine those years, years of *ja Fräulein, ja, bitte, entschuldigen Sie*, years of pale Johnnys and freckled Fritzes and hairy Hermans, towheads all, who take pretty Mary dancing and roller-skating and sometimes downtown on the El to the movie theaters on State Street to see Clark Gable, and who buy popcorn and ice cream for her and, later, cups of coffee which she then drank with cream, and who hold her small hand and look up at the Chicago sky as they walk with her along the dark city streets to her father's flat on Fremont. Not *one* second thought? I cannot believe it. And whenever I interrupt to ask, she waves me away like I'm an insect flying between her eyes and what she really sees. I fold my arms, but I listen.

She was sweeping. This story always begins with that detail. With broom in hand. Nineteen years old and employed as a milliner and home one Saturday and she was sweeping. By now both her parents were old. Her mother had grown round, ripe like a fruit, like she would. Her father now fashioned wood. A mound of fluff and sawdust grows in the center of the room and she is humming, perhaps something from Glenn Miller, or she might have sung, as I've heard her do while ironing on the back porch, when from behind the locked back screen door there was suddenly a knock and it was my father, smiling.

She never tells the rest of the details. But this was the afternoon he proposed. Why he chose that afternoon, or even afternoon at all, are secrets not known to me. I ask her and she evades me. *Ask your father.* I ask him and he says he doesn't know. Then he looks at her and laughs, his eyes smiling, and I can see that he is making up some lie to tell me. I watch her. Because I loved her so much I couldn't wait until that night, he says. My mother laughs and shakes her head. No, he says, I'll tell you the truth this time. Now you really know he's lying. I was just walking down the street and the idea came to me. See, it was awful hot. His hand on his forehead, he pretends he had sunstroke. My mother laughs less.

There were problems. Another of her stories. They follow one after the next like cars out on the street—memories, there is just no stopping them. Their marriage would be mixed. Not in the religious sense—that would have been unthinkable—but in terms of language, origin, tradition. Like mixing your clubs with your hearts, mixing this girl from Liechtenstein with this boy from Sicily. Her family thought she was, perhaps, lowering herself. An Italian? Why not your kind? And his family, likewise, felt that he would be less than happy with a non-Sicilian girl. She's so skinny, they told him. *Misca!* Mary's skin and bones. When she has the first baby she'll bleed to death. And what will she feed you? Cabbages? *Marry your own kind.*

At their Mass someone failed to play "Ave Maria." Since that was the cue for my mother to stand and then to place a bouquet of flowers on Mary's side altar, she remained at the center altar, still kneeling, waiting patiently for the organist to begin. He was playing some other song, not "Ave Maria." The priest gestured to her. My mother shook her head.

She was a beautiful bride, and she wore a velvet dress. You should see the wedding photograph that hangs in the hallway of their house in Chicago. Imagine a slender brown-haired bride in white velvet shaking her head at the priest who's just married her. No, the time is not yet for the young woman to stand, for her to kneel in prayer before the altar of the Virgin. This is her wedding day, remember. She is waiting for "Ave Maria."

She is waiting to this day, for the organist never did play the song, and the priest again motioned to her, then bent and whispered in her ear, and then, indignant, crushed, the young bride finally stood and angrily, solemnly, sadly waited for her maid of honor to gather the long train of her flowing velvet dress, and together the two marched to the Virgin's side altar.

She tells this story frequently, whenever there is a wedding. I think that each time she begins the story she is tempted to change the outcome, to make the stupid organist suddenly stop and slap his head. To make the organist begin the chords of "Ave Maria." That kind of power isn't possible in life. The organist didn't stop or slap his head.

I wonder if the best man tipped him. If my father was angry enough to complain. If the muscles in his jaws tightened, if his hands turned to fists, if anyone waited for the organist out in the parking lot. I am carried away.

Details *are* significant. Literally they can be matters of life and death. An organist makes an innocent mistake in 1946 and for the rest of her life a woman is compelled to repeat a story, as if for her the moment has not yet been fixed, as if by remembering and then speaking she could still influence the pattern of events since passed.

Life and death—

I was hoping the counterpart wouldn't be able to work its way into this story. But it's difficult to keep death out. The final detail. Always coming along unexpectedly, the uninvited guest at the banquet, acting like you were supposed to have known all along that he'd get there, expecting to be seated and for you to offer him a drink.

My father called yesterday. He said he was just leaving work to take my mother again to the hospital. Tests. I shouldn't call her yet. No need to alarm her, my father said. Just tests. We'll keep you posted. My mother is in the hospital. I am not Meursault.

I must describe the counterpart, return, begin again. With 1947, with my mother, delirious, in labor. Brought to the hospital by my father early on a Saturday, and on Monday laboring still. The doctors didn't believe in using drugs. She lay three days, terrified, sweating. On Monday morning they brought my father into the room, clad in an antiseptic gown, his face covered by a mask. She mistook him for one of the doctors. When he bent to kiss her cheek she grabbed his arm and begged him. Doctor, doctor, can you give me something for the pain?

That Monday was Labor Day. Ironies exist. Each September now, on my older sister Diana's birthday, my mother smiles and tells that story.

Each of us was a difficult birth. Did my father's family know something after all? The fourth, my brother Bob, nearly killed her. He was big, over ten pounds. The doctors boasted, proudly, that Bob set their personal record. The fifth child, Jim, weighed almost ten-and-a-half pounds, and after Jim the doctors fixed my mother so that there wouldn't be a sixth child. I dislike the word *fixed*, but it's an appropriate word, I think.

When I was a child my mother once took Diana and me shopping, to one of those mom-and-pop stores in the middle of the block. I remember a blind man who always sat on a wooden milk crate outside the store with his large dog. I was afraid of the dog. Inside the store we shopped, and my mother told us stories, and the three of us were laughing. She lifted a carton of soda as she spoke. Then the rotted cardboard bottom of the carton gave way and the soda bottles fell. The bottles burst. The sharp glass bounced. She shouted and we screamed, and as she tells this story she makes a point of remembering how worried she was that the glass had reached our eyes. But then some woman in the store told her she was bleeding. My mother looked down. Her foot was cut so badly that blood gushed from her shoe. I remember the picture, but then the face of the blind man's dog covers up the image and I see the wooden milk crate, the scratched white cane.

The middle child, Linda, is the special one. It was on a Christmas morning when they first feared she was deaf. Either Diana or I knocked over a pile of toy pans and dishes—a pretend kitchen—directly behind the one-year-old child playing on the floor, and Linda, bright and beautiful, did not move. She played innocently, unaffected, removed from the sound that had come to life behind her. Frantic, my mother then banged two of the metal dinner plates behind Linda's head. Linda continued playing, in a world by herself, softly cooing.

What I can imagine now from my mother's stories is a long procession of doctors, specialists, long trips on the bus. Snow-covered streets. Waiting in sterile waiting rooms. Questions. Answers. More questions. Tests. Hope. Then, no hope. Then guilt came. Tony and Mary blamed themselves.

Forgive the generalities. She is a friendly woman; she likes to make others laugh. Big-hearted, perhaps to a fault, my mother has a compulsion to please. I suspect she learned that trait as a child, being the youngest of so many children. Her parents were quite old, and as I piece her life together I imagine them strict, resolute, humorless. My mother would disagree were she to hear me. But I suspect that she's been bullied and made to feel inferior, by whom or what I don't exactly know, and, to compensate, she works very hard at pleasing.

She tells a story about how she would wash and wax her oldest brother's car and how he'd pay her one penny. How each day, regardless of the weather, she'd walk to a distant newsstand and buy for her father the *Abendpost*. How she'd be sent on especially scorching summer days by another of her brothers for an ice cream cone, and how as she would gingerly carry it home she'd take not one lick. How could she resist? In my mother's stories she's always the one who's pleasing.

Her brown eyes light up, and like a young girl she laughs. She says she used to cheat sometimes and take a lick. Then, if her brother complained, she'd claim the ice cream had been melted by the sun. Delighted with herself, she smiles. Her eyes again twinkle with light.

I am carried away again. If it were me in that story I'd throw the cone to the ground and tell my brother to get his own damn ice cream.

You've seen her. You're familiar with the kind of house she lives in, the red brick two-flat. You've walked the tree-lined city street. She hangs the family's wash up in the small backyard, the next clothespin in her mouth. She picks up the squashed paper cups and the mustard-stained foot-long hot dog wrappers out in the front that the kids from the public school leave behind as they walk back from the Tastee-Freeze on the corner. During the winter she sweeps the snow. Wearing a discarded pair of my father's earmuffs. During the fall she sweeps leaves. She gets angry when the kids cut through the backyard, leaving the chain-link gates open, for the dog barks then and the barking bothers

her. The dog, a female schnauzer mutt, is called Alfie. No fero-
cious beast—the plastic BEWARE OF DOG signs on the gates have
the harsher bite. My mother doesn't like it when the kids leave
the alley gate open. She talks to both her neighbors across both
her fences. Wearing one of Bob's old sweaters, green and torn
at one elbow, she bends to pick up a fallen autumn twig. She
stretches to hang the wash up—the rows of whites, then the col-
oreds. She lets Alfie out and checks the alley gate.

Summer visit. Over a mug of morning coffee I sit in the
kitchen reading the *Sun-Times*. Alfie in the backyard barks and
barks. My mother goes outside to quiet her. I turn the page,
reading of rape or robbery, something distant. Then I hear the
dog growl, then again bark. I go outside.

My mother is returning to the house, her face red, angry. Son
of a B, she says. I just caught some punk standing outside the alley gate teasing Alfie. She points. He was daring her to jump at
him, and the damn kid was holding one of the garbage can lids
over his head, just waiting to hit her. My mother demonstrates
with her hands.

I run to the alley, ready to fight, to defend. But there is no one
in the alley.

My mother stands there on the narrow strip of sidewalk, her
hands now at her sides. She looks tired. Behind her in the yard
is an old table covered with potted plants. Coleus, philodendron,
wandering Jew. One of the planters, a statue of the Sacred Heart
of Jesus. Another, Mary with her white ceramic hands folded
in prayer. Mother's Day presents of years ago. Standing in the
bright morning sun.

And when I came out, my mother continues, the punk just
looked at me, real snotty-like, like he was *daring* me, and then
he said come on and hit me, lady, you just come right on and hit
me. I'll show you, lady, come on. And then he used the *F* word.
She shakes her head and looks at me.

Later, inside, as she irons one of my father's shirts, she tells me another story. It happened last week, at night. The ten o'clock news was on. Time to walk Alfie. She'd been feeling lousy all day so Jim took the dog out front instead.

So he was standing out there waiting for Alfie to finish up her business when all of a sudden he hears this engine and he looks up, and you know what it was, Tony? Can you guess, of all things? It was this car, this *car*, driving right down along the sidewalk with its lights out. Jim said he dove straight for the curb, pulling poor Alfie in the middle of number two right with him. And when they went past him they swore at him and threw an empty beer can at him. She laughs and looks at me, then stops ironing and sips her coffee. Her laughter is from fear. Well, you should have heard your little brother when he came back in. Boy was he steaming! They could have killed him they were driving so fast. The cops caught the kids up at Tastee-Freeze corner. We saw the squad car lights from the front windows. It was a good thing Jim took the dog out that night instead of me. She sprinkles the shirt with water from a Pepsi bottle. Can you picture your old mother diving then for the curb?

She makes a tugging gesture with her hands. Pulling the leash. Saving herself and Alfie. Again she laughs. She tells the story again when Jim comes home.

At first the doctors thought she had disseminated lupus erythematosus. Lupus means wolf. It is primarily a disease of the skin. As lupus advances, the victim's face becomes ulcerated by what are called butterfly eruptions. The face comes to resemble a wolf's. Disseminated lupus attacks the joints as well as the internal organs. There isn't a known cure.

And at first they made her hang. My mother. They made her buy a sling into which she placed her head, five times each day. Pulling her head from the other side was a heavy water bag. My father put the equipment up on the door of my bedroom. For years when I went to sleep I stared at that water bag. She had to hang for two-and-a-half hours each day. Those were the years that she read every book she could get her hands on.

And those were the years that she received the weekly shots, the cortisone, the steroids, that made her puff up, made her put on the weight the doctors are now telling her to get rid of.

Then one of the doctors died, and then she had to find new doctors, and then again she had to undergo their battery of tests. These new doctors told her that she probably didn't have lupus, that instead they thought she had severe rheumatoid arthritis, that the ten years of traction and corticosteroids had been a mistake. They gave her a drugstore full of pills then. They told her to lose weight, to exercise each night.

A small blackboard hangs over the kitchen sink. The markings put there each day appear to be Chinese. Long lines for these pills, dots for those, the letter *A* for yet another. A squiggly line for something else.

The new doctors taught her the system. When you take over thirty pills a day you can't rely on memory.

My father called again. He said there was nothing new. Mary is in the hospital again, and she's been joking that she's somewhat of a celebrity. So many doctors come in each day to see her. Interns. Residents. They hold conferences around her bed. They smile and read her chart. They question her. They thump her abdomen. They move her joints. They point. One intern asked her when she had her last menstrual cycle. My mother looked at the young man, then at the other doctors around her bed, then smiled and said twenty-some years ago but I couldn't for the life of me tell you which month. The intern's face quickly reddened. My mother's hysterectomy is written there in plain view on her chart.

They ask her questions and she recites her history like a lit-
any.

Were the Ohio doctors right? Were they prophets? *Please give
her to us. Maybe we can experiment.*

My father and I walk along the street. We've just eaten, then
gone to Osco for the evening paper—an excuse, really, just to
take a walk. And he is next to me suddenly bringing up the subject of my mother's health, just as suddenly as the wind from the
lake shakes the thin branches of the trees. The moment is serious, I realize. My father is not a man given to unnecessary talk.

I don't know what I'd do without her, he says. I say nothing,
for I can think of nothing to say. We've been together for over
thirty years, he says. He pauses. For nearly thirty-four years.
Thirty-four years this October. And, you know, you wouldn't
think it, but I love her so much more now. He hesitates, and I
look at him. He shakes his head and smiles. You know what I
mean? he says. I say yes and we walk for a while in silence, and I
think of what it must be like to live with someone for thirty-four
years, but I cannot imagine it, and then I hear my father begin
to talk about that afternoon's ball game—he describes at length
and in comic detail a misjudged fly ball lost in apathy or inepti-
tude or simply in the sun—and for the rest of our walk home we
discuss what's right and wrong with our favorite baseball team,
our thorn-in-the-side Chicago Cubs.

I stand here, not used to speaking about things that are so close
to me. I am used to veiling things in my stories, to making things
wear masks, to telling my stories through masks. But my mother
tells her stories openly, as she has done so all of her life—since
she lived on her father's farm in Ohio, as she walked along the
crowded 1930 Chicago streets, to my father overseas in her letters, to the five of us children, as we sat on her lap, as we played

in the next room while she tended to our supper in the kitchen. She tells them to everyone, to anyone who will listen. She taught Linda to read her lips.

I learn now to read her lips.

And I imagine one last story.

Diana and I are children. Our mother is still young. Diana and I are outside on the sidewalk playing and it's summer. And we are young and full of play and happy, and we see a dog, and it comes toward us on the street. My sister takes my hand. She senses something, I think. The dog weaves from side to side. It's sick, I think. Some kind of lather is on its mouth. The dog growls. I feel Diana's hand shake.

Now we are inside the house, safe, telling our mother. Linda, Bob, and Jim are there. We are all the same age, all children. Our mother looks outside, then walks to the telephone. She returns to the front windows. We try to look out the windows too, but she pushes the five of us away.

No, she says. I don't want any of you to see this.

We watch her watching. Then we hear the siren of a police car. We watch our mother make the sign of the Cross. Then we hear a shot. Another. I look at my sisters and brothers. They are crying. Worried, frightened, I begin to cry too.

Did it come near you? our mother asks us. Did it touch you? Any of you? Linda reads her lips. She means the funny dog. Or does she mean the speeding automobile with its lights off? The Ohio doctors? The boy behind the alley gate? The shards of broken glass? The wolf surrounded by butterflies? The ten-and-a-half-pound baby?

Diana, the oldest, speaks for us. She says that it did not.

Our mother smiles. She sits with us. Then our father is with us. Bob cracks a smile, and everybody laughs. Alfie gives a bark. The seven of us sit closely on the sofa. Safe.

That actually happened, but not exactly in the way that I described it. I've heard my mother tell that story from time to time, at times when she's most uneasy, but she has never said what it was that she saw from the front windows. A good storyteller, she leaves what she has all too clearly seen to our imaginations.

I stand in the corner of this room, thinking of her lying now in the hospital.

I pray none of us looks at that animal's face.

# Close-Ups

SANDRA THOMPSON

From *Close-Ups* (1984)

The Number One Idol is dead. His face in the obituary: white hair on white paper. He is smiling, and his eyes veer off the page. I recognize the gaze. I had tried to follow it there, to some sad, precious thing. I try to follow it now, but I stop short, my eyes remaining on the page.

I hadn't seen him in twelve years. I hadn't spoken to him. We didn't write. Had he lived twelve years more, I wouldn't have seen him. He never left Ohio, and I wouldn't go back there. So much is made of death; I wonder if it matters. I wonder if it matters whether it is now or was then that he, in his great gray overcoat, walked into the classroom and said, "This is a good day to stay home and eat crackers in bed," and immediately we were all in bed with him, close up to the watercolor-wash blue eyes whose white brows slanted upwards, slightly evil, to those neat ears that lay flat against his head and pointed heavenward, that voice like syrup-over-pebbles in our ears, in our mouths. He died, and I felt like a hatchet had struck my ankles.

My arms wrapped around books, I blow deep into my scarf, wooly breath coming back to warm my face. My legs are bare between knee socks and skirt. The pleats sway, scraping my raw skin. Beside me is my friend Miranda. We walk past the county jail. We walk past the post office and guess which of the old men who laze on its steps have tails hidden in their pants. We walk past the bus station, across Route 23, to the chapel and Haig's eight o'clock. We whisper about our idols. There are semi-idols: a black man with a mustache like sleek cat's tails who wears a starched ROTC uniform; a blonde boy with pale brow and tortured dark eyes whose face we have cut from *Photography Annual.* Haig is the only Full Idol. Number One. Legs crossed in a caduceus, I sit in the middle of the front row, not close enough to his face, to his smile, to his gesturing empty hands. There is a heartbreaking tear in the elbow of his unironed, yellowed shirt. It cries out for us.

After curfew we slip out of the dormitory and sneak to his house, three blocks from where we sleep. We gape at the Victorian monster. In its front window there is a large woman wearing a green bathrobe, ironing. It is her: Clytemnestra. (So he has called her in class.) We giggle, we are so weird, we grab each other's hands, and I feel a chill that cannot be part of our game. I turn from Miranda and run, run three blocks back to the dormitory to the side door we've propped open with a copy of *Clarissa,* and wait, panting, for Miranda.

When it happens, I can't tell Miranda. When it happens, it is no longer a game. When it happens, I don't know the words or the names. His name. I can't call him Dr. Haig. I can't call the Number One Idol just plain Jim. I can't say his name, and if, when we're not alone, I want to speak to him, I have to tap him on the shoulder or stand right in front of him as if I were addressing a deaf man.

Across the lawn he walks, almost rolls, as though there are ball bearings on the soles of his feet. He is unshaven, a gray-white

frost on his cheeks and chin, and he wears a gray overcoat, un-
buttoned, that lifts and falls in the wind. His hair is pure white,
and very short; it lies close to his head and sticks down in little
prongs onto his forehead. He smokes, letting the ash from his
cigarette drop onto the front of his coat. "Good morning, Deborah Jane," he says, taking in the campus with a sweep of his
hand.

He pulls his Chevy van into the driveway of the wrong house; it
is the one next door to where the green woman had been ironing. "What about the neighbors?" I ask. I mean, what about *her*.
I mean, promise me I won't be killed.

"The garage is attached to the house," he says. "We'll go
straight in from there." On the concrete steps at the door from
the garage to the house, he lays his hand on my neck, and, in his
face, close up, in the frost on his cheek, in the jowls that have just
begun to slacken, I feel his age.

I won't do it in the house. She is all over it. In the books, in the
linens, in the worn rugs. She hangs at the hall stairs, as homecoming queen three years before I was born. She has square
shoulders and jaunty dark hair. It is twenty-two years later and
she has been mad off and on for ten. There are children. The
youngest, Nellie, cries from inside her fever, "Stay here and be
my mommy." I kiss her at the hairline, run three blocks back to
the dormitory where the doors have already locked shut.

The motels are green. Low, flat green shacks on the backroads.
The rooms have small square radios with static on every station.
We sit crosslegged on the bed, listen to fertilizer commercials,
drink Jack Daniels Sour Mash, and play Jotto. The hair on his
chest is gray-white; little tufts of white hair spring from his ear
lobes. His face is flushed, broken veins in his cheeks like fine pen
lines. His dazzling mouth pouts as he sucks on a pencil tip. On

the eve of the marriage I make to escape him, he will telephone and breathe one word: "eerie." The perfect Jotto word: three out of five letters are the same.

We hide out in the next county. At a roadhouse, a local is expert at sleight of hand. Haig likes to drink with the broken-down old boys, drinks with the keeper of the county zoo, with the one-eyed postmaster, with this magician whose mean little face has been softened by whiskey. His palm follows the errant fifty-cent piece under the table, behind Haig's shot glass, inside my blouse pocket. Haig buys him a short beer. "And she," he says, nodding toward me, the sliver of his mouth turned up on a grin, "is she your granddaughter?"

"I'm his wife," I say, placing my hand on the table, on the third finger, a dimestore band.

The magician disappears. I talk fast; I can't get to our future too fast: we move to New York City where people are sophisticated, Haig writes a best-selling thriller, we drink and fuck a lot, are rich, happy, and notorious.

"No, my love," he says. "Our ending will be like this: I will order you to leave me for your own good, and you'll do it. You'll marry a lawyer" (and the way he says "lawyer" we could lie down in the grass and rest between the syllables) "or, God forbid, a stockbroker, who will support you in the manner to which you were accustomed—before you knew me. You will have two children, each with freckles on his nose like on yours. I only hope you'll remember me with some fondness—"

"No!" I cry. Across the booth, I grab his neck with both hands, press my palms into his skin to firm it.

He writes the first three pages of the thriller.

Someone blabs. Clytemnestra returns from the asylum with names, dates, places. She crashes into the kitchen of the rooms

Haig has rented above the campus bookstore. She is large, in a brown coat, and with teeth like pilings of a rotted dock. She stalks the circle of the kitchen table. She walks behind me, puts her hands on the back of my chair, and shoves it, the wooden legs making a shrill scrape on the linoleum. "So this is the one now?" she says. (Will he let her kill me?)

Haig stands with his back to us, at the counter by the sink. We have run out of Jack Daniels and he is pouring cooking sherry into a jelly glass.

She lowers herself into the chair next to me at the table. "You don't think you're the first, do you?"

Haig turns to her, his glorious face awash. He is gray and tired, and when he speaks there is in his voice too much kindness. "I love her," he says.

Her unkempt face leers close to mine. "What color eyebrow pencil is that you have on, sweetheart?"

"Smoke," I tell her.

I want her to die, I want her to be happy, I want to pack us all off somewhere where it's safe.

"I love you." I run my hand down the jagged scar on his thigh. Bayonet, Italy, World War II. What is a bayonet? I try to remember from the late shows. He rolls down the shot-up Italian hill and is nursed by Italian whores. Anna Magnani. Six months after V-E Day my mother lifts me above the barricades to Eisenhower, who kisses my cheek with his clean, dry lips. We make love eight times. He cooks meatloaf with hunks of potato mixed in, and as I eat he watches me, and smokes and smokes. His emphysema is threatening. Clytemnestra is threatening. The college is threatening. The nuns are threatening to take his small daughters. We sit on borrowed sheets and play Scrabble until it's time to make love again. I win with sure one syllables in play after play while he searches for the single, stunning word.

————

Clytemnestra takes to passing by campus in the van, trying to run me over. Around every corner I see her, high up at the wheel, a cigarette hanging from the ruins of her teeth. She is driving for blood. She rats on me to my housemother. She rifles the files in the Registrar's Office and grabs my I.Q. She leaks it to him; hers is higher, thus erasing my breasts, their pink nipples, and my smooth thighs. I dream I am onstage at graduation and as the president steps up to hand me my diploma, just as my fingers are about to grasp it, at the edge of the campus lawn she steps down from the van, takes out a rifle, and shoots me through the heart.

The zoo keeper corners me in the bus station. He buys me coffee and says, "You should look up *emphysema* in a medical dictionary in the library. Your man is very sick. He is straining his lungs. He is straining his heart. You stop him drinking! Stop him smoking! Stop him, Deborah Jane, or he'll die." The zoo keeper squats down in the jackal's cage: "Eat roughage for bulk: lettuce, cabbage, a nice cole slaw. All this raw meat's no good for you."

I am backed against the white wall, inches from the door. Haig sits at the kitchen table in the darkening room. The downward lines in his face turn black as the face lights up in the flame of the kitchen matches he strikes, one by one, and flicks at me. His chest heaves. His shirt is unironed, is ill-buttoned, one tail hanging inches below the other. His face is florid, his cheeks heavy, his blue eyes, slits. We glare at each other. Neither of us can move.

The cross-examination:

Q. Do you love him?
A. Yes.
Q. Will you stay with him?
A. Yes. No.

27

Q. Well?

A. Yes I've poured myself into him and left nothing over. No he's skipping to the grave and pulling me alongside—

Q. Yes or no?

A. I have one foot on either side of a gaping split in the quake-reft ground, my legs are spreading wider and wider—

Q. Yes or no? Yes or no? Yes or no?

Haig and I sit in a rowboat in the middle of a green lake. He has let the oars lie slack in their sockets. I am wearing a smock with tiny pink flowers on ivory, two pigtails and bare feet. Haig's gray cuffs slosh in the water in the hull of the boat. He has worn the same shirt for three days: yellowed white. His face is yellow-white, set on his shoulders like a bloated moon. He coughs, takes a swig of Big Cat, coughs again. Underneath me, the hard seat seesaws with the undulations of the water. I dive into the thick green lake, swim in quick, clean strokes, and surface where the boat is a yellow speck between water and sky.

After Haig's death, I dream a portfolio of his papers has been forwarded to me in the mail. It includes a book he has written: I can't see the title, but the dustjacket is shiny and smooth and green, and on the back cover, in a black and white photograph, is Haig, in his gray overcoat, walking, springing, on his ball-bearing feet; as he goes forward off the page, his face, glorious again, is three-quarters turned back, smiling at me.

# A Little Something

WENDY BRENNER

From *Large Animals in Everyday Life* (1996)

Helene is young, brown-haired, and intelligent, but not necessarily an attractive person. She knows that her expressions change too dramatically; she can't seem to hold her face still like people on TV, or even most people she meets in real life. She tends to take things personally, like the time she was sunning in her square of a front yard, feeling puffy in her new bikini, and she opened her eyes to the Goodyear blimp, humming serenely overhead. She dresses well, knows how to wear a suit, but she's also aware of how easy it is to put together a wrong ensemble. It tires her out, just thinking about it, or about how easy it is to say the wrong thing. She works hard at life, but believes herself to be lazy and obsessive; she knows she is not necessarily a pretty person.

She works downtown in the Loop, in the planning department of a firm that publishes astrology guides and pocket cookbooks. This involves phoning freelance artists and figuring out how many recipes or astrological forecasts will fit on a page. To brighten her work space she tacks up photos of men who remind her of Joe, the man she is in love with. There's Jack Nicholson, a local talk show host, and an unidentified magician from an ad for vodka. It's not that she doesn't have photos of Joe himself, but there's something exciting, amazing even, about finding his likeness in someone else. Connection is implied, connection and fate. Her co-workers needle her about this; a divorced editor named Jan, in particular, takes issue with Helene in a smilingly sardonic way. "Do you actually *believe* this zodiac stuff?" she says.

"No," Helene says quickly. "It's just exciting to think that there's a connection, however random . . ."

"But why can't it be just as exciting," Jan says, "to think that there's no connection at all? That's what *I* call exciting."

Helene has no answer for this, but on the whole she feels lucky to be part of the close, energetic crew of people at this company. Outside of work she feels a little unanchored. But at the office, for eight and a half hours each day, even though her mind starts to repeat itself as she labels, counts, and copies, she is secure in ritual.

Joe is twelve years older than Helene, between jobs but unalarmed. He literally doesn't sweat over things. His body barely even has a scent of its own, beyond soap. Helene thinks this is because he refuses to move fast enough to perspire. It's a small rebellion of his; he seems exempt from the rush of city living, but really his spirit gets by, undiluted, sneaking around in his slow body. He still believes, in his late thirties, that he can get away with whatever he pleases. He lets his spine hang in a lazy posture of truth, for anyone who cares to notice, and of course Helene notices. Joe has a favorite, comical houseplant, a dimestore jade tree, that he claims reminds him of her. The plant fell apart once when he repotted it, but now it grows so rapidly it seems to stretch upward before his very eyes, with the same awkwardness Helene seems to suffer when she's over at his place, trying so hard to act offhand. He says he expects someday to catch her stumbling around in a pair of dress-up pumps three sizes too large.

They met at O'Hare International, in a cocktail lounge where a small crowd was waiting out a blizzard. It was just before Christmas, and the low-ceilinged room was dimly lit with strung bulbs. Everyone in the lounge was watching a news program on the wall television about a woman who'd been trapped under a piece of construction machinery for seven hours, but who'd lived and learned to walk again. People were turning to each other over their drinks to exclaim about this miracle. An airline worker wearing a weighty jumpsuit sat next to Helene. "I know of a club about a mile from here," he said softly. "It only costs three bucks to get in and they got a pool that's hot as a bathtub." Helene nodded and kept her eyes on the TV. The airline worker shrugged and started telling her about his father, who'd died recently in an auto wreck. "It's just plain hard," he said. "You only get one father."

Helene tried to think if anything this difficult had ever happened to her, but nothing had. Her parents were clever agnostics who didn't believe in sadness or the unknown. Her mother, for instance, could tell you what they'd be having for dinner three weeks from now. Helene imagined that when it was her parents' time to die they would manage to make a rational decision out of it somehow, just as they chose what vegetable went with pork chops or what color carpeting to put in Helene's old bedroom when she moved out. Unreasonable occurrences such as auto wrecks kept their distance from Helene's parents. On the other hand, so did miracles. For that matter, so did Helene. The airline worker was still watching her hopefully. She coughed and turned away, and there sat Joe on her other side, looking ageless and arch and familiar. He gazed at her as though he'd been gazing at her on and off for years.

"If you think that's bad," he said finally, "listen to what happened to me. I went to buy a goldfish this morning and the bus I was on ran right over a cat. Broad daylight. Killed it." Helene felt her face fall, out of her control. "But wait," he said, "that's not all. I got to the aquarium store and it was all boarded up! Apparently the old man who ran the place got *hit by a car*, running across the street for lunch. Can you believe it?"

Helene shook her head. She couldn't tell if he was actually self-pitying or just trying to get her to talk. It seemed that he might be neither. "Well," she said, "I was at the YMCA the other day and I overheard two little girls in the locker room, and one of them said, 'You look like a woman,' and the other one said, 'I do?' and the first one said, 'Yeah.' It was wild." Helene knew she was striving for non sequitur. Joe looked surprised and slightly touched. They exchanged names and she took note of his bad complexion and the precise way his lips came together. "Are you waiting for a plane?" she asked. Her own flight was grounded, not because of the blizzard, but mechanical trouble.

"I'm trying to get out of the country," Joe said. Helene noticed his dark whiskers, dark lashes. "I'm on standby for half a dozen flights," he said. "Anywhere warm. And you? Wait—let me guess. You're a college student, right? Home to the folks for Christmas? No—I'll bet you're going to Palm Beach with five friends who look exactly like you, only blonder, right?

"Well, close," Helene said. "Phoenix. But I'm not a student." She was making her yearly visit to an old high school friend whose parents ran a guest ranch.

"Always good to get away for the holidays," Joe said. "Go somewhere hot and foreign, where people don't get so worked up."

Helene sipped her vodka and 7-Up and silently agreed. She loved the tropical, slowed-down feel of life at her friend's ranch, even though she knew it was inauthentic, produced by a paid staff for the tourists. There was something, nevertheless, about the palmettos and prickly pears and the birds that ran up and down on the footpaths that seemed to mock the guests and all their serious human activities. Helene supposed if you grew up surrounded by these crazy plants and wild pigs and coyotes howling like sirens in the night you might not feel so starved for extremity. You might just calm down and get on with your life. At any rate, she always came back to the Midwest. She had to admit that what she loved about Arizona was probably only the novelty; you couldn't base your whole life on what the foliage happened to look like. "So what do you do for a living?" she asked Joe.

He told her he was the voice of time; he had made a local telephone time recording. They'd paid him a fortune for that, he said, and before that he had worked in a burlap bag factory that burned to the ground. He wore a stylish double-breasted suit, Helene saw, and he took his cigarette smoke up through his nostrils. "Are you also an artist?" she asked.

"Oh, Christ, no," he said.

Embarrassed, Helene glanced at the TV, on which an interviewer was now leaning forward toward his guest, saying, "So, do women *dig* conflict?" "You know," Helene said, "I don't go around picking up men in bars."

"Don't sweat it," Joe said. "You think innocents are any more *pure* than we are?" He paused dreamily for a moment, then said, "You're just a little something God sent me."

No one had ever said anything like that to Helene. She slid her napkin out from under her glass immediately and got a pen out of her bag and wrote down her phone number for Joe. When her flight was announced he kissed her on the forehead and wished her good luck back at college. She was halfway down the long corridor to her gate, her heart pounding, before she realized she hadn't corrected him. She thought of a phrase from one of the astrology guides she'd worked on: *When the student is ready, the teacher arrives.* At the gate a group of noisy, bright-jacketed teens were jittering around restlessly, clutching homemade posters that read WELCOME HOME, AMBER!! IF YOU'RE TAN, JUST GO BACK!!! I was never that cynical, Helene thought. I don't ever want to be that cynical.

Before Joe, Helene had only one other boyfriend. He was

younger than Joe and much more ambitious. His life's work, he knew at twenty-five, was in the public sector. He was very principled about certain things. He made Helene feel ridiculously important and minuscule at the same time. "I'm so proud of you," he'd say to her, "with that little job of yours." Once they had an argument which ended with him standing over her, kicking her in the side. The argument started over a TV program Helene liked, and ended with him shouting at her that she must learn to live in the real world. She thought, at the time, that he was trying to help her.

Remembering that time in her life makes Helene's stomach turn as though the earth has suddenly reversed in its orbit. She wishes she could pull the rug out from underneath her memories. She is smart enough to know about things like taking charge, responsibility, Oprah Winfrey, about independence being the redemption of the modern woman. But certain of her longings she cannot seem to eliminate. She would just like to *locate* her faith, get it down to a science, like packing her lunch each night. Jan, at work, seems disgusted with her. "You know what you need to work on?" she asks Helene rhetorically. "Your relationship with your*self*." Another of Jan's favorites is: "We all cause our own happiness and unhappiness, and the sooner you accept that, the better." But Jan might as well be from Mars as far as Helene is concerned. She lives alone, Helene knows, and is constantly modifying her diet, eliminating sugar, adding brown rice, as though health is a mountain that need only be climbed, as though appetite is of no consequence whatsoever. She is active in small political organizations that support distant and obscure causes, and she often urges Helene to "get outside" herself and come to a protest or a rally. At the office, Jan snaps Polaroids at parties, keeps the money for the football pool, and gets mildly involved in everybody's business. Helene supposes she herself is too self-involved, too busy tallying, stockpiling, looking for various affirmations, to get up much steam for Jan's type of activities. She supposes Jan has a point. Helene is, after all, tired of so much craving.

Early one morning, an unassuming spring dawn, Helene gets up and goes into Joe's chilly bathroom. She has slept at his apartment only two or three times so far. There on the edge of the sink sits his bar of soap, plastered with dark short hairs from his head. She feels like she's seen his diary, or a hidden scar; she can't believe his body let this happen. She can't believe the soap let this happen. She can't believe she's allowed to see this. By the time she tiptoes back into the bedroom it is filled with light. She eases under the comforter, unsure if Joe is conscious. "What happened to you?" he mumbles.

"I found salvation in your bathroom," she says, trying to make it sound like a joke. She watches Joe slip so easily back into sleep, and quiets her heart, trying, as hard as she's ever tried anything, to match his slow deep breathing.

Joe has been engaged to be married twice in his life. The first time was to a precocious girl who wanted him to help her hold up a Circle K store just outside of Amarillo. He didn't go through with that plan, but they did drive all over Texas together in a Vega loaded with half-empty liquor bottles and assorted ammunition. Every town they stopped in they charmed people. The girl wore a football jersey that said "Mikey" on the back, and Joe wore a string tie that fastened with an enormous lump of turquoise. Men in filling stations kept calling him "Mikey" when he paid for gas. Eventually, the girl decided to go back to school, and made this clear to Joe one night by throwing a folding chair at his head. He recovered and met an internationally known runway model at a party in Houston where he tended bar. The model's father was a Nigerian statesman who had survived the revolution there, money intact. He seemed to like Joe's offhand wit, or perhaps his taste in clothing; at any rate, it was decided that Joe would marry the runway model, who was actually only seventeen. This engagement lasted three weeks and then the model shaved her head and tried to shoot her father. Her father bought Joe a one-way plane ticket to a Northern city. This was all going on in Joe's life at the same time Helene was a ten-year-old making God's eyes out of yarn and sticks at summer camp.

Joe doesn't recall the exact moment he first laid eyes on Helene, or anyone else, for that matter. It's been a long, long time since he was surprised at the way people entered and exited his life. Some people might even consider him detached—a doctor once told him: You refuse to dip your toe in the stream running right outside your own front door. It's unfortunate, but that's how it is. There are a thousand ways to get by, Joe knows, and nine hundred and ninety-nine of them involve messing other people up. Truthfully, he doesn't feel unfortunate at all. One thing he's noticed is that if there's anything worse than bad memories, it's the insidious good ones. Remembering too far back makes his heart feel like a balled-up washcloth. His heart hurts, his head aches, it hurts to look out the window and smell October coming. Who needs that kind of pain? Not Joe, who once stood on the roof of the Sears Tower wearing only a loincloth, and another time served paella to Natalie Wood. When you let go, life is one fabulous day at a time.

He wishes Helene could learn to relax, though he doesn't see it as his business to teach her. He wishes she wouldn't think about their ages. He knows she thinks a lot about loving him, what it means to love him, and he wishes she wouldn't. His love for her isn't anything he thinks about; it's like a birthmark— he would never doubt its permanence. One night he broiled a chicken for their dinner, and when he cut half from his plate for her she stared at him so intensely he told her to stop it, she was being too romantic about the whole thing. But this was a mistake; he doesn't want to tell her how to act. He would no more patronize her than patronize his own big toe. "Think about moving in with me," he says. When he sees her expression, he says, not unkindly, "Jesus, here we go." But then she laughs, and he thinks: *Maybe there is hope.* He can't focus on all her fears, all her trying, who she thinks she is or who she tries so hard to be. He sees only Helene, and senses the inevitable unknown, waiting, as it always does, for the right moment. Which is okay with Joe, because he can wait forever.

Summer is over, and Helene is not sleeping well. She wakes up in the middle of the night and believes she is missing a self. She's positive there were two, and now there's only air next to her in the bed. One is supposed to be the child, and one the woman. Which one is still here? She hasn't decided whether or not to move in with Joe, and it's driving her nuts. During the day she rushes impatiently through her rituals; she spends less time on her hair, less time at lunch, and less time actually working. She finds ways to streamline, to take shortcuts in her work. She is definitely hurrying, but hurrying toward what?

"You sure are jumpy," Jan says.

"I know it," Helene says. "If I could just figure out what to do about the Joe situation . . ."

"Oh, situation schmituation!" Jan says. "You're still *in* love with him."

"What are you talking about?" Helene says.

"You've got to get past *that*, if it's going to work," says Jan. "Every relationship should have its disillusionment." She picks nonchalantly at the edge of Helene's desk blotter.

Helene is suddenly annoyed. "There's a big difference between you and me," she says. "You're divorced!"

"The difference between you and me," Jan says, "is that I know how to have a good time."

Lately Joe has been suggesting that they shop for furniture, but Helene has a revelation: she suggests they go buy that gold-fish he's been wanting. They drive way out in the west suburbs on a mild Saturday in September. The day is clear and warm, but rather fainthearted—the smell of fall is everywhere. They drive so far they have to pay three tolls. From the outside the Pet Castle looks like a regular building, but inside the decor is lush and confusing. Neither Joe nor Helene has ever seen anything like it; it looks like both an enchanted forest and a Swiss chalet. Walnut beams crisscross overhead, and a waterfall rushes down from the second level. Tropical birds scream from the rafters, and the pond is crowded with goldfish. Joe looks disappointed.

"What is it?" Helene asks.

"I don't know," he says glumly. "In a setup like this, they can never catch the one you want."

"Maybe they'll let you catch it yourself," she says. "Do you know what you're going to name it?" She's assumed Joe is the kind of person who comes up with witty names for pets.

"Nothing at all," Joe says. "If you name them, they just die. That's the whole secret behind goldfish."

Helene nods and walks away so he won't see her looking taken aback. She squeezes between customers and rows of cages. Excited children keep bumping into her.

An animated woman with a tiny terrier under her arm is chatting with a salesperson. "My puppy's fine now," Helene over-hears. "The instant we get in the car, he just goes right to sleep." The salesperson nods vigorously. "That's as it should be," he says with a heavy European accent.

Helene finds the kittens, her favorites. There are at least twenty of them, squirming and crying in a big glass showcase lined with newspaper. They climb all over each other trying to get close to her. She sees one kitten step right on another kit-ten's face. This is not a good advertisement for cohabitation, she thinks. The European salesperson arrives at her side and says, "You want to hold?"

"Oh, no thanks," she says. It would just make it impossible. Once she held it, she'd have to keep it. And she doesn't even know where she'll be living in one month's time. If only they were literate, Helene thinks suddenly. She wouldn't mind having a pen-pal here at the Pet Castle. But what could you write to a kitten? How would you explain to it why it couldn't come live with you? The salesperson wanders off and the kittens mew frantically. Helene wonders if they are as innocent as they appear to be. "I doubt it," she says aloud.

From behind her, a small raspy voice says: "I doubt it."

She whirls around, and there's a smug black myna bird on a perch. "What the hell," she says. The bird edges toward her, then edges back. "Tell me something else," Helene says, but the bird is silent. It bobs its head, shakes out its shiny black wings, lifts its feet and sets them down, one small round eye trained on Helene. It is definitely telling her something, but what, *what*? But maybe its strange movements are enough; maybe this, the fact that she and the bird are speaking to each other, is all she is supposed to know. She turns and sees Joe up on the second level, grinning at her and waving a goldfish in a plastic bag. Maybe this is what life will be like with him, she thinks. One small miracle after another.

# The First Baseman

## DANIEL CURLEY

From *Living with Snakes* (1985)

She had long dark hair that she pulled straight back and tied with a piece of bright, heavy yarn. It gave her face a forward-straining, eager look—something like a figurehead, very, very quiet. Just the same there was nothing wooden about her. Although her expression rarely changed—as far as I can remember, she never smiled—she was simply relaxed and alert. I assumed she was intelligent as well. I also assumed she was gentle, compassionate, and very loving. I was, of course, madly in love with her. And the first time I stood beside her I realized she was fully six-foot-two in her baseball shoes.

I'm an even six-foot myself—well, although it's not generally known, five-foot-eleven and fifteen-sixteenths inches. That sticks in my craw because I always wanted to be six-foot, and I've been led to lie a lot about it.

Every night after work I was out at the softball park, hoping her team would be playing. I got into the habit of hanging around the refreshment stand to buy her a beer after the games. Each night she looked mildly down at me and thanked me and drank her beer. The next night I would be back in the stands with the odd husband, a boyfriend or two, a scattering of babies. The center fielder on her team—great arm, strong and accurate—used to leave her baby on a bench there bundled up in one of those things Indian women use, a carrying board of some kind, and when she wasn't in the field or at bat she would whip out a breast and feed it.

My first baseman was marvelous. She played as good a first base as I have ever seen, very close to the bat, more than half-way down the line, crouched, ready, arms hanging, weight just balanced. I really worried about her playing so far in. In cricket there are positions very close to the bat called silly mid-on and silly mid-off. Well, she played a silly first base, but she was very quick. Great hands. The greatest. I've seen men sit and catch flies with their hands. I even knew a man who could pick them out of the air between his thumb and forefinger. And there is the legendary samurai who could snap them up with chopsticks. I doubt if she had ever heard of chopsticks, but she was in that league.

I came very late to women's softball, but I had watched a lot of baseball—I'm a frustrated first baseman myself. That is, I was slow to react and couldn't hit. Anything else? But I know what is good just the same, and she had it all. She could hit. She could run. When she stood up to an umpire, it was her jaw she stuck out, not her chest, although I had checked that statistic, too, of course. But when I watched her play I only thought exactly what I thought when I watched Joe DiMaggio: Christ, how beautiful. Perhaps all the time I had been wanting to be in love with a really great first baseman and didn't know it.

Well, I bought her a beer—I swear it—just the same way I would have bought a beer for Joe DiMaggio if he had really been there and willing to accept a beer. I think I did anyway. It's hard to tell for sure. I did think it over. I thought it over long after I knew she went to the refreshment stand after every game. I asked myself: Look now, if this was Joe DiMaggio would you buy him a beer if he was really here? Or is it that buying a beer is what you do for a woman?

The next night I bought a beer for the winning pitcher in a game in the men's league. He was in the executive training program of the bank where I cash my checks and just about the only person in town I know. A couple of nights after that I bought one for the third baseman on the Indian team. He had done something I admired—envied actually. He was playing way in with a runner on third and fielded a hard smash perfectly and faked a throw to first. The runner broke for home and was tagged out before he could stop. It was really great.

And then I said to my first baseman, "Can I buy you a beer? You had a great game." It seemed just right. I couldn't see a thing wrong with it. Actually, there was supposed to be one more step after I bought the beer for the Indian third baseman. I wanted to test my feelings by buying for someone on the Indian women's team. That team was, after all, my first love. I went night after night to see them play. They were all fat and jolly, and I enjoyed their games because they enjoyed them so, even their own strikeouts, their own errors. But when it came right down to action, I couldn't buy any one of them a beer. It wasn't only that I couldn't find one of them to tell she had a great game. There was also the matter of a sneaking doubt that even if I could buy her a beer I wouldn't dare buy a beer for a white woman. I didn't want to know that. Then when I discovered that I could in fact buy a beer for my first baseman, I was no longer interested in buying a beer for anyone else.

"Thanks," she said. She raised the can to me. I raised mine to her. I never was one for small talk. That accounts for a lot, I suppose—accounts for the fact that we went on the same way for about a month. And I swear when I watched her play, it was as if she truly was Joe DiMaggio. When I saw her in the post office, though, it was different.

Each morning on the way to work I checked my mailbox. I had noticed her in there picking up mail for some office. She wore a jacket and mini-skirt I recognized after a while as the uniform of the tellers at my bank. She was impressive all right, but I didn't think much about her until I saw her play. Then I began to time my visits to the post office more carefully. My day would be off to a very bad start if I didn't see her squat and open the big bank box on the lowest level of boxes. The splendor of her thighs in nylon—which I never thought about when I saw them bared on the field—the swell of her breast when she reached through the box to pick up the canvas pouch from the floor—oh, I was nearly out of my mind. I couldn't tell if I was in love with a first baseman or a woman. Curiously, we never spoke in the post office. We avoided each other's eyes. I never said, "I dreamed of your plays." It wasn't strictly true anyway. I just lay awake and reran the entire game and bits of other games as well, but it was as good as dreaming.

At the end of a month of beers she said, "You're quite a fan, aren't you?" She leaned back against the counter with both elbows. I couldn't have been more pleased if she had shot a stream of tobacco juice at a passing rat.

"Oh, yes," I said. "I wouldn't miss a game."

"What will you do now the season is over?"

That was something I had been trying not to know. The thought had crossed my mind from time to time, but I had managed pretty well to assume that the season would go on forever. "Buy a TV, I guess," I said.

"There'll be basketball," she said, "but that's a long way off."

"What will you do?" I said.

"Run after work," she said. "Allow myself an extra beer."

"Does that start now?" I said. I made a slight gesture with my can.

"Training is now relaxed," she said. It was as near to a smile as I ever saw on her face.

"Well—" I said.

"They're closing up now," she said. And we had to step forward to avoid being hit by the hatch coming down.

"There are lots of places," I said.

"I can't go dressed like this," she said

I was desperate. "Look," I said. It was all slipping away—what there was of it. "If you were Joe DiMaggio, I'd ask you to my place for a beer."

"But I'm not Joe DiMaggio."

Things were rapidly getting worse. "I mean, you don't know me."

"DiMaggio wouldn't know you either."

She sure wasn't making it easier for me. "I mean, well, you're a woman."

"Yeah," she said.

"I mean, you have to be careful."

"So does DiMaggio," she said. "You might turn out to be some kind of queer."

"Oh, no," I said.

"I said *might*," she said. "But that would make it all right for me to go to your place."

"Yeah," I said. I felt a little sick.

"Or I might not be interested in men—look how big I am."

I must have looked as stunned as I felt.

"I guess you're interested in women," she said. "And I only said *might*. You have to touch all the bases, you know."

That put her one up, because in spite of her *might* I still didn't know if she was interested in men. I wished to hell she had kept quiet. It had never occurred to me in spite of her size and in spite of the way she could make me forget when I watched her play.

"Put up your hand," she said.

I was caught off guard and flung up my hand to ward off a blow.

"No," she said, "like this." She had her elbow resting on the broad shelf of the refreshment stand outside the closed hatch. She wanted to arm-wrestle.

"ok," I said. I put down my elbow and clasped her hand—it

was not at all like clasping a man's hand. Immediately she began to put on pressure. Nothing sudden. Just letting me know she wasn't wasting any time. For a while then she let me build up the tension, and she just held. My arm began to tremble. Then she pressed my arm down. It didn't seem to take a special effort. I couldn't feel a tremor in her arm. Surely there was no change of expression on her face.

I laughed—or tried to. "Step right up and call her Joe DiMaggio," I said.

"Make that Joan," she said. "OK," she said, "now we both know that, let's forget about it, OK?"

"Sure," I said, although it wasn't the kind of thing I was likely to forget.

"Now, do you still want to go to your place for a beer?"

"Oh," I said. "Yeah. Sure."

At the door of my apartment building I noticed that I automatically stepped back so she could go first and that she as automatically went on ahead. She clumped up the stairs in her baseball shoes as if she were on her way to the Yankee locker room. But those tight-ass shorts going on before were a different matter altogether. Those bare legs. On her right thigh there was a large angry scrape where she had slid into second, a picture-book slide. I was about to say I hoped it wasn't too sore—Gee, Joe, that's some raspberry—but I stopped in time. Not that she probably would have minded. In fact, I suppose she would have been more likely to knock me down if I had said something that showed I hadn't been enjoying her legs.

I told her to make herself at home while I went to the kitchen. When I came back with two bottles of beer—I wouldn't have given DiMaggio a glass—she had taken off her spikes and was coiled into my easy chair, very womanly.

"Did you see that play in the third inning?" she said.

"The pick-off?" I said.

"Right."

"She was out," I said.

"She never got back to the bag," she said. "I was back there and took the throw before she got turned around."

"Nice pickup," I said.

"Worst throw she's made all year." Her right hand, hanging over the arm of the chair, made a little scooping motion—she was left-handed, something else I liked about her—and she seemed quite pleased with herself.

"The umpire was out of position," I said.

"He was looking at the shortstop's ass," she said. "The creep. I know him."

"Well, anyway," I said, "now you can sit back and figure your batting average."

"Three eighty-seven," she said.

"Including tonight's game?"

"Sure. I went two for three. I figured it at the bank this afternoon on the machine."

"You mean you really planned two for three?"

"Of course not." She frowned at me. "I figured 0 for one and one for one and 0 for two and one for two and two for two. Like that."

"So it was a good season," I said.

"I wanted to break four hundred," she said.

"So did DiMaggio," I said.

"The last four-hundred hitter was Ted Williams," she said.

"Right," I said. "Four-0-six in '41."

"Right," she said. We drank to that and were silent in admiration of the Splendid Splinter.

I couldn't think of any way to go on, so I had to go back. "Jesus Christ never batted four hundred," I said.

"He had a bad year," she said.

"Babe Ruth said that."

"I know," she said, "about the president."

"That was why the Babe made more money than the president," I said. We looked at each other for just a second as if we had exchanged the secret handshake. Then we took small drinks of our beer.

"Did you ever play?" she said at last.

"High school," I said.

"I thought so," she said. "Not since then?"

"I hurt my shoulder," I said. "I can't throw."

"Tough luck," she said.

"I was diving for a shot over the bag—I didn't even get it."

"First base?" she said.

"Right," I said.

"Left-handed?"

"Right," I said. "I mean, yes." We exchanged another small look. "I wouldn't dare play the way you do."

"I've got good reflexes," she said.

"Great hands," I said. She held them up and we both admired them. They were long and slender, very very long fingers. What people call artist's hands. They were lovely and soft looking, and I knew exactly how strong they were.

"What kind of hitter were you?" she said.

"Not much," I said. "I usually managed my hit a game."

"Say two-fifty."

"About that," I said.

"It might have got better if you could have worked on it."

"Oh, sure," I said. "Have another beer?"

"Why not?" she said. I brought the beer. "I work at it all the time. Study films of my swing. Films of great hitters. Williams for one. Around the first of the year I'll start in the batting cage over at the college. Next year is going to be the four-hundred year."

"Right on, brother," I said. She didn't notice, and I didn't either—or at least not much.

We drank all the beer in my refrigerator. Before I could offer to drive her home, she said, "I'll jog home now. It helps me sleep."

Next morning I fumbled with my mailbox and watched her fill the bank's pouch. Those thighs. Those silken knees. And hands, quick and light and sure, bright red nails. Her loose hair swinging low so that I couldn't see her face. When she stood up she turned the other way and walked briskly out of the post office. Her spike heels very loud on the marble floor.

# Big Bend

BILL ROORBACH

From *Big Bend* (2001)

That night Mr. Hunter (the crew all called him Mr. Hunter) lay quietly awake two hours before the line of his thoughts finally made the twitching conversion to mirage and hallucination that heralded ease and melting sleep.

Primarily what had kept him up was a worry that he was being too much the imperious old businessman, the self he thought he'd conquered, even killed in retirement, the part of himself poor Betty had least admired (though this was the part that brought home the bacon). This area of worry he packaged and put in its box with a resolution to ask only questions for at least one day of work, no statements or commands or observations or commentary no matter what, to Stubby or anyone else, no matter what, questions only.

Secondarily, Stubby, who was now asleep and snorting in the next bunk of their rather nice but rustic staff accommodations here at Big Bend National Park. Stubby was not hard to compartmentalize, particularly: Mr. Hunter would simply stop laughing with or smiling at or even acknowledging Stubby's stupid jokes and jibes, would not rise to bait (politics primarily), would not pretend to believe Stubby's stories, especially those about his exploits with women. Scott was Stubby's actual name, his age fifty-three, an old hippie who'd never cut his ponytail or jettisoned the idea that corporations were ruining the world and who called the unlikely women of his tall tales "chicks" and "chiquitas." Strange bedfellows, Stubby and Mr. Hunter, having gotten the only two-bed room in the worker's dorm by dint of advanced age.

Thirdly, Martha Kolodny of Chicago, here in blazing, gorgeous, blooming, desolate Big Bend on an amateur ornithological quest. Stubby called her Mothra, which at first was funny, given Ms. Kolodny's size and thorough, squawking presence, but which was funny no longer, certainly, given the startling fact of Mr. Hunter's crush on her, which had arrived unannounced after his long conversation with her just this evening and in the middle of a huge laugh from the heart of Ms. Kolodny's heart, a huge and happy hilarious laugh from the heart of her very handsome heart. The Kolodny compartment in his businesslike brain he closed and latched with a simple instruction to himself: *Do not have crushes, Mr. Hunter.* He was too old for crushes (sneakers, he'd called them in high school, class of 1945). And Ms. Kolodny not the proper recipient of a crush in any case, possibly under forty and certainly over one hundred fifty pounds, Mr. Hunter's own lifelong adult weight, and married, completely married, a stack of two large rings on the proper finger, large gemstones blazing.

Fourthly, fifthly, sixthly, seventhly, eighthly, up to numbers uncountable, many concerns, placed by Mr. Hunter carefully one by one in their nighttime lockers: the house in Atlanta (Arnie would take care of the yard and the gardens, and Miss Feather would clean the many rooms as always in his absence); the neglect of his retirement portfolio (Fairchild Ltd. had always needed prodding, but had always gotten the job done, and in the last several years spectacularly); the coming Texas summer (he'd lived through hot summers in more humid climes); his knee (but his knee hadn't acted up at all—he was predicting, and predicting was always a mistake and a manufactured basis for worry and to be abolished except when proceeding from reasonable evidence, of which there was none in this case, his knee having been perfect for nearly thirty years since surgery after hyperextension in tennis).

Many concerns, more and less easily dismissed, and overshadowed all of them by Bitty (he always called her): Betty, his wife, his girl, his one and only love, his lover, his helpmate, his best friend, mother of their three (thoroughly adult) children, dead of stroke three years. They'd planned all they'd do when he retired, and when he did retire she died. So he was mourning not only her loss but the loss of his long-held vision of the future, the thought that one distant day she would bury him. No compartment big enough to compartmentalize Bitty, but a kind of soft peace like sleep when he thought of her now and no longer the sharp pains and gouged holes everywhere in him and the tears every night. Count your blessings, Mr. Hunter, he had thought wryly, and had melted a little at one broad edge of his consciousness, and had soon fallen asleep in the West Texas night.

The United States Forest Service hired old people—senior citizens—as part of their policy of nondiscrimination based on age and so forth, pleasant jobs at above minimum wage. And because they didn't accept volunteers for the real, honest work that Mr. Hunter had decided to escape into for a salutary year, he signed on for pay, though he certainly didn't need the money. And here in Texas Mr. Hunter found himself, rich as Croesus and older, shoveling sand up into the back of the smallest dump truck he'd ever seen, half shovels so as not to hurt his back, and no one minded how little he did: he was old in the eyes of his fellows on the work crew, a seventy-something, as Stubby razzed him, $6.13 an hour.

The crew was motley, all right: Mr. Hunter, assumed to be the widower he was, assumed to be needy, which of course he was not. In fact, the more he compared himself to his new colleagues the wealthier he knew himself to be: Dylan Briscoe, painfully polite, adrift after college, had wanted to go to Yellowstone to follow his ranger girlfriend, was assigned here last summer, lost girl, met new girl, spent winter in Texas with Juanita from Lajitas, a plain-spoken Mexican-American woman of no beauty, hovered near Mr. Hunter on every job, and gave him his crew name because constitutionally unable to associate the word Dennis with such an old geezer; Freddy, a brainy, obnoxious jock taking a semester off from the University of Alabama, fond of beer, leery of Mr. Hunter, disdainful of Stubby, horrible on the subject of women ("gash," he called them collectively), resentful of work, smelling of beer from the start of the day, yet despite all well-read and decently educated; Luis Marichal, the crew boss, about whom much was assumed by the others (jail, knife fights, mayhem) but of whom little was actually known, who was liked awfully well by all, despite his otherness, for saying "Quit complaining" in a scary voice to Freddy more than once and who for Mr. Hunter had a gentle smile always; finally, Stubby, short and fat and truly good humored. Nothing had needed to be assumed about Stubby, for Stubby told all: he'd recently beat a drug habit, was once a roadie for the Rolling Stones, had been married thrice, had a child from each marriage, had worked many tech jobs in the early days of computers, had fallen into drink after the last divorce or before it, then cocaine, then heroin, had ended up in the hospital four months in profound depression, had recovered, had "blown out the toxins," had found that work with his hands and back made him sane, and sane he was, he said. This work crew in Texas had made him so.

$6.13 an hour all of them, excepting Dylan, hired on some student-intern program with a lower payscale, too shy to ask for parity, and of course excepting Luis, who'd been crew here many years though he wasn't thirty, and was foreman—Luis made probably nine bucks an hour, with four young kids to support. And in a way excepting Mr. Hunter, who in addition to his $6.13 an hour from the Seniors-in-the-Parks Program was watching his retirement lump sum grow into a mountain in *eight figures*. His $6.13 and a great deal more he was feeding purposefully back to Luis in deals on genuinely exquisite paintings by Luis's tubsome wife, improbably named Cleopatra, religious tablitas of the sort Bitty had loved so well, and so Dennis Hunter.

And Dennis shoveled sand with the rest of them, a wash of sand from the last big rain that had made nearly a dune in the shoulder of the road for a hundred yards, a dune dangerous to bicyclists and this a national park, so the crew shoveling into the small dump truck, Luis driving, if rolling the truck ahead a few feet at a time could be called driving. Dennis Hunter in comfortable and expensive relaxed-fit jeans, shoveling, which he preferred to the jobs the other Senior Program folks got: cashier at the postcard stand, official greeter, filing associate, inventory specialist, cushiony nonsense along those lines.

"Fucking say-and," Freddy said. "Endless fucking say-and. Why don't they drive down the backloader?"

"Then only one person would have a job," Stubby told him with elaborate superciliosity. "Five of us are cheaper than the machine to run. Even ten would be. Don't you wish your only job away, Homecoming King."

"Fucking endless fucking desert of fucking say-and," Freddy said.

"Quit that bitching," Luis said.

"Spic," Freddy said, under his breath such that Mr. Hunter heard. No excuse, an educated boy like that.

"It is nice and cool today," said Dylan, peacemaker.

"What kind of work would you most prefer, Frederick?" said Mr. Hunter slyly.

"Love slaaaave to Sharon Stone," Freddy said unwryly.

"She's like, my age," Stubby said.

"She wouldn't like no Freddy," Luis said.

They shoveled a while and Dylan was right; it was a good day for it, cool under high cloud cover, a rare day of breezes in the desert. Around them here in April after a wet winter all was in bloom: prickly pear, cholla, century plants, scores of others, colors picked from the sunset and the sandstone cliffs and the backs of birds.

"Lovely here indeed," Mr. Hunter said.

"I'd fuck her so fie-est," Freddy said.

"I'm not so sure women like it fast," Stubby said slowly.

"From Freddy, fast is the only way woman gonna like it," Luis said. "The faster the better, and gone."

Freddy grew redder, but didn't say it. He'd said it once early on and Luis had scared him, just a look in his eyes that Freddy was not going to forget. Alabama football: tough. Texas border town: tougher.

Stubby put a cheek on the handle of his shovel, grew dreamy in a way familiar to all of them: "Sticky Fingers tour one time I swear I was crating the JBL's when this little spacey chick comes up under the tower and squeaks, like, Where's Mick? and she was so sincere and I go, Mick's already in the Concorde flying home, baby, and she goes, You *know* him? And I did know him a little, of course. I go, He's a nice man, a little vain. And I look down and realize she's got her shirt off and she's got these goofy little boobs and she's dancing and taking her pants down. If Mick's not around, she's thinking I'm good enough!"

"Yeah, right," Freddy said.

"And she goes, The show got me so hot. And we go back behind the speakers and I swear her goofy little bush is trimmed off shape of a heart and she's sopping as the bog end of a beaver pond and I take her behind those crates and . . ."

"Penthouse Letter," Dylan said, risking all, and Mr. Hunter laughed for him, and Luis, though Mr. Hunter and probably Luis had no idea what the referent of the joke actually was. Dylan needed the laughs badly, soaked them up.

The Stones groupie turned out to be a long story, her twin sister and all, and everyone teased Stubby and threw shovelsful of sand up into the bed of the small dump truck, none of them working hard, but together making progress down the road, exposing its shoulder wetly.

"Oh Lord, I gotta dip this thang," Freddy said.

"You take off the gas cap," Luis said.

"Fuck a truck," Stubby said, and everyone laughed and laughed, as if this were the wittiest crack ever made.

Such an inefficient team! The likes of which would in the past have made Mr. Hunter smolder. But he shoveled as lightly as anybody and did not laugh at Stubby's stories and thought of Martha Kolodny for no reason he could make sense of, her laugh from the center of her heart and soul and her large frame that oughtn't to be alluring to him at all but was indeed. And her braininess—intelligence always was sexy to him. She was smart as Bitty and as quick, though Bitty would have called her noisy.

Luis said, "Dylan, what about you? Who is your perfect *mujer*?"

And Dylan blushed and said, "Juanita," with evident pride and huge love for her.

And everyone at once said, "Juanita from Lajitas," which was fun to say and which had become a chant and which they knew Dylan liked a lot to hear. Not even Freddy from Alabama would say anything that might harm Dylan-boy's spirit at all.

"You are like me," Luis said. "A steady heart and a solid love."

And Stubby, damn him, said, "Mr. Hunter, what about you?"

"Have you noticed that I'm only asking questions today?" said Mr. Hunter.

"But I saw you stalking Mothra. Mothra, Queen of the Bird-watchers Bus. She's a cute one, she is. Tall drink of water, she is. I'll bet she was one athlete in her day! Iron Woman! Anchor in the Freestyle Relay! Bench press 200 pounds, easy. What do you say, Mr. Hunter? You were gabbing with her nearly three hours yesterday in the parking lot there. You were! No, no, sir, you were! You're a better man than I! More power to ya! She won't give me the time of day, you she's laughing and shouting and joking! And she was scratching her nose the whole time, which Keith Richards once told me is the sure sign you're going to get a little wiggle in."

And all work (such as it was) ceased. Mr. Hunter made a game smile and smiled some more and enjoyed the breeze and the attention, really. He asked a question: "Do you know that right at the beginning of Plato's *Republic* there's a discussion of just this subject, of love and sex? And do you know that one of the fellows sitting around Socrates says something like, *I saw Sophocles*—the old poet, he calls him—*I saw the old poet down in town the other day, three score and ten, and I asked him: At your age, Sophocles, what of love?* And do you know what Sophocles told that man? Sophocles told that man: *I feel I have been released by a mad and furious beast!*"

The crew stood with eyebrows raised a long time, absorbing this tale from the mysterious void of time that was Mr. Hunter's life.

After a long silence, Stubby said, "Oh, fuck you."

Mr. Hunter knew what Stubby meant: the implied analogy was faulty. And Stubby was right. Martha Kolodny was certainly on Mr. Hunter's mind, Martha Kolodny of all women, and the mad and furious beast had hold of Mr. Hunter certainly. And though it wasn't like he'd had no erections in the past affectionless three years, the one he'd had this morning had caught his attention surely. And it wasn't all about erections, either, it was that laugh from the heart and the bright conversation and something more: Martha Kolodny could *see* Mr. Hunter, and he hadn't been seen clearly in three years nor had his particular brand of jokes been laughed at nor had his ideas been praised, nor had someone noticed his hair like that (still full it was, and shiny, and bone-in-the-desert white), nor looked at his hands so, nor gazed in his eyes.

At the Thursday Evening Ranger's Program a very bright young scientist lectured about Mexican fruit bats with passion, somewhat mollifying Dennis Hunter's disappointment. Oh, in the growing night the assembled travelers and Rangers and tourists and campers and workers (including Stubby) did see bats as promised. And among the assembled listeners there were a number of birders from Martha Kolodny's bus. But Martha was not among them.

Dennis Hunter lurked on a back bench in clean clothes—Hong Kong–tailored white shirt, khaki pants, Birkenstocks (ah, retirement), eight-needle silken socks—trying to remember how long Martha had said her birding group would be here. Till April 17, was the date he remembered, almost his second daughter's birthday, his second daughter who was, yes, about Martha's age. Five more days, only five. That bats don't get in your hair, that they have sonar, that they are rodents—all this was old news.

Then there was a sweeping presence and a suppressed laugh from deep inside the heart of someone's capacious heart and Martha stood just beside him. "May I sit?" she said. This was a whisper, but still louder in Dennis's ear than the Ranger's lecture. She sat on his bench and slid to his side like an old friend, got herself settled, deep and quiet, perfume expansile, put her chin in the air and raised her eyebrows, seemed to try to find her place in the stream of words as the passionate Ranger introduced a film.

The heavy narration covered the same ground the lecture had, with less fervor and erudition, but the pictures of bats were pleasing to watch, all sorts of camera tricks and lighting tricks and slow-motion tricks and freeze-frames and animation. Bats streaming out of Carlsbad Caverns, not eight hours from here. "Always wanted to see that," Martha said, leaning into Dennis. "Always, always."

"I thought for you it was birds," Dennis said.

Martha put a hand to her nose, scratched. "Whatever has wings," she said. Her other hand was on the bench close between them, and she leaned on it so her head was not a breath away from Dennis's. He smelled her shampoo, coconut and vanilla. Her henna-red hair, braided back into a thick lariat, her strong chin, the strong slope of her nose, her deep tan, her wrinkles from laughing from the heart of her, her wide shoulders, loose white shirt—all of it, all of her, was in his peripheral vision as he watched the film, which was more truly peripheral though he stared at it, her many scents in his nostrils, inside him.

Last night they'd taken care of the small talk: Martha Kolodny was an arts administrator, which title Dennis pretended not to understand, though he knew well enough what it meant: she was the kind of person he'd disdained in his years as marketing wizard at Pfizer (years he then told her about). He'd felt the truth talking to Martha of something Bitty had said once: he had really grown up after sixty-five. Martha had patiently explained that she ran a grantswriting office that helped provide funding—not such huge figures as Martha seemed to think—for several arts organizations, the Chicago Lyric Opera among them. Dennis Hunter could surely appreciate the Lyric Opera if not so much the private foundations that made individual grants to artists smearing excrement on flags and Bibles.

Martha herself had once danced—modern dance—with high hopes. She was too *big*, she had said daintily, "My teachers always said I was too *big*." And she had laughed that laugh that came from the heart of her heart and smote Dennis.

Her husband was a medical scientist at Northwestern, both a Ph.D. and an M.D. His first name was Wences. He was first-generation Polish. He was working on neuroreceptors, about which Dennis knew a thing or two, from years with the drug company. The couple had no kids, for they'd married rather late, after (at her age) kids were impossible. Wences and she barely saw each other. For them, the passion had fled. "I'm caught," she had said. "I'm caught in an *economic arrangement.*" Her eyes had been significant, Dennis thought.

The film ended abruptly. The Ranger-scientist took the podium in the dark that followed. A spotlight hit his face. Martha sat up, looked at Dennis fondly; that was the only word for how she looked at him, like an old friend. She whispered, "One Batman joke from this boy and we're out of here!"

And in a television voice the Ranger said, "That's the Bat Signal, Robin."

"That's it," Martha said, feigning great shock. She rose and took Dennis's hand and pulled him ungently to his feet and the two of them left the natural amphitheater and were soon striding along a rough path that led into the Chisos Mountains night.

"I knew you'd be at the talk!" Martha said.

"I'm not there now," Dennis said.

She said, "I can't get you out of my head!" She was breathless from the walk. They pulled up at the end of a looping path that looked out over the great basin of the Rio Grande under brilliant stars, under coruscating stars.

"I shoveled sand all day with the boys. Thinking of you."

"I love when you grin just like that," said Martha hotly

But you are married, Dennis thought to say. He held the words back forcibly: what if she didn't mean anything romantic at all? What an awful gaffe that would be!

They looked out into the blackness of the valley and up into the depths of space and were quiet a long ten minutes. "Mexico over there," Dennis said.

"You know you can rent a canoe and paddle across the Rio Grande to Mexico for lunch? No customs inspection necessary."

He said, "Someone did say that. And at the hot springs, apparently, you can swim across pretty easily. But no lunch."

"Unless you brought your own," Martha said.

"And the hot springs are very nice, too, I hear. Nice to soak in, even in the heat, I hear." He'd heard all this from Freddy in the grossest terms, Freddy who said it was the place he'd bring a *bitch*, if there were anything but *stanking* javelinas around here.

"Do you hear that snorting?" Martha said, as if in league with his thoughts.

"Javelina," said Dennis. He couldn't help the grin. Javelina was the Spanish for what Americans called banded peccaries, Dennis knew, like little pigs, partially tame, sturdy little wild pigs that patrolled the parking lots and restaurant dumpsters around here for scraps. They were more cute than threatening, though there were stories of mayhem among tourists as scary as the bear stories in Glacier Park.

"There's worse in Chicago," said Martha, meaning just that she wasn't afraid.

"In Atlanta we have bombers and disgruntled office workers," said Dennis.

"Somehow I knew you'd be here," said Martha softly.

"I would like to kiss you," Dennis said. He'd forgotten entirely how this sort of thing was done, knowing just that now—this he'd read—now in the twenty-first century, one got permission for everything, each step, before proceeding.

"I told my husband I wouldn't mess around with anyone while I was in Texas," Martha said. Then, less lightly: "That's the shambles our marriage is in."

"Well, Martha, darling, a kiss is certainly not necessary to a good friendship," Dennis said, glad he'd asked and not just acted to a rebuff and embarrassment, though he was embarrassed enough.

But Martha kissed him, full on the lips, and he was glad for the Listerine he'd swilled and glad life hadn't ended and glad to remember all the electrical connections and brightened cells and glowing nerves he indeed was remembering from the bottom of his feet to the tip of his tongue as he kissed her and was kissed.

They talked and necked—no better expression for it—for an hour under the stars.

"Well," Dennis said, "I'm afraid, despite best intentions, you have kissed in Texas." He felt badly for Wences Kolodny.

"But I have not messed around," breathed Martha.

"On technicalities are the great cases won."

She said, "Do you want to take a little swim to Mexico tomorrow?"

"I'll unpack my swimming trunks."

"I said nothing to Wences about messing around in Mexico."

"That isn't funny to me," Dennis said.

But they kissed till near eleven, when the Chicago birders' bus loaded quickly and headed back to the birders' hotel on the outskirts of the enormous national park.

Dennis walked back to the workers' dorm with feelings he hadn't had in fifty years, pain both physical and metaphysical, elation sublime, ambivalence scratching and snarling like some enraged animal under his squeaky cot.

Mr. Hunter no longer had the physical strength of his estimable colleagues on the work detail, but they had not his old man's stamina. With his steady work all day he outperformed the college boys, though Stubby could do more than the whole crew did all of most days in a single hour when he got inspired, which he did just before lunch this day, Friday. Stubby worked like a dog and demon and an ox, worked as if possessed: every cliché applied. He said, "We don't want Luis in trouble if this sand ain't up and off the road, boys!" They'd got about a quarter of it up the day previous, and already by noon this day two quarters more.

And this day, my God, it was hot. Plain, blazing sun. Mr. Hunter wore $400 chinos and a Gramicci T-shirt. His enormous Mexican straw hat (two hours pay at the tourist store in Terlingua) bobbed about his head to general hilarity, a foolish hat, but it kept him from falling over with heatstroke. The rest of the boys wore shorts and baseball caps, no shirts, and roasted in the sun, all of them except Dylan, who covered himself well against skin cancer years hence and advised the same for all, daily. Freddy the Homecoming King was going to be one spotted and speckled and scarred old geezer if he ever got past forty running his car dealership or his insurance agency: already he was burned crimson and sweating angrily. Stubby's Herculean flinging of sand into the little dump truck seemed to have caught the corner of Freddy's competitive instinct, and Freddy's competitive instinct trumped his more general laggardly nature every time. The kid *worked*, he actually *worked*. He said, "Fucking say-and!"

Luis shoveled too: that sand really did need to be up today, for Monday they started trail maintenance, and no excuses. Mr. Hunter got to sit in the truck and roll it forward down the slight hill in tiny and perfect increments, pumping the heavy clutch, worrying about his knee, then sitting there in the dry heat, no breeze, drinking from the great cooler of water, dispensing water to the other men when they came to his door.

At lunchtime the younger crew climbed on top of the damp load of sand for the ride back up into the mountain. Mr. Hunter slid over so Luis could drive. And the wind was pleasant, if hot, and the view was spectacular: otherworldly landscape, baked sand, a plane of cactus, bright cliffs of sandstone and limestone, old reefs in yellows and purples and blues and reds.

Mr. Hunter said, "Before I leave here, Luis, I would like to commission Cleopatra to do a large painting along the lines of the one you showed me in the Boquillas chapel. With that hunched angel hovering over Mary, do you know? And the little bald man."

"Santo Sebastiano," said Luis, crossing himself. "I will suggest it to her."

"I mean truly, the same size as the one you showed me in the chapel."

"That is large, Mr. Hunter. Where in your room could it go? And this would be a hard work for Cleopatra, weeks of time. For the chapel it was a gift, but you are not Jesus." He smiled like the only visitor to a hospital bedside: pity and sorrow and self-satisfaction.

"I am only a man, it's true. But I will pay five thousand for the painting, and extra to pack it and arrange for shipping to Atlanta."

"Did you rob a bank?" Luis loved to probe Mr. Hunter's wealth. He alone among the crew had noted the cut of the clothing, the whiter skin where an embarrassingly rich watch had lain, the quality of even the work shoes Mr. Hunter wore on detail, the gold covering all his back teeth, the tidy precision of his knee scars, this mystery of a rich man at common labor.

Mr. Hunter smiled with Luis: "Your wife's paintings are worth no less."

The crew dumped the small truck's twelve yards of sand at the head of the Gorge Trail, where next week they'd make use of it repairing a season of washouts and collapses and violated switchbacks. And one hundred yards up the trail, in the shade of a juniper tree, sitting each upon his own rock and looking out over the long gorge to a sliver of the Rio Grande and thence into Mexico, the crew ate lunch, each in his style: Stubby a huge sandwich of cheeses and sprouts and peppers and who knew what vegetarian excesses on thick bread he'd baked himself; Dylan a plain tortilla wrapped around beans; Luis a small feast packed in a series of paper bundles by Cleopatra, tortillas and three kinds of beans and slivers of meat and roasted peppers and whole tiny avocados and an orange and several whole tomatoes and tamales in cornhusks and more, always more; Freddy, poor bigoted kid, a single enormous bag of barbecue potato chips from the PX and his usual ungrateful snacking from Luis's bounty. Mr. Hunter didn't eat lunch, not anymore, but had a few samples of Cleopatra's cooking, marvelous.

As the crew settled down into what should normally have been something like a siesta, Stubby turned to Mr. Hunter. He said, "Where did you and the bird lady go last night when you left the lecture so early?"

"Why is it you ask?" Mr. Hunter said wryly, as the attention of the crew fell pleasingly upon him.

"I was only worried, is all," said Stubby, even more wryly.

After a long silence Luis grinned and said, "Tell us, Sophocles, old poet, what of love?"

"Love!" Stubby said. "You should have smelled our room in the night! What perfume! And perfume, my brothers, does not rub off without some rubbing!"

Still wryly—there was no other safe tack to take—Mr. Hunter said, "Do you imply that it is wrong for an old man to seek romance?"

"Not s'long as it's with an old lady," Freddy said.

"She's not as old as all that," said Stubby. "She's not yet my age, and I'm a youth, as you can see."

"Is she over forty?" Dylan said helpfully. He got embarrassed, bit into his burrito, looked out over the dry valley of the Rio Grande.

"Ah, forty!" Stubby said. "Forty is the youth of old age and the old age of youth!"

Freddy said equably, "How old are y'all, anyway, Mr. Hunter?" He leaned a long way, gave a short smile, reached and took another of Luis's tortillas.

"Three score and fourteen," Mr. Hunter said. "Seventy-four. The youth of death, I would say, if pressed."

"Y'all? No way. You don't fucking look it!" Freddy said.

And Dylan, too: "You don't even look sixty!"

And Stubby: "You do to me! You look sixty as hell, and that's a compliment!"

"What of love, Sophocles?" Luis said again.

Mr. Hunter could not help himself. He beamed. He said, "Do any of you really believe my private hours are any of your business?"

Stubby: "Do we not have the right to learn from those older than us and do you, Mr. Hunter, not have the duty to teach us?"

"Tay-ake her to Viagra Falls," Freddy said.

"Mr. Hunter has twice the cactus you have, hombre," said Luis.

"It's not all about sex," Dylan said.

"Thank you, Dylan," said Stubby. "And do tell us: What is it all about?"

"Blow jobs," Freddy said animatedly.

Dylan shrugged Freddy's coarseness off. He thought of Juanita (this you could see in his reverent face). He said slowly, "Closeness. Is what it's about."

But Mr. Hunter didn't mind that some part of this was indeed about sex, and that sex was certainly perhaps some of the closeness he was missing, and further, had the enlivening notion that sex and he might be in the same place this evening if he got off work early enough. But then there was the trouble, the trouble that had awakened him so early this morning and that would not be shut off in its compartment: "Gentlemen, let me state the problem: Martha is married. And my conscience tells me not to proceed, even as my heart says go."

"And what of thy pecker?" said Stubby, triply wry.

"My pecker says go," said Mr. Hunter, which made everyone

laugh. He had never spoken like this to them and indeed not in his life.

"Then listen, brainiac," said Freddy: "Go for it!"

No laughter at this. Just an expectant turning to Mr. Hunter, who said nothing, sagging a little.

"Listen to your conscience," said Luis. "Listen well. If you spoke this way of Cleopatra, I would kill you just for speaking. For the doing I'd kill her, as well."

"Then y'all'd be single again, at least," Freddy said.

"Hey, I don't know," Stubby said. "This woman, this bird-watcher, Mothra, obviously she's looking for something her marriage isn't giving her. She's taking power here. She's taking care of her needs. She's unfulfilled. Who's to say she should honor this husband, who apparently does not honor her?"

Dylan said, "But she made a promise."

"What is the nature of the promise we make in marriage?" Mr. Hunter said. He tried to sound wry, playing Socrates, but this was too close to the heart of his worry, even under a tree in hot shade.

Dylan said, "That we should love, honor, and obey."

"The flesh is weak," Luis said opprobriously.

"The flesh has a job to do," Stubby said.

"I say, go for it," Freddy said.

A long silence in the windless day, punctuated erratically by the squawks of Mexican jays.

"I don't see how," said Mr. Hunter.

Freddy: "Well, the boy kisses the girl . . ."

And the crew, except for Luis, laughed. He said, "And what of your wife in heaven? What will happen when you see her there?"

"You're not really saying that," Stubby said, incredulous. "It's till death do you part. Man, come on."

"I agree with Stubby," Dylan said. "But still, the woman you're talking about is married!"

"Y'all should just go up to Juarez," Freddy said helpfully. "Soak that nut."

"It's not sex he's after," Dylan said bravely.

"Sure it is," Stubby said. He picked up a stone, weighed it, then flung it with an elegant arm into the chasm below them. "Get real. A man alone, a woman who likes him. I'm with Freddy: go for it."

"I notice that you say 'it,'" Dylan said. "But what of the woman, who is not an 'it'?"

"Go for *her*," Stubby said, conceding Dylan's point.

"I don't see how I really can," Mr. Hunter said.

"There are many women in the world," Luis said. "You do not need to break God's law."

The others, except Mr. Hunter, hadn't seen Luis as religious till now. The air grew more serious. Everyone stared off, each in his own thoughts.

Until this from Stubby: "Actually, there's probably more here than the moral question. You've really fallen for this chick, you know? How are you going to feel if it goes further and then— boom—she's off to Chicago and back to her husband? Leaves you alone! That's going to be a blow, Dennis!"

"When Tina broke up with me . . ." Freddy said. The others waited, but that was all he managed. Freddy looked off into the sky, and for the first time you could see his heart in his face and think of him as tender.

"There might be that kind of price," Stubby said.

"This is good advice," said Mr. Hunter. "I don't know if I could stand the aftermath of any one-night stand."

Stubby slid off his rock, leaned back against it, closed his eyes. Dylan lay down, chewing a twig. Luis stood, stretched, patted Mr. Hunter's shoulder, walked up the path to be alone. Luis prayed after lunch, Mr. Hunter knew. Freddy you might think was softly weeping if you didn't know what a tough customer he was.

Mr. Hunter had made up his mind: no married woman for him.

Martha an athlete, Stubby had joked, and so she was: forty-seven years old, Dennis Hunter's height and weight, and walked with the physical confidence of an athlete, looked in her shorts and stretch top as if she might jump up and fly at any moment. But in Dennis's little rental car her folded legs seemed delicate and soft. Her skin was beautiful to him, and her smell, and her voice. "I couldn't sleep all last night," she said.

"I could barely work today," he said.

The other talk on the hour's drive to Hot Springs Canyon was about the landscape of the park, and they didn't need to say much for looking at that landscape, the great buttes and cliffs and mesas miles away and unmoving. Martha read from her guidebook: "The park is 708,221 acres."

Dennis Hunter hadn't known that.

She read: "The Rio Grande was known to the Spanish conquistadors as the Great River of the North, and to the early pioneers as the River of Ghosts."

"I'm told this was Comanche territory," Dennis said. Luis had said so.

Martha nodded her head, then shook it, then nodded it. "Comanche country," she repeated, saying it from the heart of her heart, where her laughter came from.

Oh God, and Dennis felt his heart flowing out to her entirely, yet not leaving his rib cage at all. They drove slowly through the great basin of the River of Ghosts, past the Chisos Mountains. A pickup truck zoomed up from behind, passed easily, zoomed out of sight, New Mexico plates. Dennis thought about how easily he could declare his love and ask dear Martha her intentions. Perhaps Wences was out. Perhaps a split was imminent. How ask? Dennis said, "Chisos means something like ghostly in the Apache language." Luis had told him that, too.

Just quietly driving along, looking at the landscape. "Yes, it is," Martha said. "Ghostly, all right." She put her hands up in a gesture of amazement. She'd taken off her rings. "Living things don't belong here. Not people certainly."

Dennis felt himself and the car almost lifting off the pavement. Not that he was faint, not at all; he felt more present if anything, floating car and all, with warm blood in his air-conditioned face and something humming in him, thighs to lungs. She'd taken off her rings. Dennis had never taken his ring off, not once for any reason, not since the night it went on his finger, June 11, 1947.

He said, "I've seen javelina, mule deer, pronghorn antelope, and a gray fox since I've been here. Also, Luis showed me the droppings of a bobcat and a raccoon and owls."

And just then a roadrunner zipped diagonally across the road in front of them, stiff posture a little comical, even somehow portentous, even to pragmatic Dennis.

Martha Kolodny shifted a little toward him, really interested in what he'd seen and what he knew. She said, "I've seen a lot, too: roadrunner, elf owl, Harris's hawk (I saw a pair), Inca dove, ladder-back and golden-fronted woodpeckers, verdin, a hooded oriole maybe, pyrrhuloxia, vermilion flycatcher, a varied bunting (I think, I hope, my prize of the trip), an ash-throated flycatcher, canyon wrens (I heard them only), other wrens, a curved-billed thrasher, sage thrashers, many sparrows, a great-tailed grackle."

"You've got the list by heart," Dennis said, afloat in adoration.

She smiled, plainly pleased with his fascination and infatuation. She said, "All new additions to my life list and not one of which is found in Chicago, or much of anywhere but here."

In the small canyon where the hot springs lay they walked in the hot sun along sea-bed cliffs, striated layers of the ages thrown up by earth forces at odd angles. Martha heard immediately a great horned owl, and got it calling to her by hooting saucily. Dennis Hunter floated, he floated along the dry path and felt that Martha floated, too.

Together they inspected the abandoned ruins of the old hotel and store there, the hotel and store Martha had read aloud about from her booklet. Together they found the petroglyphs she'd read about, and walked along the path, a Comanche path that had become a commercial enterprise's trail to the hot springs, now but a park path for tourists. Martha took Dennis's hand. He wanted to declare his love. How old-fashioned he knew he was! She'd laugh at him, he thought, and this laugh would come from her teeth and not her heart.

The path descended between thick reeds and willows and the canyon wall. Soon Martha stopped, put a finger in the air. "Hear the river?"

Yes, Dennis heard it, a rushing sound ahead. Martha's hand in his, dry hands casually clasped, pressure of fingers in a small rhythm, a pulse of recognition: something profound between them.

A group of four British-sounding tourists with wet hair and mussed clothing came up the path. Their presence explained the one other car back at the end of the dusty and eroded canyon road. Dennis let go Martha's hand, oh, casually.

Approaching, a tall man with wire glasses said, "There's an owl up in the cliff." He pointed high in the sandstone bluff. "Just there."

Martha saw the big bird immediately, and pointed to it for Dennis's sake. When he saw it he was amazed at its size. He'd been seeking something smaller.

"Bloke's calling a mate," said the tall Britisher. His friends nodded.

A pretty young woman said, "We've heard her response."

And the owl, on cue, hooted spookily. Across the river came another bird's hoot.

Martha took Dennis's hand and pulled him along. "River of British Ghosts," she said.

Dennis couldn't get the words as the Rio Grande came into

view: "Doesn't it . . . isn't it . . . doesn't this just . . . *tickle* you?" That was pathetic. He thought and tried again: "This little sprite of a muddy river, this ancient flow, this reed-bound oasis? That this is the famous border?"

"Dennis, I don't know what to do."

"That that is Mexico over there?"

"May I see you in Atlanta?"

They stopped there on the plain and dusty rock—flat, polished sandstone, solidified mud really—they stopped and held hands and looked at the river and could not look at each other.

She said, "What is this between us?"

Dennis could think of a word for what was between them. It was passion, nothing less, on the one hand, and her husband, nothing less, on the other, both between them and no way to say a word at this moment about either. He let a long squeeze of her hand say what it could, then pulled her along. Brightly, he said, "I expected gun turrets and chainlink fence and border stations."

"Well, there's nothing but desert for hundreds of miles. They just don't watch much here."

Pleasingly, no other soul occupied the hot springs, a steady gush of very hot water rising up out of a deteriorated square culvert built a century past. The buildings were gone, swept away by floods, they must have been. But one foundation remained, and formed a sort of large bathtub, well, enormous, maybe the size of a patio. In the hot air of the day the water didn't steam at all. A kind of soft moss grew in there.

Martha sat on a rock and took her shoes off. Dennis liked her feet. He wondered if Wences liked her feet. He liked her knees very much. He liked that she was so strong and big, he did very much, so unlike Bitty, who was a bone. He liked the fatty dimpling of Martha's thighs in her black shorts. She dipped her feet in. "Wow, hot," she said.

"Maybe too hot for today?" Dennis said.

"No, no, it's wonderful! And then the river will feel cold," she said. "A blessing," she said. Then: "Well, no one's around." And she pulled off her shirt, just like that, and clicked something between her breasts to make her bra come loose, and shed it, then stepped out of her shorts and then her lacy panties (worn for him, he was startled to realize) and slipped into the hot water in a fluid motion, Dennis more or less looking away, looking more or less upward at the cliff (cliff swallows up there).

"I'm not sitting here alone," Martha said.

So Dennis tried a fluid kind of stripping like hers, but ended up hopping on one foot, trying to get his pants past his ankles, but stripped and hopped, and slid into the hot water, self-conscious about his old body, the way his skin had got loose, the spots of him.

"It's love between us," he said, which was not the same as declaring love. "And that you are married," he said.

"No touching in Texas," said Martha, far too lightly.

The water was shallow and she sat up to her waist and barebreasted in the hot water and not exactly young herself. The hot water was gentle and very hot and melted them both, turned them red like lobsters.

"Swim," said Martha. And she climbed out of the pool down old steps into the river and dropped herself into the current. Stroke stroke out of the current and she was standing on the bottom again, waist deep. She was forty-seven and married and standing waist deep and naked in the Rio Grande River not twenty feet from Mexico. Dennis felt her gaze, thought of his knee, considered Wences, heard Luis's stern voice, heard Freddy's (*Go for it*), heard Bitty's funny laugh, thought of his three children, heard his daughter Candy (*Daddy, I know mother would want you to date*) and followed Martha, climbed in the river after her, enjoying the cold of it after the scalding spring. Stroke, stroke, stroke, he was being swept away in the current, pictured himself washed up on a flat rock dead and naked miles downstream. But

Martha got hold of his hand laughing and they stood waist deep together in the stream rushing past, silty, sweetly warm water.

"I'll get our stuff," Martha said.

She swam back and bundled everything—large towels, clothes, binoculars, bottle of wine—and easily swam with one arm in the air till she was back by Dennis Hunter's side, holding the bundle all in front of her chest, dry, and if not absolutely dry, what difference? It would dry in seconds in the sun and parched air.

Suddenly she said, "The American Association of Arts Administrators conference is in Atlanta this June." They stood in the flow of the river. "I could stay a week with you," she said. "Maybe more. It's June. Two months from now, only."

"After that?" Dennis said.

Solemnly: "We shall see what we shall see." Then she laughed from the heart of the heart of her and Dennis laughed and stumbled and they made their way through the water to Mexico.

"I hope no one shoots us going back," Dennis said.

They made the rocky shore in Mexico and walked, not far, walked in Mexico until they were out of sight of the hot springs across the river, and right there under the late sun she spread the blanket and right there hugged him naked and the two older Americans in Mexico kissed and Dennis Hunter was a young man again—no, really—a boy in love, a tanned and buff shoveler of sand, a repairer of trails, a knower of animals, a listener to birds, anything but a widower alone in Atlanta the rest of his miserable days, miserable days alone.

# Sawtelle

DENNIS HATHAWAY

From *The Consequences of Desire* (1992)

Charles lay awake in the pale light of dawn thinking of his partner, Ben, and of the predicament—Ben's wife messing around with the neighbor kid, a nineteen-year-old who went to junior college and lifted weights and rode a Ninja. What, exactly, did Ben need? Advice? Sympathy? Charles shut his eyes and saw the yellow frame of the house that he and Ben had begun that week to wire, a big two-story house whose unfinished state seemed to mock his faith in the certainty of domestic arrangements. He listened to the slow rise and fall of his own wife's breath and its very regularity made him nervous. She had never given him reason to suspect that she could be unfaithful, and yet as he lay in the fading darkness, listening to the unchanging rhythm of her breath, he felt somehow distrustful, betrayed.

Driving his truck into a spreading flare of sunlight, Charles thought of how the news about Ben's wife had come as such a surprise, and what this meant about his own perception of reality. "You remember that night we went to the Aztec?" Ben had said to him, interjecting the question into the middle of an argument started for no reason that Charles could see, other than sheer contrariness, over the proper place to drive the ground rod for the electrical panel. Ben had managed to squeeze a lifetime's worth of portents into an hour that Charles could not recall as remarkable in any way, with the possible exception of the fact that Ben's wife had ordered a hamburger from the American part of the menu, claiming that Mexican food gave her indigestion. "It's coming right at you," Ben had said to Charles, his eyes glittering as if with fever. "Right at you in plain goddamn sight, but you can't see it, then smackeroo!"

Charles guided his truck through traffic beginning to clot into the morning rush, trying to review in his mind a list containing the conduit, connectors, the other things he needed to pick up at the supply house. He felt apprehensive. He wished almost desperately for the Ben of old instead of the Ben who showed up late and made dumb mistakes and lost his temper three times in a single day—once with the general contractor, once with the architect, and once with Charles, who surely took it more personally than the other two. He pulled into a parking lot crowded with vans and trucks. Against his will, he began to imagine how his wife would spend her day—drive their daughter to school with the baby strapped in the back, drop the baby at the sitter's and go to her exercise class, come home and eat lunch and put the baby down for a nap, spend a couple of hours doing company bookwork. Irritated by sudden unfounded suspicion and the clogged parking lot, he blew his horn at the driver of a van who was taking too much time to back out of a space.

At the counter inside he saw the faces of strangers, heard the unfamiliar voices of men he suspected of bidding low just to get some work, men who made it hard for those like Charles and Ben who had long since paid their dues. By the time he gave his order to the man at the counter he was unreasonably angry. The man was young, blonde, his hair pulled back into a ponytail. Charles wondered why a woman the age of Ben's wife would be attracted to such a man, hardly more than a boy. The young man didn't know what he meant by a servicehead coupler and Charles said, loudly enough for everyone to hear, that whoever worked the counter ought to at least know the names of the things they had in stock. "Let me talk to Leo," he said, but Leo, the manager, was on the phone, and Charles said, "Fuck it. I'll get it later," and walked out feeling at least as stupid as the kid, or Ben, for having lost his temper.

The house was going up on a leveled-off ridge above a canyon dense with chaparral, and on a clear day the view encompassed newly whitened mountains, the crowded-together buildings of downtown, and the long tan curve of the beach. This wasn't such a day, however; as Charles backed his truck inside the chain-link fence surrounding the house he could see nothing but a bluish haze beyond the tops of the eucalyptus trees that grew at the foot of the canyon. Ben was already there, his truck backed up to the pile of lumber scrap that the general contractor had promised to have hauled away, a high, messy pile that forced them to circle around, to waste a dozen steps to get inside the house. Through the space where a window would be Charles saw Ben bent over and small beneath the high, vaulted ceiling, nailing boxes to the studs. The face of Ben's wife passed vividly through his mind and he felt a chill of unease, wondering what he would say or do if he ran into her.

He skirted the pile of trash and entered the house. Just inside the doorway he saw a box nailed to a stud on the wrong side of the layout mark that he had made, but he decided not to say anything, not yet, anyway. Ben had shown up on time and was working instead of moping around or complaining or trying to start an argument, and for the moment at least Charles felt relieved, almost happy. He looked up at Kevin, the apprentice, who was on the ten-foot ladder drilling holes in the joists. He hadn't braced the drill the way that Charles and Ben had taught him; if the bit grabbed in the wood the handle could snap around and skin his knuckles, or sprain his wrist, or if he was really unlucky, break something. Charles thought, why isn't Ben on the drill and

Kevin nailing up the boxes, which is an easier job, less conducive to the chance of injury? He decided not to say anything, though. Who knew what might set Ben off? It must be tough, he thought. He imagined his wife, in the bed still warm where he had slept, in carnal embrace with the blonde young man at the supply house. Jesus, he thought.

"Hey," said Ben.

"Hey." Charles dropped the coil of conduit that he had carried in from his truck. Looking at Ben, whose mouth was a thin, hard line, he recalled for no obvious reason the moment, working as a journeyman in the union, that he had witnessed the aftermath of an electrocution. Christ, he said to himself, feeling a reprise of dormant emotion—fear, sadness, a queasy sickness in his gut. Get off it, he told himself, stop feeling so damn morbid. Again he thought of his wife, alone in the house, and again a feeling of betrayal seized him. But he was certain of her fidelity. Their marriage, like most, had gone through a rocky period or two, but in the year since the baby had come she had seemed content, less likely to complain about the hours he worked or other things that were out of his control. As for himself, he had never thought about adultery in any realistic way, had never considered acting out the fantasies that arose from urges temporary enough to suppress, to ignore.

He watched Kevin lean too far with the drill instead of getting down to move the ladder. Kevin wasn't a bad kid, he showed up on time, he didn't jerk off instead of working, he wasn't really dumb, but did have trouble absorbing the things that Ben and Charles tried to teach him. He was always nodding, humming, his body twitching to what Charles imagined was the music that they had forbidden him to play on the job site, heavy metal that was like a drill going right through Charles's head. When Charles gave Kevin instructions he sometimes had the urge to shout in order to cut through the noise inside the head that never seemed to stop nodding, swaying, rocking with a beat. He decided to bring Kevin down off the ladder before he got himself into a really dangerous position.

"Shultz was here," said Ben, arranging eight-penny nails heads-up in his palm. He was staring past Charles, through a wide opening that would become a doorway in the wall, out to where a mound of yellow earth rose beside the bowl-shaped excavation for the pool. Shultz was the general contractor, a man no older than Charles and Ben who drove a brand-new Bronco with a cellular phone and wore a beeper on his belt. "He wants us to get the feed in for the pool equipment. Today."

"Tell him to give us a trench." Charles felt in a hurry to get Kevin down off the ladder.

"He says it's in our contract." Ben picked up a box and held it in his other palm, staring as if it were something he had never seen before. Maybe he had gotten over losing his temper, Charles thought, and would now be in a state suggested by this oddly flat, unemotional tone.

"Shit," said Charles.

"Says we provide our own trench."

"Christ," said Charles. He had written the contract, and surely had excluded any trenching, because it took a jackhammer to get through the earth here, decomposed granite, hard, yellow, flaky stuff the hills all around were made of. A copy of the contract was in his briefcase in the truck. He wanted to get Kevin off the ladder, but instead he went to the truck and got out the contract and saw the line that his wife had typed stating that "others shall be responsible for trenching" and how someone had x'd out the word "others" and typed "subcontractor" above it. He shut his briefcase, breathing consciously, slowly. He went back inside, averting his eyes from the pile of scrap that made him go out of his way. He ordered Kevin off the ladder. He told Ben that Kevin should be nailing up boxes, that Ben should be on the ladder with the drill. He stared at Ben until Ben opened his hand and let the eight-penny nails rain to the floor. Ben was normally neat, almost to a fault, but Charles decided not to say anything about the nails. It was a bad example for Kevin, who stood watching, waiting to be shown what to do, but Charles felt the situation was somehow fraught with danger. He was afraid that Ben might explode, and that he might explode in return, and something might happen that both of them would regret, that would in some way be irrevocable.

"I'll go down and rent a jackhammer," he said. "I'll pick up a couple of laborers on Sawtelle." He took a deep breath and his chest felt tight. "How deep do we have to go?"

"Foot." Ben looked away again, staring at something, or nothing, an unpleasant picture in his head, his wife with the neighbor kid maybe.

"Foot-and-a-half," Charles said. "We'd better check the code."

"Twelve inches," Ben said. He said it with an obvious smirk and smutty tinge to his voice, as if describing a fabulous male member. The neighbor kid, thought Charles, feeling irrational. What did Ben's wife see in him, if it wasn't something like that? Sex. She was a year older than Charles, and to Charles's point of view Ben had always treated her at least as well as she deserved.

He got in his truck and drove a little too fast down the cool, shaded canyon toward the invisible mass of the city. Ben had two kids, both in school, and Charles wondered if they knew or understood what their mother was up to. He thought of his own daughter, a pretty, outgoing girl, and the thought of her carrying around the knowledge of her mother screwing a teenage boy made him feel turgid, almost ill.

At the bottom of the canyon he stopped at a minimarket and bought an orange juice and a newspaper to read at lunch and a six-pack of Cokes for everybody. The girl who took his money looked about eighteen, a little plump, a Latina with black eyes that glistened. Her fingers brushed his palm as she gave him his change and he felt a flutter in his chest. Back in the truck, in the slow, clotted traffic, he thought, yeah, it's easy enough to imagine. Getting it on with a girl like that. He knew that Ben, a few years back, had messed around with a woman whose house they had installed some smoke detectors in, a woman in the middle of a divorce, on the lookout for an immediate thrill that had materialized in the form of Ben, a decent-looking guy who could turn on a kind of charm that certain women seemed to find irresistible. To expect fidelity from Ben's wife and not from Ben was in some fundamental way unfair, he knew, and yet her violation seemed far more reprehensible than Ben's. Maybe she had known about Ben and the woman and had waited all this time for a chance to get her revenge. But Ben believed that she was unhappy. Why, he didn't seem to know.

Charles got a jackhammer at the rental yard and headed east, turning within the shadow of the elevated freeway onto a street lined nearly solid on either side with men who whistled and waved when they saw his truck, making him feel exposed, as if he were some sort of parade. He drove slowly, looking for two men alone. Men in larger groups stepped off the curb and beckoned aggressively, but Charles kept moving; he knew that if he stopped the men would immediately surround his truck, pound on the windows, and jump uninvited into the back, forcing him to pick out two from a dozen all desperate to be hired without even knowing what they would be asked to do. Finally he saw a pair by themselves, one short and stumplike, the other taller and thinner, with a straw hat shading his face. Charles pulled quickly to the curb, gestured with his head, and the men climbed into the back of his truck without the exchange of a single word. He swerved back into the traffic as others ran, shouting and waving their arms, toward him.

At the first stoplight the man with the hat leaned close to the open driver's window and said, "How much you pay?" He had to say it three times before Charles understood.

"Five," called Charles over his shoulder. *"Cinco."*

The man said nothing further, but then, heading into the cool shade of the canyon, Charles heard voices, and laughter, and he thought that things were askew, these men whose lives were surely fraught with hardship laughing together while he and Ben moped and sulked like adolescents who have every conceivable comfort but nevertheless decide that life is miserable and unfair. He tried to imagine getting up each morning to stand on the street with hundreds of other men, hoping against all odds to be noticed and hired to dig a ditch. With family, wife, and children, thousands of miles away. I'm lucky, he told himself. I'm doing what I want to do. I'm happy. It's just that sometimes nothing goes right. And this business of Ben and his wife had unsettled him, made him feel that everything he assumed to be predictable was suddenly up in the air, subject to the vagaries of chance, as in an earthquake, when the ground that everyone has always believed to be solid, immutable, begins to quiver and shake.

He showed the men how to run the jackhammer. With a shovel he drew a line in the dust. He knew only a smattering of Spanish, but communication on this level was a simple matter of handing over the shovel, pointing, and saying, *"Aquí."* He penciled a mark on a scrap of wood, showing how deep he wanted them to go. Eighteen inches. He was right. He began to think that Ben wasn't really holding up his end of the business, but then he stopped himself, he didn't want to feel disgruntled, disappointed in anyone. Not in Ben, who had the ability to keep track of thirty circuits in his head, who could always say with utter confidence which wires were neutral and which were hot, who could gaze upon the total chaos of an unwired panel and see all the circuit breakers in place, neatly labeled, doing their job. With all the conduits in, with all the wire pulled and the ends twisted and spliced inside the boxes, Charles would be able to stand in a room and see a kind of elegant simplicity and inevitability in the path the conduits took through the studs and joists, a reflection of an idea that had never existed on paper, only in

Ben's mind. To the owner of the house, of course, and to the architect, even to the general contractor, what mattered was not the craft or art of the work but the fact that a particular light go on when a certain switch was flicked, that current flow from an outlet to an appliance, that the job be finished without delay, without any extra charges.

Charles thought of an old man in the union, a foreman for whom he and Ben had worked, first as apprentices, then as journeymen, abiding his temperament because they had known, Charles guessed, that he had something important to teach them. "You don't be sloppy," the old man had said. "You don't cut corners just because your work is going to be covered up. You be even more careful, because you are the only ones who know what you have done."

They ate lunch outside, in the back, sitting on brittle yellow grass beside the crater that would become the pool. Charles had driven back down the canyon to the minimarket to buy burritos for the laborers. The clerk with the pretty black eyes had smiled at him, causing a little bump in his throat that seemed to sink down through his body on the way back to the house and became a leaden lump of dismay. Already they had fallen behind, at least half a day, and at the pace they were going they wouldn't get done for another week and a half and would be lucky if the money they got was enough to cover their labor and the materials.

Charles glanced at Ben, who had that look again, as if he were watching a movie inside his head. "We've got to pick it up," Charles said, uneasy, aware that Ben might lose his temper, start up his truck the way he had done on Monday after getting into an argument with Shultz and the architect, roar out in a storm of dust, and disappear. Charles looked at the laborers, dozing in a wedge of shade cast by a deck that cantilevered at an angle from the second floor of the house. "The son of a bitch changed the contract. I ought to call a lawyer," he said.

"You signed it," Ben said, in the flat, dry tone that he seemed to have adopted for the day.

"Yeah. He's still a son of a bitch."

"Read before you sign."

"You're telling me."

"How much?" They both looked at Kevin, stretched out in the sun asleep. He stayed out too late at night, drank too much beer, Charles guessed. But so did he, at that age. Who am I to judge? he thought. Kevin. Ben's wife. Anybody.

"Ninety for the jackhammer," he said. "Eighty for the laborers. If they get it done."

"They won't." In four hours, perhaps a third of the trench had been dug. The flaky ground was getting harder, too, the closer they got to the pool.

"Three fifty," said Charles.

"Your time," Ben said. "And gas."

"Four hundred." Charles felt irritation like sweat itching on his skin. He got up and went over to the jackhammer, which lay beside the trench in the thick, grainy dust that coated everything. He picked it up and squeezed the trigger, giving off a burst of noise that made the laborers sit up straight, blinking. He let the jackhammer drop and turned to see Kevin, still dead to the world, and Ben standing above him, foot drawn back as if to deliver a kick to the ribs. Christ, said Charles to himself, at the same time he heard Ben's low voice say, "Get up, asshole."

It was just a matter of time, Charles knew, until Kevin quit. Kevin was a decent kid, despite his flaws, but he would never be able to grasp the importance of something that would end up being hidden inside the walls. What did it matter if you had one too many bends in the conduit? At the worst you would have to pull a little harder to get the wire through. Why did it matter that all of the conduits going into a box were lined up side by side and not crossing over one another? Why was it such a big deal if a home run took a few more feet to get the panel than it needed to? Why was it so important that the boxes were all straight, level, set at exactly the right depth in the wall? Didn't the drywall crew come along and knock everything out of whack, anyway? Who cares about something nobody can see, as long as it works?

Charles followed Ben into the house, hearing voices in Spanish, then the rattle of the jackhammer. He could smell the yellow dust. If Kevin quit in the middle of the job they were screwed. He found Ben in the kitchen, staring in distaste at the wall where the plumbing for the sink was roughed in, where they would have to put in circuits for the garbage disposal and the dishwasher.

"Plumbers," Ben said, the word like something sour he was about to spit out on the floor. "How are we supposed to get in there?"

"What's new?" said Charles. So the plumbers didn't give a crap about the electricians. Neither did the heating men, the carpenters, the cement men—nobody seemed to give a crap about anyone else. It wasn't always this way, Charles said to himself. Things used to be different, didn't they? With a clarity abrupt and startling he saw in his mind his mother, in a housedress, standing beside the young man who had lived next door, a young man who never seemed to wear a shirt, not even on the coldest winter days. He saw his mother and the shirtless young man in the kitchen of his parents' house, standing a little too close to one another. Charles blinked. Was this a memory, or just a piece of fiction floating up out of the feverish matter in his head? His father and mother had always seemed to love each other, in a reserved, undemonstrative way. He looked at Ben. If it wasn't for Ben's predicament he wouldn't have had such a repellent fantasy. They wouldn't be standing there, staring at the sloppy plumbing, unhappy with each other, with everything.

"You've got to lighten up," said Charles, feeling rushed, wanting to get past this scene and whatever was likely to follow. "He's just a damn kid."

"I don't care," said Ben.

"What do you mean?" Charles saw that the plumbers had notched a stud so deeply that it was nearly severed, no longer able to support anything. The building inspector would jump on that in a second. It's not my problem, he thought, I'm not going to say anything to Shultz. But it will hold things up, become an excuse to delay a payment. "What do you mean, you don't care?"

"I don't give a shit about anything," Ben said, in a low voice that made Charles think of the noise a tomcat makes in prelude to a fight.

"Yeah," said Charles. He was no longer willing to pussyfoot around; things had gone too far now, they had to come to a head. "Well, do something about it then. Kick her out and get it over with." He didn't want to look directly into Ben's face. His eyes followed the black pipe up the wall to where it disappeared through another sloppy notch in the two-by-four plates. "Or tell her you want to go to a marriage counselor. It's not the end of the world. I mean, it happens. You still love her, tell her whatever's wrong you want to figure it out, get past it. Don't take it out on Kevin. It's not his fault."

"She said she stopped."

"Huh?" Charles heard an acquiescent, possibly defeated tone in Ben's voice. I don't want this kind of thing in my life, he said to himself, I want us to grow old together, have grandchildren, buy a camper and travel around without any baggage or clouds from the past hanging over us.

"She said last night that she stopped. That she wasn't going to see him again."

"You believe her?" Charles wondered if *he* did.

"Yeah."

"Well . . ." Charles felt the swollen atmosphere around them suddenly deflate, but it didn't necessarily feel like a relief. It was too inconclusive. Ben would forgive her, everything would go back to being the way it was before—was that the end result of all this turmoil? He listened for sounds to indicate that Kevin had taken the initiative to do something without being told, but all he could hear was the sound of the jackhammer echoing slightly through the unfinished rooms. He grinned at Ben, feeling for some reason embarrassed. "Well," he said, "I guess you're happy."

"About what?" said Ben.

Yeah, thought Charles, about what?

"What do I do?" Ben went on, in a voice with all the previous menace drained away.

"Do about what?" said Charles.

"I walk out of the house and there he is, across the street. I want to kill him, buddy, I really do."

"Don't do that," said Charles, with a stir of panic that brought again a glimpse of the electrocuted man. "That would be really stupid. You have to forget about it."

"You're shittin' me."

"Listen, Ben." Charles felt as if he were talking to Kevin, not quite able to get through the invisible howl of guitars and thrash of drums. "You want to stay at the house for a few days? Let things cool off? You can sleep in the den."

"A man has a right to defend his honor," Ben said.

"Jesus, Ben." Charles thought with dull resignation that they might as well roll it up, call it a day; whatever they had accomplished to this point would probably be wrong and have to be torn out and done over in the morning.

"A man has a legal right," said Ben.

"To kill somebody? Come on."

"You catch your wife and somebody in the act, you have the right to do whatever you want. To both of them."

"Where did you hear that?" Charles observed with unease that Ben's body had begun to sway, that his eyes had begun to roll back and forth like loose green marbles. In his imagination Ben fell to the floor and foamed at the mouth, his legs drawn up and arms disarranged like those of the electrocuted man. How do I deal with this? he thought. Would he have to call the police? Go to the kid, warn him that his life was in danger? Tell Ben's wife to get away? Perfectly normal people went crazy. You could read about it from time to time, somebody running amuck, shooting people, wives, kids, strangers. Was Ben going crazy? How could he tell?

"Come stay at the house," he said. He decided that it was his imagination, not Ben, that had run beyond the bounds of reality. "As long as you want." He took his eyes off Ben and saw a plume of black from a point where the plumbers had nearly set fire to a stud with their soldering torch. "If she says she's not going to see this kid anymore, then it means she wants you to stay together. She wants to work it out."

"Why couldn't it have been you?" he said.

"Me?" Charles was startled. He got along all right with Ben's wife, but she was a little loud, a little aggressive for his taste. She tended to treat Ben like one of her kids. The only time Charles had ever thought anything at all about her was the first time the four of them had gotten into Ben's new hot tub without their clothes, a moment in which alcohol and a few puffs on a joint had combined to afflict him with an adolescent lust. He wondered what Ben was trying to suggest.

"I get up early and sneak out of the house," Ben went on, in an injured, lugubrious tone. "I don't want anybody to see me."

"Sure," said Charles. "That's understandable." He heard Kevin, the shuffle of feet in their direction. They had to wrap this up. "Just don't take it out on Kevin, okay? You can stay at the house. Let things cool off. Get this job wrapped up." He saw Kevin's lopsided grin between two studs, his head nodding to the concealed cacophony of sound. "We've got to get this job done, Ben. We've all got to hold up our end. You, me, Kevin."

At the sound of his name Kevin grinned, clapped and then joined his hands and shook them as if in self-congratulation. "I picked up the nails," he said, the tone of his voice suggesting unqualified happiness. "What's up now? What happens next?"

At five o'clock, in the fading light of dusk, Charles went outside and saw that the trench had nearly reached the pool. "You finish," he said slowly, emphatically, "I pay ten dollars more." The man in the straw hat nodded and said, "*Sí. Está bien.*" The other man said something that Charles did not understand. He headed back to the house where Kevin was rolling up the cords and putting the drills back into their cases. He would have to take the men back, and then the jackhammer, and it would probably be seven o'clock before he got home. This was the only bone of contention between himself and his wife, his spending so much time on work, getting home and having to shower and make telephone calls and attend to matters of business just when their daughter was wanting to be read a story before going to bed. He had promised more than once that things would change, that having Ben as a partner would take off some of the load, but nothing had changed, not really, except that so many people had gotten into the business, foreigners, fly-by-nighters, guys without the proper license, without insurance, bidding low, trying to get a piece of the business that was booming because it seemed that everybody had decided to build, to remodel, to put up something on every vacant lot, on every acre of empty land.

He thought about asking Ben to take the jackhammer back, but decided not to rock the boat. Ben had worked hard all afternoon, had seemed to get his focus back where it belonged, on the complex scheme of the wiring that he carried inside his head. Ben had even left Kevin alone. He told Charles that if they all worked Saturday they could get the conduit in and that on Monday Charles could pick up the wire. "Let me know," Charles had said again, "if you want to stay at the house." Ben had nodded, but said nothing.

Now Charles watched Ben's truck bounce over the ruts and onto the asphalt of the twisting canyon road. Kevin had already left, burning rubber, going too fast for the road. He was okay, though, a decent kid when all was said and done. Ben, too. He was okay. A good guy. He wouldn't hurt anybody, not deliberately. Charles gestured to the men to put the jackhammer in the truck. The rental yard closed at six and he would have to hustle. He didn't like to speed on the canyon road. Some idiot could come flying around a corner on the wrong side, or back out of a driveway, and he wouldn't be able to stop the truck. Why are you so nervous? he asked himself. So worried about things that are unlikely, matters of pure chance?

He could hear the men in the back of the truck, their voices muffled by the glass of the window that he had rolled up against a chill that descended when the sun went down. In a week it would be Thanksgiving. Then Christmas. He wanted to get his daughter a bike for Christmas. And a rocking horse for the baby. He could still remember the rocking horse he had when he was a little kid and what a thrill it had been the first few times he had gotten on it. He thought about the men in the back. He regretted the fact that he couldn't speak their language and therefore ask them about themselves, about their families, whether they had wives, children. Probably they did, he thought. Still in Mexico. Or somewhere else. El Salvador. Guatemala. Places he had never been and wouldn't be likely to go. He had given each of them fifty dollars, seeing in his mind the money as a bite out of an apple that was the profit deserved by himself and Ben. He had resented giving the men the hundred dollars, and then he had felt ungenerous. It wasn't their fault that he hadn't read the contract after Shultz had given it back to him. Shultz made money because he was smart, he didn't have any obligation to tell Charles that he had crossed out the word "others" and typed "subcontractor" above it. That was the way business was done now, and Charles would have to learn the rules of this game.

The two men in the back of the truck had worked without a single break after lunch, and he wished, briefly, that he could pay them even more. What kind of Christmas would they have? he wondered. Ben had said that these men didn't have it so hard—because a lot of them lived together and sent most of what they made to Mexico so that when they went back they would be rich, because of the fact that dollars could be exchanged for so many pesos. Rich? He somehow doubted it. And what kind of life could it be, living so far from your family, crowded with a bunch of others into a place meant for two or three, standing on the street every day, trying to attract the attention of someone like himself, who had a dirty, tedious job, a ditch to dig?

He turned onto Sawtelle, saw the deserted sidewalks littered with wrappers, cans, things that men had earlier dropped there. He pulled to the curb. The truck bounced as the men got out and he rolled down the window.

"*Gracias,*" he called, aware of some deficiency in his pronunciation.

"*Más trabajo?*" the man in the straw hat said. "Tomorrow?"

Charles recognized only "Tomorrow?" He shook his head. "No. Sorry."

"Okay," said the man, with a smile. The short man smiled, too; they waved and drifted into the night, becoming shadows beyond the greenish glow of the streetlights. I ought to have asked them where they live, thought Charles, maybe I could have dropped them off closer to home. He had no idea where such men lived. And he wouldn't have known how to ask this question. At the stoplight he looked at his watch. It was after six. He would have to return the jackhammer in the morning and pay for an extra day. He should have asked Ben to return it, because he had just thrown away ninety dollars, just like that, like trash into a can.

He turned in the direction of his house. The ninety dollars would eat at him, along with his failure to notice that Shultz had altered the contract, and the knowledge that if Ben did something crazy he would be responsible, because he hadn't warned the neighbor kid, or Ben's wife, or the police. But he was sure that Ben wouldn't do anything crazy. It was entirely possible to talk about blowing someone away in the emotion of hurt and jealousy without ever having the intention or inclination to do so. Charles knew that if he caught his wife in bed with somebody he wouldn't go into the den and get his shotgun out of the gun safe and start blowing heads off; he would possibly threaten or even want to do so but that would just be emotion, the terrific hurt of betrayal by somebody he had always trusted. What would he do, though?

He pushed the truck to fifteen miles an hour above the limit, feeling a sudden, panicky desire to get home and see his wife, kiss her and tell her that he loved her; kiss the baby, too, and hug his daughter, tell them how much he cared about them. They might wonder what was going on, but that was okay. He was lucky, he realized, thinking of the men with their wives and children in Mexico or some other country, out of sight, beyond the range of touch, of love. He just wished that Ben would come to the house, at least for the night. He realized that he hadn't said anything to his wife about this business of Ben's wife and the neighbor kid, and he wondered if she knew. She and Ben's wife weren't really close, but they got together now and then, talked on the phone. He realized that he was in a hurry to get home to tell her himself, to put his own interpretation on the situation, before she started thinking that it was all Ben's fault. Maybe Ben hadn't been paying enough attention to his wife. Maybe he didn't listen to her, a complaint that Charles vaguely remembered hearing that night at the restaurant. But how did that justify bedding down with a kid, making a fool out of Ben, screwing up their lives?

He backed the truck into the driveway, up close to the house where thieves or vandals wouldn't be likely to bother it. The windows were lit in the kitchen and living room and when he got out he heard the baby squall. If the baby had been fussy all day his wife would be irritable, and probably have something to say about his being so late again. Then the baby stopped, abruptly, and he heard the distant voice of his wife, calling his daughter's name in a tone that might have been plaintive or simply neutral, he couldn't tell. He had been in such a hurry and now he felt himself dawdle, to delay going inside. The faces of the girl in the 7-Eleven, the young man in the supply house, the laborers, the kid on the Ninja, all appeared in his head and made him feel anxious, as if he was being forced to make some kind of choice. The kitchen window was up a few inches and he heard his wife say clearly, "Your father's home." He checked the lock on the toolbox of the truck and then headed for the side door of the house. "Your father's home." She had said it without any particular emphasis, a matter of fact, and as Charles turned his key in the door he suddenly felt lighter, less anxious, less estranged, more confident of the future, whatever it might turn out to be.

# The Widower's Psalm

DEBRA MONROE

From *The Source of Trouble* (1990)

She was fifteen years and seven months old and a man named Harlan came up with a construction crew from Texas to work on the water tower. Even the grown women talked about Harlan, how debonair he was in the coffee shop, how he shot pool like a shark. He kept a silver three-toned travel trailer on the edge of town. After his car skidded into a telephone pole one night and he was instantly killed folks went inside the trailer to find out who his kin were so they could send for them. They found good liquor, gold satin sheets on the bed, and a photo of Harlan lying on those sheets, bare-chested, hands behind his head.

That's the photo they put in the paper.

But Harlan was twenty-two and Linda wasn't sixteen yet when he climbed the water tower and painted LINDA ON MY MIND, the name of the Conway Twitty song, in six-foot letters on the side. He got fired and ran out of money and that was the way he came to end his days in Cherryvale. The water tower stayed like that until they tore it down: a robin's-egg blue cylinder jutting into the sky on spindly legs with black and uneven letters curving around it. Linda's stepfather beat her the morning he first looked up and saw her name there, then locked her in the shed for three days. Everyone knew. She was the only Linda in town.

I was delivering newspapers when I first saw her. She was leaping through the sprinkler in the front yard to her ramshackle, unpainted house. She was wearing a red plaid swimsuit and water glistened in beads on her legs and her ponytail hung like a rope on her back. Her family never paid for the paper but I delivered it anyway.

Sometimes, in the attic of their shed, I laid in a pile of hay while she rubbed slivers of ice on my chest. (She was the nurse and I was the soldier.) Then Sammy Manwell moved to town and she tended his wounds, not mine. She went me away to fetch things and drive the enemy back, and when I returned she and Sammy were gone from the haystack and the spot where they'd been laying when I left was flattened out. I kissed her once, between the LP gas tank and the cellar stairs, and she asked me for money for gum.

I was with Sammy one day when she stood on her back steps in a white dress and said she'd recently come to realize what love was and it wasn't what she had with Sammy. He ran his bicycle into a tree. She loved several movie stars, the man who ran the Ferris wheel at the fair, the doctor when she had the mumps, Harlan when she was fifteen.

The summer I turned sixteen Sammy was in Wichita working at his uncle's store and Linda and I rode our bikes to Pilgrim's Creek and laid on a flat rock underneath the limbs of a wide oak tree. She unhooked my overall straps, one at a time, then peeled my clothes away. I lay naked on the rock and she bent down and delicately kissed the tip of my pecker, which seemed red and strong and spear-shaped to me then. She guided my hand underneath her skirt to the inside of her cotton pants. "Sherm," she said, "see? This part of me always stays cool."

On prom night the year Sammy and I were seniors and Linda was fourteen she wore a dress made of coral-colored shiny material with little yellow beaded pineapples on it and her cleavage showed plump and neat and the earrings in her ears sparkled bright as her front tooth, which was silver.

My date was Arleen Sanders.

The four of us stayed at prom long enough to dance only a few times beneath the swirled crepe paper on the gymnasium ceiling and Linda said we should go to her house because her stepfather was gone and she had the key to the cabinet where he stored the liquor. He was always gone on Saturdays. We drank choke-cherry juice mixed with Southern Comfort, slices of orange floating in the tall glasses, and Linda turned the radio up loud. She dabbed whiskey behind her ears and on her wrists. She lifted up her skirt and dabbed whiskey behind her knees like it was perfume.

I was in the front room on a dark green, prickly sofa kissing Arleen when Linda's stepfather burst in, ran to Linda's bedroom door, and yanked it open. Linda stood with her eyes wide, arms in an *X* across her chest. Then she reached for her dress, unzipped and hanging around her waist, and held it to her as she ran through the front room and out the door. Sammy followed, tucking his shirt in his pants.

Linda's stepfather threw rocks at the car as we sped down the driveway. He yelled, "Whore!" Arleen had to be in by midnight so we took her home. Linda cried for a while. Then she and Sammy and I drove to Pilgrim's Creek and sat on the rock and watched the water crash. The moon shone like a disk on the creek's surface and Linda stood up. "I'm going swimming," she said.

Sammy said it wasn't warm enough.

I said we didn't have any swimsuits.

Linda said, "I'm going in wearing my skivvies." She unzipped her dress and dove in wearing her white underpants and her bra with its old-fashioned cone-shaped cups. "Scaredy cats," she yelled, treading water.

Sammy and I stood on the rock, Sammy wearing a blue sportscoat, holding the bottle of Southern Comfort. I hung my clothes on a tree and dove in after Linda. An hour later the three of us walked upstream and waded out to the ledge where the water fell. "I know it's deep enough down there," Linda said, "if we jump in the middle and not to the left and not to the right. And if we don't try to dive."

She jumped first, disappearing, then reemerging and shooting downstream. We all jumped many times: the current expelled us, then transported us away. But when Linda leapt into that pocket of water for the last time Sammy reached out to pat her on the hips. He reached to pat her in that split second when she was not on the ledge and not plummeting into the water, but poised in the air.

She landed facing the falls.

Sammy and I watched her flail. We watched her long mahogany-colored hair spiral, spiral around slowly, then faster, then faster and faster. "What the hell is going on?" Sammy yelled. "What's she doing?" He dove in after her.

She reached for him and by the force of that exertion slid out of the eddy. He slid in. I watched her float downstream. And I watched him struggle and jumped in after him. I hung onto a rock with one hand and with the other I pulled him out. We drifted downstream and Linda clung to a branch. "Help me," she said. "I'm tired."

She laid on a pebble-covered beach then, her chest heaving, and we knelt over her. "I was ready to give myself up to that underwater grave, Sammy," she said, "and your white arm flashed by in the green water and I decided to live."

A man came by to fish that morning and was so frightened by the sight of the three of us wet and bedraggled on the creek bank that he drove to a phone and called the police. The sun was high and we passed delivery trucks and farmers on tractors as we rode back to town in the squad car. Linda got locked in the shed for three weeks. Sammy got sent to Wichita to live with his uncle. Everyone was sure he'd be a basketball star there but one night he got drunk and broke into an ice cream parlor that showed coin-operated dirty movies and he stole some bags of quarters. In the morning, sober, he went to return the money and the police, waiting for him there, arrested him.

When Linda was fifteen Arleen Sanders said, "You don't advertise something that's not for sale." Linda had just walked past wearing a halter she'd made by tying two blue bandannas together.

Linda's voice was soft and pretty but when she got drunk it was raspy; and before, when she said mean things, it was accidental but now it wasn't. We were standing around a pickup with a keg in the back, and in front of eight or ten people she said to Arleen, "If I had a bladder the size of yours I'd give up beer and wouldn't try to act like I was putting on lipstick every time I walked around the corner to pee." To me she said, "Sherm, you wear that same damn green-checked shirt every Saturday night. Can't you spring for something new?"

Then Harlan came to town and I ran into Linda every Saturday night and most weeknights at the corner tap, My Place it was called. Harlan had convinced the owner to let her in and most of the time she sat on a barstool talking to him while Harlan shot pool. She smoked cigarettes, drank a shot of whiskey every fourth beer. Every drink the owner didn't pay for, Harlan did. Or I did, sometimes.

One afternoon when I didn't have to work and Linda had less inclination than usual to go to school we decided to drive to Pilgrim's Creek. I pulled up in front of her house in my truck and she burst out the door and tottered down the sidewalk in a one-piece swimsuit and heels, carrying a straw bag. We sat on the rock and she painted her toenails and said Harlan wanted to marry her and his grandmother was going to give them her farm and move to an old folks home. She said, "And when I get that place and make it mine I'm not going to pick one color for my decor. I'll put in it everything of every color that strikes me pretty, and if I put enough colors together—red, blue, pink, gray, yellow—it'll all match. Doesn't that sound nice?"

Harlan climbed the water tower that weekend and was killed in that crash before Linda's stepfather let her out of the shed. My boss's wife—I was pumping gas then—told me about that photo of Harlan they put in the paper and where it came from. They'd found photos of Linda lying wrapped in those gold bedsheets too.

So Linda quit school and worked at the Mercantile. She dated the salesmen who came to town and one of them took a picture of her dressed in clothes from the line he sold, a picture I still have: her hair coiled high, wearing a satin dress and pearls, she holds a seashell.

I asked her to go to the harvest dance with me and the weather turned cold and we stood on the sidewalk and watched people drinking and twirling around in the blocked-off street. Sammy Manwell appeared. "Sammy," Linda called. She ran into the street to meet him. He looked heavier than he used to be and he had a beard that was darker than the hair on his head and he looked sloppy. His shirt wasn't tucked in his pants. "You came back," she said.

And the three of us sat on a bench at the end of the street and I asked Sammy where he'd been. In jail, he said, serving time for possession of marijuana with intent to sell.

Linda said, "But did you smoke it?"

He passed us a joint. It was my first, Linda's too. "God," she said. She held her head in her hands between her legs and her hair spread like a fan on the grass. She said, "Sherm, don't let me drive." She stuffed her keys up my sleeve between my wrist and coat cuff.

The neon cross on top of the Presbyterian church glowed. Sammy said, "Think of what that must have cost—the cross, I mean."

Linda said, "It did cost a lot, I heard."

Sammy said, "They could have spent the money planting food. Or getting ready for the nuclear fallout."

Linda said, "But it's so pretty. Don't you think so, Sherm?"

Sammy said, "It's a monument to the human belief that what lies ahead is an improvement."

I walked away. I went downtown and danced with Arleen Sanders until my shirt stuck to my back and sweat streamed down my face from under my hat, and then I followed her home and made love to her in her trailer. "Finally," she said. She fell asleep with her head on my chest and I looked out the window, at the driveway, the streetlight and, beyond that, the flat horizon and the starless sky.

I drove home at four and one of those storms, where the snow falls lightly and dusts the edge of the road and the sagebrush white, was just beginning. I found Linda huddled in the doorway to a downtown store, her skinny, nyloned legs looking cold below her parka, smashed paper cups, food wrappers, and napkins strewn around her. Harlan once said to me, "She's so unspoiled, a small-town girl." And when we were in high school Sammy said he loved Linda because she seemed older than him. My father said, before he died, "A pretty girl is everything everyone wants her to be." Also, "You have a claim when you stake it."

I married Linda right away. "We'll hang a cowbell on the bedsprings and wait outside the window to hear it ring," someone yelled. A flash went off in my face. Everyone was drunk. We drove to the motel. The wedding night was not what it should have been.

I was working at the gas station then and I got so dirty every day it took me half an hour to clean up and my hands and fingernails never came clean. It seemed right that Linda should quit her job at the Mercantile, but we didn't have enough money so I took a second job in a small building on the edge of town. I'd passed by that building all my life and wondered what kind of business they did. They collected bills. It was my job to go around in dress pants and a good shirt and tell people to pay a little every month if they couldn't pay the whole thing.

Sometimes Linda had dinner waiting for me. I knew most everyone whose door I knocked on. And when I came home at night I was tired and didn't want to talk. I sat on the porch of the house we rented and stared at the setting sun. "Did you ever think about dying?" Linda said. "I mean, everyone has to die but I just thought about it for me the first time ever. Never hearing or touching or smelling or thinking again. And it gave me the jeebies."

One night I was looking for something to read and I found Linda's Bible from her Sunday School days, her name stamped in silver on the cover. The words sounded pretty: "Walketh not in the counsel of the ungodly. Bringeth forth fruit in season; thy leaf shall not wither."

I looked up. Linda was standing in front of me in a navy blue and white polka-dot dress with a white apron. She held a dust-rag. She said, "Sherm, I dust and dust every day, and each night the wind whips up again and blows the dust back in the house. The house must have cracks in it. I can't stand it."

She started bartending three nights a week. The corner tap had a new name, The Why Stop Inn. I stayed home and sat on the porch and enjoyed the smell of the evening, the soil as it cooled that first hour after sunset, the cicadas singing high and electric in the trees. One night, on a whim, I drove to town. Cold air hit me in the face as I opened the door to the bar. "Hey close that," someone yelled. "Make it latch. Keep the hot air out."

Linda was standing in front of the dart board and next to a table with a pitcher of beer and two glasses, and she held a bunch of darts in her hand. Ollie Jensen, who works at the grain co-op, stood behind her with both of his hands on her hips.

She set the darts down and walked toward me in that fast way. She always wore heels. "Sherm," she said, "Ollie's been teaching me to shoot." She kissed me, took off my hat, and hung it up. "Sit down," she said, "and drink some beer."

Ollie Jensen sat on the barstool next to mine. "Does he know about that dead raccoon?" he said.

Linda smiled. "You'll have to ask him."

Ollie said, "She says that on the road to your place there's a dead coon hanging on an electrical pole."

Linda said, "There is, Sherm. He's been hanging there for two weeks and he's going to drop any day. It's across from Dick Fall-ey's place."

I shook my head. "I guess I let my mind drift when I drive," I said.

Ollie said, "I hope he don't let it drift when he's doing some-thing else." He slid off his stool and walked around the corner of the bar and put his arms around Linda.

She said, "Sit down, Ollie." She pushed him away and poured

another beer. I told Linda I'd see her in a little bit and I left. I slowed down as I passed the Falley place and something dark and small was hanging from the top of a pole across the road and swaying in the night breeze. At home I sat on the porch with the Bible. "Why do the heathen rage," I read, "and imagine a vain thing?"

When the 4th of July was just around the corner I told Linda I'd like to go to Bartlesville for the weekend and stay at a motel and eat in a restaurant. "Just the two of us," I said. But there was a dance and she had to bartend on the sidewalk and she was going in early in the pickup and I was supposed to come by later in the car.

The sun rose high and gold. Steam hovered over the fields. "See you later, Sherm," Linda said. And the screen door slammed. I read the paper, then looked through it again for news I'd missed: who'd lost the most weight at T.O.P.S., Area Deaths. I showered, put on a short-sleeved shirt and my best hat, and drove to town.

Linda was standing in front of the stage when I got there. Ollie Jensen was there, Arleen Sanders, and the owner of The Why Stop Inn. Linda stood with all of her weight on one leg, on one high-heeled white patent leather sandal, with her arms folded, and she was chewing on her lower lip.

I looked in the same direction she was looking. Tom Horn, a drummer from Pratt, was standing with his hands on his hips, drumsticks sticking out of his back pocket, a cigarette hanging from his mouth. The expression on his face was unpleasant to me.

Then a boy asked Linda to dance. She danced, and she danced with Ollie and the owner of The Why Stop Inn. I drank beer and everyone looked hot. That band finished and came down from the stage and Tom Horn walked over. Linda smiled, then left to pour beer. He followed her and sat at the plank-and-sawhorse bar, staring.

Linda tapped me on the shoulder. "Sherm," she said, "I'm going into the street to dance with Tom Horn."

I went to the park to play horseshoes. When I came back I couldn't find Linda. "Have you seen her?" I asked. No one had. And I found her on a side street, sitting with Tom on the tailgate of our pickup. I said, "We're going home now."

She said, "But I'm supposed to bartend."

I said, "Either you're coming or you're not." I walked away.

She started to follow me, and Tom Horn grabbed her by the belt and jerked her toward him and caught her in his arms. She turned her face to his and laughed. "Sherm," she said, over Tom's shoulder, "wait." I went back to the street and drank whiskey in my beer and danced with Arleen Sanders.

I looked up and saw Linda and Tom Horn.

Linda met my eyes once, then never looked at me again. I watched her bobbing and swaying, I watched her light blue shorts bob and sway in that crowd, and her navy blue sleeveless top was damp and sticking to her sides, and her hair was curly right at the temples. Tom Horn's hand rested in the curve of her back.

Arleen said, "Just ignore them."

A man on stage said, "We'd like to dedicate this song to the pretty ladies of Cherryvale."

I walked over and pushed Tom out of the way. "Whore," I said to Linda, "don't come home."

And I went inside The Why Stop Inn where it was cool and I drank until closing time. Then I went home. I found Linda on the way, on the highway, standing next to our stalled pickup. "I hit a coyote," she said. Parts of it were hanging off the grill: flesh, and pieces of fur. "We'll leave the truck here," I said. We drove home in the car and I gave her my handkerchief because she was crying.

She said she was going to take a bath.

She stood in front of me in a yellow kimono, sipping lemonade through a straw, and she said would I please take a bath with her. She'd draped a rose-colored scarf over the lampshade to make the room dark and she was brushing her hair. She unhooked my pants. She cupped my parts in her hand and laid her face against them. She rubbed her cheek against them and said, "Please, Sherm."

I said, "I'm tired." I went outside and sat in the rocker. I stared at the sky and in a little while I opened the Bible. "All the night I make my bed to swim," I read. "The harried ones cry out. Make no tarrying, O my God."

I fell asleep.

I was in a snow-covered national park, hunting. As the dream continued, I was not a hunter but one of those scientists who protect the animal from people who want its horn or pelt, or the oil from its secret gland. And I was sitting near a stream and in the distance I heard voices, people coming to get it.

"The coon fell off the pole," Linda said. I woke up.

And I thought I should walk in there and lift her out of the tub and carry her somewhere and make love to her, a red candle burning by us, her long wet hair hanging down and wrapping around me. I also thought that men would never quit looking at her and she would always look back and it was only a matter of time before she left. I went into the bathroom to tell her this.

She was sunk under the water, her eyes closed, lips parted. Her hair floated on the surface in mahogany-colored whorls and her breasts were high and white. I bent down, lifted her up, and breathed into her.

Her eyes fluttered open and she described this dream: "I was in these green woods and I was going to lay in a pool and you woke me. I'm going back there."

I said, "What's in the green woods?"

She didn't answer.

The coroner said afterwards she couldn't have spoken at all except in my imagination, my state of shock. But that's what I remember, also that the scarf she'd draped over the lampshade started to smoke and I pulled it away and turned the lamp off. And when I'd turned off every light in the house, I went back into the bathroom and lifted her up out of the water and carried her away. Her hair hung like seaweed over my arms and water dripped on the floor as I carried her away.

They asked me for a picture they could put in the paper and I sorted through many: Linda as a child, Linda and Sammy standing next to their bikes, Linda holding a seashell, Linda in a plaid blouse and tight blue jeans, standing next to a tractor. Finally, I chose a photo of her taken on the day she went with her high-school class to Wichita to see the refinery. Her arms linked to other arms, her shoulders one set in many, machinery lumbering behind her, she stands alone, a flourish, a cipher. She was buried in a white dress with seed pearls and I helped the undertaker arrange its long folds in the casket. I was wearing a black suit, the only suit I own, and as they lowered her into the ground I looked up and saw the water tower, pale blue and nearly invisible against the sky. The letters had faded. "Many that sleep in dust shall awake," the minister read. It seemed, for a minute, that I had climbed the tower and pained Linda's name, that refrain: On My Mind.

# Tidal Wave Wedding

ANNE PANNING

From *Super America* (2007)

Rob had seen it happen so many times since coming to Hawaii, he immediately picked up on the telltale signs: a handsome, sunburned young couple combed the beach hand in hand, the woman in tears, the man determined and morose. A sympathetic group of onlookers helped the two honeymooners search in vain through the damp, sparkling sand: a lost wedding band. Rob, a lean and stylish hairdresser with bleached white hair, waded out of the water with his big blue flippers flapping against the current. His snorkel mask gripped tightly to the top of his head like a small yellow bonnet, and he approached the couple, hoping to help.

"Did you lose something?" Rob asked, and pegged the man instantly as military. The haircut was undeniable: a closely shaved neck, a half-inch buzz up to the ears, and a gentlemanly, little square patch at the top, parted to the side. Rob removed his flippers and tried to remain steady as the strong waves lapped against his calves.

"Oh, God. Yeah, my wedding ring," the man said, and massaged the empty spot on his left finger. He was pale and muscular with small blue eyes and a tank of a chest; every time a new white wave broke against the shore, his eyes searched desper-

ately among the glimmering white sand and nuggets of battered
coral. He pressed his hand to his forehead. "God, we just got
married, you know, and—shit—it was my dad's wedding ring—
he's dead. Is that it?" He reached down into the sand with two
fingers but pulled out a deceivingly shiny pebble. "Fuck, we're
never gonna find it. Trish is really bummed—you can't blame
her—" He turned to search for his new wife, and Rob noticed
the smooth ripple of muscles flexing from his back to his ribs.
He was well built and reminded Rob, in a way, of his partner,
Jeremy, who worked out every day at the Y and was a beautiful,
solid, smooth, toned man.

"Well, let me help you look for it," Rob said, and lowered the
mask over his eyes. He pulled himself through the soft, silky water, pumping hard with his thighs to propel himself forward to
where the water shifted from pastel blue to a hard, rich green.
His hands looked pure white and delicate in the water, despite
the many nicks and cuts from the small golden scissors he used
at work, Society Salon. He didn't like the name—its connotations
too sober and aristocratic—but the owners, Claire and Ann-
Ellen, had targeted Honolulu's cream of the crop, the idle rich
who could afford the luxury of beauty and glamour. The en-
trance boasted pale granite columns, and each station was built
of custom cut slabs of green marble, special ordered from a
small island in the Philippines. It was a heavenly place to work,
as far as Rob was concerned: air-conditioning, classical music,
cappuccino served in tiny blue cups, a thirty-foot ceiling, and
three walls of windows. He was well liked there and made more
than his weekly salary in tips on any given day.

Suspended by the buoyant salt water, Rob hung over a net-
work of purple coral. He saw no wedding ring but watched a
small school of yellow-black angelfish swim past coyly like little
kids. The parrot fish were much bigger, glummer, and hung toward the bottom of the reef; as usual, Rob wished he'd brought
his spear gun. He could surprise Jeremy, who'd be tired and

sweaty from working another dinner cruise, with the beautiful blue fish, grilled, belly split, stuffed with lemon and zucchini and tomato. They would laugh, drink white wine, and massage each other's bare feet, leading them, as always, into the bedroom, painted a soothing mint green—Jeremy's idea—to help alleviate the heat. Only lately, Jeremy hadn't been much fun to be with. He was cool and distant and slunk away whenever Rob tried to talk about their future. In the back of his mind, Rob worried that Jeremy was sleeping around, seeing other people in some kind of effort to stay young, attractive, and single.

Rob turned back toward shore, raising his head briefly like a turtle to get his sense of direction; in doing so, he heard a long, wailing sound, like a fog horn. He looked back toward the ocean to check for boats or helicopters but saw none. Confused, he quickly swam to shore, peeling back layers of ocean to channel his body through smoothly. When he reached the sandbar, he unhooked his fins and yanked off his mask. He shook his head and smacked lightly at his ears with his palms and, indeed, heard the sirens.

The new husband still paced up and down the beach, and Rob noticed his wife, a short, suntanned woman in a geometric-print bikini, lying face down on their beach towel, shoulders shaking. Her hair was poorly dyed a yellow-blonde and revealed dark roots, which Rob would've liked to get his hands on. Rob approached the husband, uneager to give him the bad news. "Hey," he said, calling over to him. "Sorry, I couldn't find anything. No luck here either, huh?"

The man stood, hands on his hips. His nose glowed red from sunburn. "Nah, we looked and looked. Just—nothing." He shook his head and dug his toe in the sand. "I suppose it's impossible. I mean, it's—" and he gestured toward the horizon, purple and pink with streaky clouds. "It's the damn ocean. I mean, what we say in the navy is, it gives and it takes, so you gotta respect it."

The man fixed his eyes on Rob for what seemed to be the first time and held out his hand. "I'm Collins, by the way." They shook hands and then stood back awkwardly. "So, you live here or what?" Collins asked, and crossed his arms, looking back periodically to check on his wife lying on the towel. Rob noticed his jagged teeth, with small spaces between each one.

"Yeah," Rob said, "it's my day off. I like to get out and enjoy the water when I can." He swung the snorkel mask as if to illustrate.

Collins stuck his hands underneath his armpits and stood tall. "Yeah, I hear ya. So what do you do?"

"I'm a hair stylist," Rob answered, and anticipated Collins' dismissal.

But Collins surprised him by rubbing his fuzzy head and scratching the back of his neck. "Oh yeah? That's funny because I was thinking I could probably use a trim. Getting a little long." Suddenly, the sirens rang again, long and shrill and disconcerting. Rob wondered if it wasn't the first Wednesday of the month, testing time, but it was definitely Monday, his day off for the past twelve years.

Collins stuck a finger in his ear. "What the hell is that?" he asked.

"I'm not sure." Rob watched people gathering up their beach chairs and coolers, staring out at the water and then toting off frantically to their cars. Then it hit him. On the way over, he had heard about the big earthquake in Japan on the radio but hadn't put two and two together until now: the vibrations rippling secretly underneath the Pacific Ocean, brewing potentially giant waves that could hit the Hawaiian Islands with a fierce slap. A tsunami warning. The two lifeguards began making the rounds, clearing the beach, and soon Collins' wife came scrambling over with all their stuff in a huge tote bag.

"There's a tidal wave warning!" she said, and grabbed Collins' elbow. Her eyes were puffy and pink from crying, and her diamond ring glittered brightly. She seemed to take note of Rob warily.

"This is Trish," Collins said, and grabbed her around the waist. Her skin looked healthy and rich and dark, and soon she began crying again.

"It's just so symbolic!" she said, talking through sobs, wiping her made-up eyes with upturned palms. "I mean, we just get married, and he loses the ring? It's just too awful! How can we go on after this? I mean, it was his dad's, and it's just not replaceable!" She turned and looked out at the ocean, as if it might respond and spit the ring back out at her feet.

"Hey, I don't mean to be unsympathetic," Rob said, startled now by the evacuation going on behind them. "But I think we should probably clear out of here. You just never know with these tsunami warnings."

Collins looked uneasy and eager to leave, but Trish held tightly to his arm. He grabbed her hand and squeezed it. "Hey, baby, we better go call a cab. We're just not gonna find it, okay? We'll get another one, somewhere, I promise."

"But we can't go until we find it!" she said, and ran a hand through her short yellow hair. "Oh, it's just too awful. It's no way to start a marriage!" She kicked the sand as sadness turned to anger.

Rob, growing a bit tired of them, offered a suggestion. "Well, I don't mean to tell you what to do, but when my grandparents were honeymooning in Hawaii, a long, long time ago, my grandpa lost his ring in the ocean, too, and instead of buying him another, my grandma decided to throw her ring in, too. So they were joined at sea. Kind of romantic, huh?" Rob was chilled now and wanted to get showered and dressed. He felt his hair drying in ridiculous spikes. "That's a great idea!" Collins said. "Trish, let's do it." He grabbed the bulging red bag from her shoulder, threw it to the ground, and reached for her left hand. But she pulled away.

"No!" she said. "I love this ring! You worked so hard saving up for it, and I'm not going to throw it in the ocean. I'm sure!" She glared at Rob, turned away from Collins, and began combing the beach again, head down, body bent at an almost perfect right angle, hands clasped behind her back like an inspector.

Rob apologized to Collins, said good-bye, and walked up to his little beach spot: striped mat, fold-up yellow chair, small mesh bag for his fins and snorkel, large bottle of mineral water, book. But when he'd gathered his things and was turning toward the parking lot, he saw Collins and Trish standing in the water, arms wrapped around each other, staring out at the stormy surf, the color now of spit and bullets. Her breasts curved into his ribs; his knees nudged her thighs, and the water threatened to take them down, but didn't. It was a snapshot honeymoon moment, but somehow, Rob could not turn away. He felt a deep, hollow ache inside of him, not necessarily for what they had, or didn't have, but for what he knew did not exist: a true union of human spirits, a binding of two souls forever, without fear or pain or loneliness pending.

He breathed in the salt air and was transported, through memory's passage, to his first lover, Cesar, a wealthy, mustachioed Brazilian he had met years ago in San Francisco, when Rob was not so much a prostitute as a companion, a paid accomplice of sorts. Cesar, with his flashy eyes and black felt hats, flew Rob to Brazil, where they had lived in a luxurious tile-floored mansion in the middle of the rain forest. Rain dripped upon the shiny blue roof and slid like oil; monkeys laughed with abandon, far off. It was the jungle, Cesar had always reminded; he would then twirl his thin brown cigarettes in the air and shout, "Green!" in Portuguese. There was a maid to empty the chamber pots, a boy to cook sausages and onion with rice, an uncle to drive them to town; Rob had lived there for ten long years—a beautiful, tall, blond North American boy with aviator glasses—until something fell apart. Cesar had begun trying to control his every move. There were family riches to hold over Rob, and Cesar would sometimes punish him by withholding money for something as simple as postage stamps. He'd sought to keep Rob isolated and removed from the rest of the world, all to himself, like a bribed best friend. But Rob began slowly dying inside, withdrawing in anger and suffocation, until he finally, secretively, convinced Cesar's wealthy father to buy him a ticket back to the States, promising to stay away from Cesar for the rest of his life.

As the tsunami siren quaked across the island, the few remaining cars drifted onto the narrow highway and sped away. Even the lifeguards, after stabbing "Dangerous Swimming: Tidal Wave" signs into the sand, began to close up their orange towers. Rob stood in the middle of the deserted beach and cupped his hands around his mouth. "Collins! Trish! How about a ride?" He watched them break apart, argue, negotiate, and approach. They stood in front of Rob, beach towels saronging their hips. They were out of breath and seemed to cross their arms stubbornly, as if challenging Rob.

"Yeah, we'll take a ride," Collins said, "if it's not too much trouble. There's no way we're getting a taxi out here now." He reached into the red tote, which was back in Trish's possession, pulled out a crumpled white T-shirt, and put it on. It said: "KOOL, Kool Radio 98.5 Des Moines" in orange letters, and Rob began to make assumptions about his background.

"Thanks," Trish said, "we really appreciate it, you know, your being so nice and everything." She seemed more subdued to Rob now, as if she had given up on the ring. They all toed through the sand, burdened with heavy beach gear and regret.

They brushed off their feet and got into the small gray car. Rob shifted into reverse, hung his sunglasses on the rearview mirror, and made a right. "So, where are you staying? Waikiki, right?"

"Yeah," Collins said, and touched his lip in a way Rob found sexy. "But what's our hotel called again, honey? The Outrigger? Or Surf Rider or something like that? Or no, it's Waikiki something."

Trish leaned up from the backseat, which comforted Rob. She smelled like Coppertone and vanilla and hung her arms between the two men. "No, it's the Waikiki Grand. On Kapa—lua—God, what's that street again? I forget."

"Oh, right," Rob said, relaxing finally and sliding down in his seat. "On Kapahulu. It's not too far." With that reassurance, Trish sat back, staring quietly out the window; Rob glanced at her in the rearview mirror and made no more attempt at small talk. Collins, in the seat beside him, radiated warmth from sunburn.

When Rob reached Waikiki, there was pandemonium everywhere. Cops redirected traffic, banning all cars from the Waikiki strip. Official yellow tape was wound around large white sawhorses, making the entire beach area off limits. Rob's head pulsed with a smashing headache, and he began to wish he had not been so friendly, had not gotten involved in this couple's plight. It was just as Jeremy said: Rob was a pushover, he had to learn to say no, he had to keep to himself more. Still, Jeremy sat at the other end of the spectrum: he was a yes-or-no man, had clear-cut divisions of what was right or wrong, didn't believe in saying hello to strangers on the street, and still clung to harried, frantic East Coast habits in the middle of the Pacific. It frankly worried Rob, Jeremy's life speed: he would run across the street on red lights, finagle his way into the grocery store's express line with more than nine items, and worst of all, would give slow drivers and befuddled rental-car drivers the finger and lay on the horn if they so dared to hold him back a fraction of a second.

"It doesn't look like we're going to be able to get you to your hotel," Rob announced, and was surprised that neither of them took the news with any apparent stress or disappointment. Collins shrugged his shoulders and leaned his elbows on his knees. "Well, wait," Rob said, rolling down his window and turning off the a/c. "Let me ask this guy over here what's up." In the lilting local accent he'd picked up over the years, Rob asked a cop what he should do.

"Tsunami," the man said, and jammed his walkie-talkie into its pouch. "Nobody's going into Waikiki. If these guys are staying down here, they're evacuating to the high school in Manoa. They can get a bus by the zoo. Over there." He pointed to a group of tourists dressed in pastels.

"How long will it be until it opens up down here?" Collins asked, ducking his head low to peer through Rob's window. The cop laughed, tuned into his walkie-talkie, responded in code, turned it down, and took a step away from the car.

"Never know," he said, and started to wave them away. Traffic was building up behind them, mostly shiny new rental cars. "Gotta move along now. Could be thirty-, forty-foot waves. Never know."

"Thanks for the info," Rob said, and rolled up his window. He was starving and hoped the tsunami warning meant Jeremy had not gone out to work the dinner cruise. Perhaps he'd even be at home, cooking something Rob loved, like lemon fettuccine, or broiled salmon with that wonderful tarragon sauce Jeremy had invented. "So, I don't know what you guys want to do . . ." Rob asked, cocking his head back to address Trish more than Collins.

She seemed startled out of a daydream and ran her hands through her hair before answering. "Well, it seems pretty hopeless at this point. It's just not anything like I'd imagined it would be, you know?" Rob watched the tears well up in her eyes again, but she fought them back this time.

Rob murmured quietly in response. Collins sighed. The traffic moved so slowly, Rob held the steering wheel with two fingertips. He tried to get a station on the radio for an update on the tidal wave, but it was either slow-time hula or classic rock. "You know, I guess you guys could come to my place until this blows over," Rob offered, knowing that bringing two unknown guests into his home would illicit a silent but obvious irritation from Jeremy. "I don't live far, and I'm out of the tsunami zone, so it'd be safe. Sometimes these things blow over really quickly. They just have to take precautions. You could come over until it's all clear. It'll be better than the high school gym, believe me." Traffic lurched forward a block, two, then stopped. Tall, now-empty hotels flanked the street on either side, creating a tunnel-like dimness.

"Oh, we don't want to bother you," Collins said, and placed his big flat hands on top of his knees like a king. His fingernails were square and healthy and pink; his leg hair was golden, curly, and delicate. Rob could clearly imagine him naked, could see the firm buttocks flexing with muscle power, hollowed out on the sides where Rob would sink his hands and press deeply.

"Oh, it's no bother. My roommate, Jeremy, is probably whipping up dinner as we speak." Growing impatient, Rob changed lanes and wove his way to the right, grinding into third, and finally turned off on Hinano. Sometimes Jeremy was his "friend," sometimes "partner," sometimes, rarely, his "lover." In this case, "roommate" seemed appropriate, although anyone could guess the nature of their relationship, considering the blatant kiss Jeremy enjoyed smacking on Rob in public.

"There we are," Rob said, and felt relief to be on the nearly empty, quiet street where he lived. "This is the home stretch. Boy, you guys must be exhausted. It's been quite a day for you." He hadn't meant to remind them of their loss but knew instantly he had. Collins fingered his left hand again and squeezed the emptiness. In the back seat, Trish brushed out her hair frantically; Rob parked downhill, turning the wheels to the right, so as not to roll away.

His apartment was actually more of a double bungalow—the

owner, Webster Ming, a small, old, nosy Chinese man, lived in one half, and Jeremy and Rob in the other. A narrow concrete stairway ran up between the dwellings—Rob's door to the left, Mr. Ming's to the right. There were always rows of shoes and slippers lined up like an offering outside Mr. Ming's door. He and his wife, Letta, in addition to being landlords, also worked a souvenir stand just down the street at the weekly Kodak Hula Show. Rob guessed they probably had plenty of money, though, considering the steep rent he and Jeremy paid and the shabby, threadbare frugality evident in the Mings' clothing, car, and furnishings.

As Rob ascended the stairs, Mr. Ming stuck his head out the door, with his usual plucky gray crew cut, and beckoned. "There's a tsunami warning, you know!" he said, and hung back in his dark doorway, barefoot, wearing khaki trousers and a white T-shirt. He glanced warily at the two strangers and thumbed at them. "Who's that? You have visitors during the tsunami? That's too bad for them." Mr. Ming clucked his tongue, and Rob saw Letta Ming peer out from underneath his armpit, to see what was going on. By now, the Mings were used to a steady flow of mainland visitors lugging bags to and from Rob's apartment, though that had tapered off once they'd been in Hawaii several years.

Rob enjoyed the Mings, even though they kept increasing the rent, little by little, every six months. "No, these two are on their honeymoon—" Rob stopped and made brief introductions. "They were over at White Beach when the tsunami warning started, and they didn't have a car, so I brought them here. Their hotel's been evacuated."

Mr. Ming looked disappointed for them. "Oh, that's too bad for you. Don't worry. It will get better. The water will calm down. It always does." Sometimes Mr. Ming spoke like poetry, but other times, he swore viciously, as he did when he was losing at poker.

Rob could always tell when he was losing, too, because he could hear Mr. Ming slam his hands down on the table and start shouting, "Dammit! Goddammit already!"

Trish leaned against the railing, looking exhausted and fried, still wearing nothing but her bikini top and a towel. Bits of white sand stuck to her chest, and Rob wanted to wipe her off briskly with a towel. "My husband lost his wedding ring in the ocean today," she said, as if Mr. Ming could help her somehow. "We've got to go buy him a new one when this big storm is over. Although, it sure doesn't look like a storm to me." She glanced up at the sky, which was void of clouds and still bleeding a strong white sun.

"Sure doesn't," Collins said, and looked bored, as if he regretted accepting Rob's invitation to his home. "Looks like maybe they'll open up our hotel soon." He crossed his arms over his huge chest and seemed ready for a long delay, despite his hopeful statement.

"No," Mr. Ming said, "with the tsunami, you never know. You can't tell if it's coming or not. Once, a whole two hundred houses were swept into the ocean, just like that." Mr. Ming raised his arms high, miming the disaster, then brought them crashing down. Mrs. Ming, meanwhile, disappeared, then returned with an old cigar box. Mr. Ming, confused, turned to see what she wanted. "What? What is that?" They spoke briefly in Chinese to each other, and Rob made a motion to leave. Often, as much as he enjoyed the Mings, these exchanges in front of their doorways lasted too long.

"Well, we better get going," Rob said, and couldn't tell if Jeremy was home or not. The screen door and the interior door were both closed. "See you later."

"Just a minute," Mr. Ming called, and nudged his wife over to Trish and Collins. Her gray hair was wound up like braided bread in back and fastened high with a metal clip. Her dark eyes shone, and she wore red lipstick in the middle of the afternoon.

She displayed the cigar box with a small, curious grin on her face. "Rings," she said, and opened the box up like a mouth. "I've had these for so many years now."

Inside were rings in various sizes and colors. Most of them were tiny and silver with Chinese characters etched into them; others were thin, pale, jade, or chunky cuts of garnet wedged in cheap gold, but there were three plain gold bands in what looked like small, medium, and large.

Trish stepped forward and started browsing. "My God," she said, trying some on, "where did you get all of these? They're beautiful." She turned to Collins, who stuck one of his big hands in the box, going after the gold bands.

"Over the years," Mrs. Ming said, "I've bought and sold. Maybe you can find your new husband a wedding ring."

Rob stood back, exchanged glances with Mr. Ming, and wondered what was going on. Meanwhile, the tsunami sirens began blaring again, and Rob noticed that the Mings did not wear wedding bands themselves. Nor did he and Jeremy for that matter, although he considered them partners for life. Rob had always dreamed of a big wedding with Jeremy, out on a catamaran, all their family and friends smiling under a bright sun, a tall orange cake with lemon glaze, a case of champagne, and he and Jeremy tossing a brick into the sea for luck and longevity.

Trish watched to see if the largest gold band would fit Collins' ring finger. Mrs. Ming even got a bottle of dish soap and squeezed a drop on his finger for lubrication. Collins winked at Trish, grimaced slightly as he bore down, and managed to jiggle the ring back and forth until it finally grazed over the knuckle.

Everybody cheered. "All right!" Collins said, then picked Trish up in his arms and kissed her on the mouth. Mrs. Ming nodded her head and said, "It is meant to be."

Suddenly, Rob's apartment door opened, and Jeremy emerged. Trish slipped slowly out of Collins' arms, Collins examined his new ring from every angle, and the Mings retreated slightly back into their own doorway. "What's going on out here?" Jeremy said. He spoke from behind the screen door and didn't come out. Rob couldn't tell if he'd been sleeping or was simply in a bad mood. He wore a faded blue T-shirt, tan shorts, and a black cotton vest; his dark hair was pulled back in a short ponytail, and Rob wished, for the thousandth time, that he'd let him cut it.

Rob explained briefly the day's twists and turns. Jeremy listened, leaning one arm on the inside doorway. "Can I talk to you for a minute, alone?" Jeremy said, and drove a long glance at the others. Rob could see his sharp blue eyes flickering.

"Oh, sure," Trish said, perked up now by the new ring, by the miracle of the fit. "We have to talk business with Mrs. Ming anyway." She waved a hand at them. "You guys go ahead."

Rob left Collins and Trish with the Mings and stepped into his apartment, where the fan spun a semicircle of coolness around the room. Jeremy sat at the small kitchen table, a bag of chips and a bowl of salsa in front of him. He uncapped a bottle of Mexican beer. "You want one?" he asked Rob, and although Rob's head was pounding, he said yes, gripping the cold bottle in his hands, then touching it to his cheeks, forehead, wrists.

"So what's going on?" Rob asked wearily. "Obviously something's wrong." He took a sip of beer and let the sting settle in his mouth before swallowing. It seemed to improve the headache instantly.

Jeremy's jaw muscles flexed, his slim nostrils fluted in, then flared out, quickly, like fish gills. "Don't you know?" Jeremy asked. "Think of what's going on right now, and I have to tell you?"

Rob knew that soon he would have to deal with Collins and Trish, if only to finish what he'd started, and he knew there wasn't time for an argument with Jeremy. "Please don't make me guess," he said. "Just tell me what's wrong, and maybe I can explain." His knees cracked under the table, and smoothing his hands over his bare arms, he saw he'd gotten a good tan.

Jeremy scoffed, but acquiesced. "Ah, *hello*? There's a *tsunami* warning and sirens blasting *all* day long, and *I'm* sitting here, knowing *you're* at God only knows *what* beach, and you don't think I might be a little worried? You couldn't have called to say, 'Hey, Jeremy, don't worry. I'm on my way home'? Of course not, because you're too busy hauling around some sleazeball tourists! I mean, what the *hell* are they doing here? For all I knew, you were swallowed up by a fifty-foot wave and on your way to Palmyra Island!"

Rob paused a moment, making sure Jeremy was finished, and noticed the curve of his large biceps through his T-shirt. Rob also noticed that Jeremy did not have a tan but was quite pale from spending all his free hours in the gym. Rob sipped the beer, which was already losing its chill. "All right," Rob said, and placed a hand over Jeremy's, which sat, flat and lifeless, on the table. "You're right. You are absolutely right. I should've called. I guess I just—I got so confused when this couple lost their wedding ring, and I was trying to help them find it, and then—well, the tsunami warning came from out of the blue, and I just—I had to help them out. They didn't have a car or anything." Rob weighed what he'd said and tried to guess if it sounded valid.

"Let me ask you something," Jeremy said, and pulled his hand away. He pushed one loose black lock of hair behind his ear and leaned over the table, face to face with Rob. "Why do you *care*?"

Rob shifted. "What do you mean?"

Jeremy bowed his head in exasperation and tried again. "Why do you *care* about all these total strangers you're always helping out? Can't someone *else* do it? And what about me?" He sat back, arms crossed. "Did you ever think, when you heard the tsunami warning, hey, I hope Jeremy isn't out on the boat? I hope Jeremy's okay? Let me call and see! Don't things like that ever *occur* to you?"

It was true; Jeremy was right and had every reason to be upset. Rob sat there, unthinking, staring at their beautifully decorated apartment, the white gauze curtains, the low gray couch, the wonderful, round glass coffee table held up by brass elephants. The kinds of thoughts that Jeremy had just mentioned did not occur to Rob regularly. When he was at the beach, he was a lone man, soaking up the warmth of the sun, kicking in the froth of the salty ocean, helping people out when they needed it like a contemporary saint. Jeremy was "other" to him, close, but not self. Was this what marriage was, then, Rob wondered, to be joined so that the separation was not so apparent? Suddenly, foolishly, he had an idea.

"Jeremy," Rob said, and slid their bottles of beer aside. He held Jeremy's smooth hand, which smelled perpetually of lemons and limes, which he cut by the dozen for the cruise ship bar. "Will you marry me?" As he asked the question, Rob saw them as old men; they would hobble along the seashore together in cuffed pants and plaid shirts. Gray haired, they would salute the passage of years by drinking Scotch and kayaking the islands. They would travel to Switzerland, Bombay, Belize, and Turkey and always celebrate the Chinese New Year. "Well?" Rob said, eyes misting over with a peculiar twist of emotion. "We can just do it on our own, with all our friends. What do you say?"

"I say—" and there was a knock on the door. "Dammit," Jeremy said, rising for another beer. "I say, dammit."

Rob went for the door. It was, of course, Collins and Trish, all but forgotten already in Rob's mind. Likely, they felt sheepish about disturbing them, and hopefully they had figured out some sort of arrangements for lodging elsewhere. Rob opened the door and forced a smile.

Trish looked much more radiant than he'd remembered, and her hair sparkled golden, not yellow. Her nose was thin and elegant, and her teeth, perfectly white and straight. She still wore her bikini top, revealing the rise of modest breasts. Collins hung back behind her. "Umm, sorry to bother you and everything," Trish said, and seemed breathless. "But we just wanted to ask a big favor of you. If you wouldn't mind." She wrung her hands nervously, and out of the corner of his eye, Rob watched Jeremy turn on the television.

"Sure," Rob said, hoping, whatever it was, would be brief.

Trish leaned against the doorframe, neither in nor out, and presented her proposition. She listed things off on her fingers. "And so, Mr. Ming said with this ring—which we bought, by the way, for 150 bucks—can you believe it? an antique from China!—we should have some kind of ceremony." She paused, glancing at Collins, who was transfixed by the TV. "He's going to do the ceremony, you know, just unofficial, and so we were wondering if you could climb up Diamond Head a ways with us and be witness at our second—well, sort of our second wedding."

Rob's first thought, oddly, after hearing an undeniable snicker from Jeremy, was how the Mings could possibly climb the Diamond Head crater—so old and wrinkled and small they were. He asked Trish this.

"Oh, they do it every morning at 5:00 a.m. It's easy for them, they said. Please come," she said, and grabbed Collins' hand in a fit of passion. "You've been so nice to us and everything."

Collins and Jeremy were both involved in an NCAA basketball game, and Rob knew he should've said no, knew it would put him at even greater odds with Jeremy, but the idea sounded so spontaneous and splendid, in the midst of the tsunami sirens and the hot, humid afternoon. "Yes," he said, hoping, even, that Jeremy would hear. "Yes, I'd be honored."

Jeremy surprisingly agreed to accompany them, and Rob held tightly to his hand, even though that was a risk they didn't always take: no public displays of affection in front of the Mings, in front of strangers, in front of relatives. But up the three couples climbed, first on the lip of the paved road leading into the crater, then up the gravel path that led to the peak. The Mings led the way and did not hold hands but strode diffidently ahead, short arms swinging; Mr. Ming carried a candle in one hand and a bottle of wine in the other. Trish and Collins were next, arm in arm. Rob and Jeremy walked behind them and pressed sweaty palm to sweaty palm, gripping tightly, as if, were they to let go, the connection might slip and dry and fade.

The trail was practically deserted, due to the tsunami warnings, except for a few intrepid joggers. Diamond Head was up high enough to avoid any danger of a tidal wave, and Rob almost missed, for a moment, the threat of danger, of a huge splash that could wipe out cities. When they reached the top, after passing through the claustrophobic, dark tunnels and spiral staircases originally built for a military lookout, Mr. Ming stopped, turned around, and held out his hands, as if to prevent them all from falling down the cliff.

The view was all of Waikiki and part of the eastern shore and immense. Patches of ocean twinkled blue, green, and white, and islands of coral poked out from the surf. "Now," Mr. Ming said, without any warm-up or chitchat. Rob and Jeremy stood on either side of Trish and Collins, and Rob could still hear, despite their great altitude, the faint shrill of sirens.

Trish and Collins held hands, and Collins removed the ring, only to put it back on again when he was coached to do so. "Love long, and always remember the ocean for bringing you together," Mr. Ming said, and uncorked the wine. He splashed a little near Trish and Collins, who giggled and jumped, then he handed his wife the bottle, who drank from it, wiped her mouth, and threw it over the cliff.

"Shit," Jeremy whispered. "They can't just do that!"

"So now you are husband and wife, again," Mr. Ming whispered in a solemn staccato, and Rob could tell he was making it up as he went. "And you'll probably remember this old volcano in years to come."

Jeremy whispered in Rob's ear. "Please. This is ridiculous." But then Jeremy placed his hand on Rob's shoulder and squeezed, and this felt hopeful to Rob. Mr. Ming lit the small candle and set it on a rock.

"Now you can kiss each other," Mr. Ming said, clapped for Trish and Collins, and then turned around to kiss his own wife of forty-five years. They kissed passionately, her head turned into his. "You, too," he said to Jeremy and Rob, and waved them together with his hands. "You're already married, right?"

Jeremy and Rob looked at each other dumbfounded, confused by the question. They stammered and shrugged. "Well, not exactly . . ." Rob said.

"Let's say you are," Mr. Ming said, "and you are. Married. *I thee wed.*"

Rob and Jeremy, too stunned to know what to do, held hands and leaned against each other. Jeremy, despite his earlier anger, seemed less upset. He rubbed his bare shoulder against Rob's.

"Look," said Mr. Ming. "The tsunami's coming in!" Mr. Ming pointed down to the shore, and all three couples gripped the railing, mouths agape. The water stood like high, tight walls of beautiful light blue, then snatched down upon the sand like a cat leaping at a mouse; the hotels, the buildings were splashed with surf that crushed and tore and broke. Then up again, another taut, quivering blue wall lifted, high as a house, and went charging down the streets.

If you were one person standing underneath a tidal wave, Rob thought, you would seem small as a bug, and lonely. You could be wiped out.

# Live Life King-Sized

## HESTER KAPLAN

### From *The Edge of Marriage* (1999)

Late in the summer of 1993, a hurricane with the gentle name of
Tess smashed everything I had into a million pieces. From a window in the cement cooling house where I waited out the storm, I
watched the wind suck all the water from the pool, lift the thatch
roof from the tiki hut, and detonate the last of the beach chairs.
Square by square, the dining room patio was untiled, and just
before Tess changed course, a single wave plucked out the entire
length of dock.

Hours earlier, my staff had left for the main island, cram-
ming themselves into four tiny boats that seemed more dangerous than any hurricane. I'd told them to take what food they
wanted from the kitchen freezers—we'd lose power and it would
all spoil— but they still hid it in their bags and under straw hats.
They yelled that I was a crazy yellow-haired man to stare a hurricane in the eye. "She will think you're making fun of death,"
they warned, shielding themselves from the hot wind that was
already blowing up their bright shirts, "and death will make fun
back at you." On this island, superstitions and sightings are as
plentiful as the joints of coral that cut your feet in the sand, and
so I waved them away.

Weeks later, a few of my staff straggled up the trashed beach looking for work, but the rest had been spooked away for good and I never saw them again. During the next exhausting year, there wasn't a time when I wasn't picking up broken glass or scrubbing away the pocks and pecks of seawater and sand. I hammered shingles onto the roofs of twenty cabanas, quarried slabs of bluebitch stone, rebuilt the dock, spent all the money I had and borrowed more. When the repairs were almost finished, I got on the phone and begged every travel agent I'd ever had anything to do with in my fifteen years as owner of this place (at twenty-five I had taken over from my mother, now retired to the heart of Manhattan), to steer clients my way. They promised they'd do what they could.

Finally, at the height of my first season back in business, from behind the rethatched tiki bar, I stood for a moment and looked gratefully out at my guests around the pool. Five women from a book group ordered drinks from Tom, who was stiff and unsure in his khakis and flowered shirt, when he was used to carrying buckets and hammers and wearing nothing but a pair of running shorts bleached gauzy. I expected the women to start reading—the same book, of course—but they gazed at the water instead, hands under their thighs, trying on the unfamiliar work of relaxation. Three men I'd checked in the night before when they arrived from a day of delayed flights and too many mixed drinks were already asleep on chaises, their tight faces to the sun. The Jensen family reunion—thirteen in all—took up more than their share of space with their gear and noise. Scattered couples, including a pair on their honeymoon, filled out the small but adequate crowd. Down at the beach, an awkward man lumbered onto a jet-ski while his wife stood on the sand and shouted cautions at him.

The day was brilliant, the heat tempered by the trade winds, and for a lifting moment I heard the hymn I'd been waiting for since the day Tess tore through. Every host, every cook, every seducer listens for his particular sound, and mine was the simple noise of my existence—people at leisure. But despite the sound, I also knew I was barely hanging on to the place I loved so much. I'd left myself no margin for another disaster, and this might be the final decisive season for me. The possibility that I could fail so easily and lose all this—my life, the only place I knew and wanted to be—made me dizzy enough to crouch down and rest my forehead against iced bottles of beer at the base of the bar.

At a sudden shift in the air, I stood again. When I looked past the pool, I saw a deathly figure moving among the shadows. He took forever on desiccated, sticklike legs to move through the low seagrape trees, some of which were badly deformed from the storm. When he stepped out, the bright glare of the sun seemed to shock him absolutely still. His thin, gray lips pursed, and his eyes receded in sore, watery sockets. The hymn died instantly as eyes fixed on the man's distended belly, which urged itself against a pink shirt, and ears attuned to his labored wheeze. Men pulled their knees up, a child fussed, its mother tensed, I held my breath, stunned. Very soon, the man's wife hurried out of the shade to lead her husband to a chair; in a neon pink bathing suit, she looked obscene with health next to him.

I had checked her in the evening before—they were Cecelia and Henry Blaze, from just outside Boston. Henry, she'd explained while signing the registration slip with her own gold-capped pen, didn't travel well, they would skip dinner. Under the bougainvillea'd portico, I could just make out his bent shape among the bags Jono was piling into the cart that would buzz them to their cabana. They were staying for three weeks, Cecelia reminded me as she slipped her pen back in her purse, and she hoped the weather would hold. She was in her mid-fifties, and I could see that she'd been pretty once, but over-efficiency and some sadness had taken it out of her. Distracted by noise in the kitchen at that moment, I didn't think about the Blazes again.

Now as Henry Blaze creaked himself onto one of the pool chairs, I anxiously waited for leisure to return poolside, but I saw from the looks on the faces of the other guests that it wasn't going to come back so easily. No one wants to see reality on vacation, and this was an awful lot of reality on such a bright day. If my first thought about Henry Blaze was get him the hell out of here, my second was, is this death making fun back at me? Tess had nearly wiped me out. After everything, I was not going to let a dead man kill me now.

Before dinner that evening, I searched for my one remaining pair of long white pants and linen shirt. My cabana—bedroom, sitting room, bathroom—was the only place that still looked like the hurricane had just blown through. I had replaced the broken windows, but the roof continued to leak and the floor buckled. My bed was unmade—I didn't allow housekeeping in here—the unused half covered with papers, clothes, music tapes I had ordered through the mail, a plate and coffee cup from breakfast.

Some views might be bigger, but I liked the one from my bedroom best. A blue lozenge of water glimmered at the end of a tunnel of seagrape leaves, a less-is-more equation of beauty, and for a seductive second I was stuck on it. I heard calm among the guests, the routine clink of drinks being served on the dining room patio, the two young men I'd hired the week before joking as they put away beach equipment. I had a startling flash of Blaze among the trees, and the possibility that I might lose all this—and then where would I go?—hit me for the second time that day. The outside world seemed tremulous and without borders.

It was too late to iron my shirt once I found it, so I tried to smooth out the wrinkles as I walked to the dining room where the guests were already attempting to outdo each other with descriptions of the sunset. Relieved that Blaze was not around—I assumed he was eating in his cabana and I was spared for the moment—I entered the room as the perfectly confident proprietor.

The book group, shiny in sundresses, ordered a bottle of wine as I stood by their table, hands behind my back. I inhaled their smells that made me a little forgetful as I leaned over glossy shoulders to pour. One of the women had a wonderful, shocked laugh and a head of spiky hair I liked. At another table, the Jensens already had the waiters in a state of mild panic, which seemed to give Bob Jensen a feeling of great power. I'd seen this type before, entitled not by the having of money, but simply by the spending of it. Still, I couldn't deny that the table exuded a kind of welcome, affluent energy.

"How are you all doing?" I said, placing my hand on Jensen's shoulder. I felt the burn on his thick skin through his shirt—I wasn't surprised he'd flipped the sun the finger. He ordered a beer, while some of the older Jensens looked like they'd slipped gently unnoticed into a fugue state. It is true that this business only survives on repeats and referrals, so I brought maraschino cherries for the kids and a very cold beer for Bob Jensen.

I did the room from table to table, made up for the lags the new cook and dining room staff left. This was the head-filling work I was at ease in, the careful organization of a meal, the murmurs of diners, the matte of the red tile floor which would later be mopped down for the night. I heard tones of teasing waft out from the kitchen, and I stared at the spiky-haired woman from the book group, her dress drooping on her shoulders to reveal a glistening chest. I wondered what it would be like if she came back to my wind-whipped cabana and lay on my bed; I'd done this enough times over the years to pacify myself, but never for love. She reminded me that I hadn't stopped to read a book in a long time, and it had been even longer since I'd slept with a woman.

There was a hiss of rubber on the tile just then, and the sound made me recall riding my tricycle around the dining room in the windy off-season, skirting the tables like street corners and stoplights I'd seen in the picture books my mother gave me. But the hissing was Cecelia Blaze, or rather the portable oxygen tank she pulled behind her on a small dolly as she entered the room, clear tubing and the mask draped on a metal hook. She stopped to watch her husband in a white shirt and a pair of beltless pants step cautiously over the threshold of the dining room.

The tufts of hair on his alabaster scalp had been combed into temporary compliance. I showed the Blazes to the last empty table, between the Jensens and the book club. Cecelia ordered for both of them, and when the bisque came, Blaze sipped his loudly and banged the bowl with a large gold pinkie ring set with a red stone. Cecelia did not look at her husband, but stared at the view as she ate. I wondered what twist had led her to marry this older man—and what cruder twist had led them to plague me now.

Blaze didn't look up when I stood by their table, and I could tell he was accustomed to not responding until he was good and ready, that he'd once been in charge of people and things. Cecelia and I talked about hikes she might take, and when I asked if she were interested in a jet-ski—I was only trying to feel something out about these people, what would stir or startle them— she laughed, grateful, I think, for even this lame bit of flattery.

"How about me?" Blaze said.

It was more than I'd heard him say before, and the strength of his voice was unsettling, when I had expected something closer to a rasp or a whisper. His wife pretended he hadn't spoken at all and went back to her soup.

The book club ordered another bottle of wine, and when Blaze began to wheeze, I hurried to pull the cork and pour, to catch the eye of the spiky-haired woman, to make conversation and offer distraction. Cecelia slowly touched her mouth with a napkin and put it by her plate before she stood. A sense of urgency had gripped me and the room, which was now watching the scene with distaste. She began to fumble with the tubing from the oxygen tank, and small words tumbled from her lips. Blaze's shoulders heaved in an increasingly labored way. A waiter stopped short with his tray of melting ice cream for the Jensens.

"Here, let me help you," I offered, and bent down next to Cecelia, who was now kneeling, her skin pale against the red tiles. Her skirt was unwrapped up the length of a freckled thigh, revealing sad white underpants.

"I have it," she said, but continued to pull uselessly at the tubing.

A nervous odor rose off Blaze. I was now almost cheek to cheek with his wife, and a little desperate. "The goddamn thing's taped up," I said.

Cecelia shot me a look of disapproval. She flipped her skirt shut, sat back, and with what seemed like total, prideful indifference, tossed the problem to me; her husband was going to die in *my* dining room. Blaze shifted to the right then, and with a small, almost dainty cough, threw up his dinner. A moment later he took a full, wheezeless sigh while a splatter slid off his square knees onto the floor.

I stood too fast and motioned for my staff to come clean up; suddenly they were blind to me, and I was dizzy.

"Goddamn it!" Blaze said. For the first time we looked directly at each other, and I saw from his eyes that he wasn't really old at all. I could have felt sorry for him then—all this misery in a man just sixty—but I was even less forgiving than earlier that he'd chosen my place for this freak show of his.

After some cleaning up, Cecelia slouched her husband out of the room. I assured the book group that Blaze would be fine, though I could see them rallying as concerned women now and not vacationers. I sent Jensen another beer, which he received with a shrug, and I turned on the ceiling fan to blow the death smell of Henry Blaze out to sea.

Later, the book club played poker and scattered plastic chips on the patio floor, their tone a little off, like people having a good time at a wake. I heard the clatter of bikes and mopeds behind the kitchen as the staff heckled their way home. In the front office, I checked the computer as I did every night now, to see if new reservations had come in since I'd last looked. There was only one, and that not yet confirmed. I put my head in my hands.

"Jesus H., that was some scene with the old man tonight," Bob Jensen said, peering into the office and startling me. "Disturbing you?"

"Disturbing me? No, just shutting up for the night," I said. I wanted to tell him not to stroll where he wasn't welcome, and I knew by the way he was hanging around that I'd have to open the bar and give the guy a drink on the house pretty soon. I turned out the office light.

"So, I thought he was going to die right there," Jensen continued, as we walked outside. He shivered for a second in the heat. "You know that noise he made, like a spoon went down his garbage disposal. Kind of freaked my wife and kids. Let's not even talk about the spewing."

"Let me get you a drink, Mr. Jensen," I said, and led him to the dark tiki bar. He hoisted himself onto a stool and told me what a nice place I had. With his broad back half turned to me, he watched the anoles skitter by the pool lights and sipped his Cuba Libre.

"Okay, what I'm wondering," he said, "is maybe the old guy could eat earlier or later or in his cabana, or something. You don't think I'm being hard, do you?" Jensen said, his voice falsely sappy. "And I'm not saying he shouldn't be here at all because hey, that's his right too. I just think he could be less here, if you see what I mean. I'm sure I speak for the other guests, and I *know* I speak for the Jensens, all fourteen of us."

"Thirteen," I corrected.

"There's a set of twins," he said, and his tongue explored the inside of his cheek as though now daring me to charge him for one more person, when I'd sat him next to death at dinner. "The ten-year-olds. You probably missed them, everyone always does. Anyway, I'd like to see what you can do about the problem. This is our one vacation a year, know what I mean? We plan to make it a regular thing too, come back here maybe, if all goes well."

The fat fuck was threatening me. "Can I top you off?" I said, holding up the bottle of rum. But he waved it away, finished the rest of his drink in a final gulp, and said goodnight. I saw him jump back as a tiny emerald lizard crossed his path.

The book club quit around midnight and made their way, loopy with booze and solidarity, through the trees. Finally, I could go to my cabana. This not-going-to-bed-before-the-last-guest was one of my mother's more tenacious policies. She'd also say Blaze should stay, and bring him his meals herself if that's what needed to be done to keep him happy and hidden. It was a win-win situation financially, she'd declare—her own uneasiness inconsequential—her eye always on business and the next season. But I simply wanted Blaze gone, off my island before he ruined it. His ghostliness, his precarious hold on things, felt too much like mine at the moment.

Though it was late and I was exhausted, I walked toward the Blazes' cabana. From the path, I could see the two defiant fist-shaped rock outcroppings that towered over an eddying, unpredictable pool below, shaded violet even in the dark. I know my part of the island is inspired with natural, moody beauty, and that night I noticed how a winking luminescence seemed to rise from the coral reefs. Cecelia was playing cards on the open terrace and listening to a symphony on the only radio station we got on the windward side of the island. Henry, in a white robe, was asleep in the hammock chair, his head lolled to one side. Cecelia looked up suddenly, though I don't think she saw me hidden by the curve of the path. She looked pained, as if she'd lost something. She might have simply caught a flash off the water just then that made her want to go home as desperately as I wanted them to leave. For this, for her, I decided to let them have the night.

It wasn't until I was in the light of the bathroom back in my cabana that I noticed the spattering of spew—as Jensen had put it so eloquently—on the cuffs of my pants. I had to scrub with an old toothbrush and a cracked bar of soap to get them clean.

"You want us to leave," Blaze said the next morning when I showed up on the terrace of his cabana. Alone and in the full sun, he sat in the hammock swing again, an open book on his lap. He seemed transfixed by something out on the water.

I hadn't expected to arrive at the point so quickly, and it took me a moment to catch up. "I'm concerned about you, that's all," I said. "We have no medical facilities here that I'd trust to treat anything more than a moped bum or diarrhea. We're really not equipped to handle an emergency."

"Like death, for instance, which is hardly an emergency, Mr. Thierry. I take it your guests didn't like my performance at dinner," he said. "But now Cecelia has those nice bookish women to talk to because of me. They've adopted her, I think."

"Please, Mr. Blaze." My impatience surprised him only a little—I could tell he enjoyed revving people up and letting them whirl uselessly. "I'm trying to hold onto this place, and I do know I can't afford to have guests pull out now because they're unhappy or decide to go somewhere else next year for whatever reason. I'm not sure this is the best place for you to be."

"You mean I'm not an asset." Blaze countered my ugly lack of sympathy and squinted at the water again. "Your guests are too uptight."

"You have to understand my position." The truth was I could only ask him to leave; I couldn't actually force him out.

"I understand your position well enough, Mr. Thierry. Now look at mine."

Blaze was not wearing a shirt, and I saw how trim and beautiful his body must have been before he got sick, before he became distended, toxic and puffy in some places, deflated in others. A bracelet of thin black leather circled his wrist, a strange touch on such a pale American. I was repulsed by his body, and when I turned away I saw what he'd been looking at so intently while we talked. On the large sandbar not far offshore, the honeymooners from Philadelphia were bare-chested, their faces pressed tightly together. She was lying on top of him, while his hands circled the sides of her breasts and then the rise of her ass. Their bright orange kayaks sat nose-first on the sand, the single palm tree fanning a wasted shade over them.

"Not exactly private, is it?" Blaze laughed, a little wistfully, I thought.

I sat down on the low wall. My eyes adjusted to the darkness of the room behind Blaze, and to the squadrons of pill bottles and inhalers on the wicker bureau. Last night's oxygen dolly stood by the unmade bed. For the first time, it occurred to me that Blaze might have AIDS, with his collection of mismatched and terrible ravages. Our island is an oil well of pleasure, and I'd seen enough sick people standing in cool and furtive doorways in town to know this particular disease.

"Why did you come here?" I asked.

"You think I singled you out."

"Seems that way," I said. "There are a million islands, Mr. Blaze. You could have gone to Club Med even—they would have given you your own bikinied nurses round the clock."

"Not my thing, Mr. Thierry." Blaze looked up at the sky. "I can see the hurricane did a lot of damage here. This was the most beautiful spot on earth, and I've been to some pretty spectacular places all over the world. I remember you. I remember your mother too."

"You've been here before?" I asked, skeptically.

"Several times actually, last with my first wife, years and years ago. You must have been around thirteen then, miserable and pimply, performing an impressive repertoire of antisocial activities for the guests. You once stood on a rock and peed into the water while we were having dinner in the dining room. Your mother tried to distract us with shrimp cocktail. Jumbo shrimp, she kept saying, look at the size of their tails. All I saw was your skinny ass in the sunset. Still, I always thought it must have been paradise for you, growing up on this island. And now look at you—all business and good interpersonal skills to boot."

There were times I forgot how much I once hated this place, how I couldn't wait to get away. Despairingly fatherless, I had searched among each season's new arrivals for possible candidates. My mother gave me nothing to go on, though. She claimed to know little about who he was. Not because he'd knocked her up and disappeared, or was some married mystery, I was meant to understand, but because that's how she'd wanted it. Mother and child only, the picture of paradise. I was fathered by some resort guest who'd been turned on by my mother's independence and sharp business sense; her long toes, tanned face, and light eyes; the skittery sounds at night; this place so far from his home; the erotic heat in the dark. All she might have had of him was a credit card receipt in her files.

"Why did you come back?" I asked.

"I heard you were hurting for business, I thought I'd help you out a little."

"But I don't think that's what you're doing," I said. "You are definitely not good for business."

"I want to die here, Mr. Thierry," Blaze said, sounding as tired as he looked all of a sudden. "I was hoping you might be sympathetic."

Removed and up in his windy cabana on the bluff, Blaze stayed away from the other guests, and I had Tom bring him his meals. With Blaze out of my sight, I even allowed myself to feel hopeful and hear the hymn bounce off the bluebitch stone and pool's surface again. The Jensen kids napped by the pool. A man, still laughing, had to be brought back off the water when the breeze died on his windsurfer. The honeymooners slept past lunch; other guests settled into their own muted routines, while I willingly busied myself with work, the supplying of other peoples' pleasure. Cecelia Blaze had been encircled by the book group—they seemed a useful novelty to each other—and her appearance each morning was good news to me and a reminder that three weeks would go by quickly. Blaze would leave, sick but alive, as he had come.

So perhaps it was some blind gratitude finally, or simply curiosity during a hopeful moment, that inspired me to deliver Blaze's lunch myself one noon. Motionless and drained in the shadows indoors, he did not seem surprised to see me, though it had been days. He tentatively examined the tray with his head drawn back, as though the fish might jump up and bite him. I understood then that for someone as sick and weak as he was, the wrong food, wind, breath, dose could easily kill him.

He'd eaten some bad meat in Poona once and had nearly died from it. "My stomach ulcerated. I shit blood," he explained. He took a bite of fruit—he was not starving himself—which he chewed with his front teeth. "You don't know where Poona is, do you, Kip?"

"I haven't done a whole lot of traveling," I said. "Look, I wanted to let you know I appreciate . . ."

"Northern India. That's your geography lesson for today,"

Blaze interrupted. Did I know he was the largest importer of Indian movies to the United States? The demand was voracious, he explained, not to be believed, and then he pushed away his plate and could barely keep his eyes open long enough to see me leave. When I delivered his dinner, he was in the same place I'd left him earlier, though this time he didn't talk. His lips were chalky from something Cecelia had administered to him, and the air had a cool, ventilated feel to it.

The next day he was a little more alert, and in painfully slow sentences described for me the time he'd spent in the backs of tiny Indian import shops in Queens, Detroit, and Los Angeles, sitting on overturned milk crates with his Indian friends, drinking yogurt shakes and nibbling sweetened fennel seeds. He was hazy with fatigue, full of admiration for the exotic, lost in memory. I felt myself being drawn back to these places with Blaze—I had never known the kind of easy friendship he was describing— but still I was anxious to leave his dark sickroom with its sour, clinical odors.

In spite of my aversion, I fell into a routine of bringing Blaze his meals, perhaps to ensure that he'd continue to stay away from the other guests by satisfying his increasing need to talk. One morning at the end of his first week on my island, I found Blaze in bed, his skin a new shade of green. He'd been thinking of some of the many trips to India he'd made alone, he said, as though I'd always been standing there listening. I should imagine him, he urged, sweating with pleasure in a New Delhi hotel, burning his throat on spices in Madurai, lapping at the hot air with his tongue as he hung out a train window. His large house outside of Boston was full of bolts of silk and painted boxes he had brought back from his trips. The closets stank of vegetal sizing and the oil of polished copper. Cecelia and his two grown daughters had no interest in any of it.

"Can you picture it?" he asked. "Tell me, can you see it?"

I was born on this island, delivered by the cook's grandmother. A lime tree was planted over my placenta. As a child, I'd given names to crabs in the kitchen so they wouldn't be forgotten at dinnertime, I'd followed anoles around trees because I'd been told they led to diamonds. I knew the female pungency of every leaf and the taste of dirt and sun here, but nowhere else.

"Sure," I said, trying appease his growing agitation. "I can picture it."

Blaze was energetically angry all of a sudden, frustrated that he could not describe anything to me with true accuracy anymore: touch, smell, a spinning head, what it felt like to be completely lost. He recalled words these days, he said, only from the practice of having spoken them before. Imagine, he begged, being robbed of everything in the dank of a park underpass in Bombay by a smooth, beautiful Indian boy only moments after sharing pleasure with him. And imagine walking back to the hotel with pockets flapping empty, ribs aching from fear and a few swift kicks, spent and feeling exhilarated beyond belief, as though it was one of the great moments of life.

"I need you to understand," Blaze said.

I understood; he was talking about love. But what did I know about that, or what love would make a person do? "I have to go," I said, and turned away.

There was noise in the bathroom just then that startled us both, the dull thump of Cecelia's wet towel dropped on the floor. Blaze's eyelids fluttered at this sudden reminder of his wife. I sat down on the side of his bed. I wondered then if it was disease itself or the shame of this disease—it was AIDS, I was sure now—that kept submerging so many of his memories, a struggle either way.

Blaze lifted his head from the pillow, moved his hand toward my wrist, and then withdrew. "Do you see why I want to die now?" he said.

Cecelia came out of the bathroom, her fingers inept at the buttons on her shirt, her face pale from what she'd obviously just heard him say. She sat in one of the wicker chairs and crossed her legs.

"Don't be such a priss," Blaze said to her, having regained full breath now. He was unkind; she was long-suffering. They seemed to accept their complicity in the situation.

"He was telling me about some of his trips," I said.

"I'm sure he was." She nodded. "Did he tell you how he once forgot to walk clockwise around a Buddhist shrine?" She began to laugh, and pulled her knees up girlishly. "They nearly arrested him. Oh, I don't know, it just seems like the strangest thing to me."

"Cece," Blaze said, as though he'd been trying to get her to understand forever, "it is so much more than that."

Her face suddenly tightened as she considered him. Was she picturing at that moment her husband bent over another man, thrusting with passion? Was she wondering where his tongue and mouth had been? He must have also slept years of nights in bed with her, the comforter over them with reassuring weight, the dry kiss on the lips as equally reassuring. My husband is not queer, she would tell herself, he does not have sex with men because he is my husband. She wasn't going to indulge or spare him now—his dying was killing her too, after all. She fiddled with her hair while her eyes watered; the love of her life was retreating, and he didn't want her to come along.

That evening, still distracted from the morning's scene with the Blazes, I wandered out onto the patio. The book group, having splintered during their week, was back together for a last dinner, looking forced and tired. The spiky-haired woman touched my hand as I walked by—too little, too late, too difficult, I thought—but she only wanted me to see something.

"Look," she said, and nodded toward the sandbar where Blaze and I had seen the half-naked honeymooners days earlier. I offered a Deserted Evening package—wine and lobster at sunset on the tiny island—for an extra fee. It had been my mother's idea early on, an appreciation of the romantic streak in others. At most, there had only been a few takers a season. "God, it's wonderful to see them out together," she sighed.

At the edge of the sandbar, one of the beach boys was helping Cecelia step out of the dingy. In the evening light, her turquoise dress was diaphanous and slinked around her ankles. Blaze was hunched and uncertain as he lifted his knobby leg to climb out of the boat, one hand heavy on the boy's shoulder. He had not been farther than the terrace of his own cabana in almost a week, and this vastness must have startled him.

Cecelia smoothed a blanket on the sand as the boy left in the boat and Blaze sat down next to her. What a joke to offer up this sandbar as deserted. When you were on it, it felt alone and tiny and the single palm seemed enormous, but from the height of the patio—and from Blaze's terrace, as I had seen—it was a theater stage on which to act out this peculiar marriage. Cecelia's adjustment of her dress, Blaze's shift to one side as he removed something sharp from under himself, the splash as she clumsily poured wine—these were larger than life, lit up for all to see. Blaze had to know this.

We saw how Cecelia wanted to kiss her husband, so when he offered only a cheek, she forcefully took his face in her hands and pulled him toward her, pressing her mouth against his. No one spoke, and Jensen, with his knee bouncing at top speed, stared alternately at his own wife with her broad, peeling nose and at the Blazes. When I smelled the sizzle of garlic, shrimp, and lime juice, I hustled people in, tripping a little over my own feet.

Alone as I watched again in the almost dark, I saw Cecelia drop the dress off her shoulders to reveal her breasts. She straddled her husband, who was on his back, leaned down so her face was against his. They stayed like this for a long time, past the time I heard dinner brought to the tables and the sunset faded.

"You think they're okay?" Jensen said. He had left his family still eating, and stood next to me on the patio. He smelled of steak and pepper. Jensen had continued to poke his head into my office from time to time, giving me a moronic thumbs-up and looking for something to throw his weight against. I knew he was inflated with a dangerous amount of sun and restlessness.

"I'm sure they're fine," I told him, but I wasn't sure at all, and was immobilized by the idea that Blaze was finally dead and Cecelia, in some love/grief clutch, was frozen too. A freak high tide should suck the corpse out to sea and dump it on some other island.

"Let me help you get them," Jensen offered, nodding toward the sandbar. As we went down to the beach and pulled the dingy out, I wondered if I'd misjudged the guy all along—a man who is idle is sometimes not himself, or too much himself. Jensen easily rowed to the sandbar while I was transfixed by the napkin which bloomed from his pants pockets at each stroke.

"Jesus, her dress," Jensen said to me. "Hey there," he yelled to Cecelia. "Everything okay?" We were eddying in the water, Jensen's oars firm against the night's stronger and deeper current.

Cecelia slid off her husband ungracefully and covered herself as she rose from all fours. "I didn't want to wake him up. I guess I didn't realize how late it is."

"Time to come back." I jumped out of the boat and dragged it up to the sandbar with Jensen still sitting in it, sucking his teeth and showing no intention of getting out.

Cecelia leaned down toward her husband. When he opened his eyes, I could tell how disoriented he was by the water at eye level, the dark.

"I can't move," he said.

"Oh, come on, Henry." Cecelia put her hands on her hips. "It's late. These men are waiting. Try." She touched his leg with her foot.

"What's up?" Jensen yelled from the boat.

"I'm all gripped up, Cece," Blaze said. "I'm sorry."

Cecelia turned so closely to me I thought she was going to collapse against my chest, but it was only so she could whisper. "This happens sometimes when he's still for a long time, so you're going to have to carry him." Then she stepped back and waited, her arms across her chest with that odd indifference again.

I knelt down and lifted Blaze's head off the sand. It was the first time I'd touched him, and I was surprised by his softness. I struggled ineffectively until I called to Jensen. His eyebrows rose as though I'd interrupted him, and then he gestured for me to come close.

"Well, shit, what's wrong with him first, Thierry?" he said. "Cancer, AIDS, something catching? What, before I get my hands all over him."

I hesitated for a second and looked at his unpleasantly red face. "I don't know, Mr. Jensen. I'm not a fucking doctor."

I stared at Jensen with obvious contempt while he considered whether or not to hit me. Finally he jumped out of the boat, brushing his shoulder against mine.

"Can you sit?" he yelled at Blaze, as though he were deaf.

Blaze narrowed his eyes even further. "What do you think?"

Jensen and I managed to haul Blaze into the dinghy and lean him against his wife. A small crowd had gathered on the beach, and then, as we were lifting him from the boat, Blaze slipped away from us like a hooked but determined fish. Cecelia and the others gasped, while I wanted to throw my head back and howl with laughter, fall to my knees while the tears streamed down my cheeks. My hands went weak, my bowels and stomach quivered, and Blaze sank fast and helpless in the shallows. It was where he wanted to be, after all. I should just let him go.

But I grabbed him instead. Jensen was stunned and Blaze was an even more impossible weight now. His eyes were closed, as though he had decided to pass calmly through this humiliation and his failure. Someone had wheeled one of the wooden beach chairs down to the water's edge, and we managed to lay Blaze on it. His dripping clothes hung on the distorted angles of his body, making him look even worse than before. Jensen left, calling to his kids who were gawking over the patio railing as though he hadn't seen them in weeks. People flirted around us for a few seconds, while Cecelia sat on the end of the chair and stared out.

"I need to stay here for a minute," Blaze announced.

"I'm going to get you a blanket, a sweater, something," Cecelia said numbly. She stood and walked away.

"She's weaving—it's the wine." Blaze watched her go, and then pulled a pack of still-dry cigarettes from his shirt pocket. "Have a lighter, Thierry?"

"Jesus Christ," I said, and lit his cigarette. "You're smoking."

"Yes." He took a defiantly deep inhale, and looked pleased with himself. "Live life king-sized."

"What's that supposed to mean?"

"Something I liked in an Indian movie, *The Eighth Moon*. Seen it? A real blockbuster," he said. "Everything's about smoking in that country. The prince has just routed a coup, killed a few hundred ingrates, and so he pulls out a cigarette and lights up. 'Live life king-sized,' he declares. It sounded right."

I sat on the end of the chair where Cecelia had been. Blaze's ankle tapped at my thigh as he dragged on his cigarette.

"This outing tonight was my idea," he said, "so don't blame Cecelia. People say she's too stiff, but that's not really true. I think I didn't give her enough time when I was living—not dying, that is—but I love her. Your little island"—he waved his cigarette toward the sandbar—"seemed like it might be the right way to show her." Blaze laughed and pulled himself higher on the chair. "I have no energy to explain anything anymore, Thierry, my disease, my life, my unnatural passions, as it were. I want to die. Seems I'm not having much luck, though."

"It's a little hard to drown yourself in less than a foot of water." I turned around to look at him. "*You* live life king-sized, Blaze. My business is going under."

"Don't be such a pessimist. It shows a great lack of imagination."

"So what if I lose this place," I said, ignoring him. "I can go somewhere else."

"You don't want to do that. You'd get squashed, Thierry. You're an island boy with your ponytail and skinny legs. Your sneakers are all wrong too. What do you know about anything or anyone? Look, when was the last time you even watched television? Stay, reposition yourself, that's all—change with the times. Maybe you can call this Euthanasia Island, the getaway of a lifetime. Hospice Hideaway. Offer sunset pillow smotherings, poolside morphine drips, the feeding tube extraction. Quick turnover. You haven't been in the real world, Kip—you have no idea how popular this dying thing is." Blaze tossed his cigarette into the water. "I could make it worth your while. Repeats and referrals, the blood of the business. I know everyone, I'd bring them to you, all my friends I've told you about. You help me on my way, and I'll save your business in return."

"You're asking me to kill you," I said.

Blaze tapped his foot against my thigh again. His offer was horribly simple—if I believed him at all. I thought about how many times, after Tess tore through and I was on my knees picking up the endless pieces, I said I'd do anything to save my island. I heard water slide into the sand, heat spiral in the air, the coral reef shift and settle. All my life this sound had been my idea of a perfect night, and always would be, no matter where I ended up.

"I won't kill you, Blaze," I said absolutely. "Not even to save all this." Finally, I was more sure of this than anything else in my life.

"Euthanize is the word, Thierry. It's an act of mercy, not business." He sighed, defeated. "I've been trying to tell you that, to show you. I've told you all my stories now."

Their week over, the book club and other guests left the next day, and I was hardly surprised when Jensen checked out with them, a week early, bullying my office to accommodate his immediate change in plans, dragging his dopey family with him.

The time before a new group of guests arrived had always been a good break for me and my staff, and now I fell into it, grateful for the distraction. The staff talked in full island voices again. Together we ogled over the stuff people forgot under beds and in full view. We ate lunch in the kitchen and sloppy salad with our hands, whisked our bare feet across the floor. Staffers' children, now bravely out from among the trees, wandered around and bounced on the empty beds. I had Tom bring Blaze his meals again, so I wouldn't have to see him. On two evenings, I saw Henry and Cecelia standing on the dirt road that led to the center of the island. I didn't know where they had been or were headed as they looked up at the canopy of trees that kept the moon from lighting their way.

By the middle of the Blazes' second week, there were several last-minute cancellations and occupancy was at an all-time low. I must have seemed shell-shocked as I wandered around, and I felt I'd slipped into some kind of mindlessness. I wondered if this was how Blaze felt, giddy, knowing what would come next, a true dead end, for it was now pretty clear it was over for me. The few remaining guests began to assume the natural liberties that come with an enormous amount of space. Their irritations became public as they echoed off the bluebitch, and they were careless with their things, which I sometimes saw float away with the tide.

One morning I wandered aimlessly behind the kitchen. Inside, a tape played loudly, and I'd been drawn to the open door by the music to watch the women bent and swaying over counters, sweat on the backs of their thick necks, feet slipped out of shoes. I had known them forever, and so I was still paying them with what little I had left, but there was almost no work to do; they were playing cards, sucking on toothpicks, talking. As I watched, I remembered how once one of the staff had come trembling to me. She swore she'd just seen her long-dead father leaning against the kitchen's back door, smoking and waiting for her to get off work, and she wanted me to shoo him away, which I pretended to do. Now I felt those eyes and a hot breath in the shade and left quickly.

That evening, Tom told me the Blazes were waiting for me on the patio. Cecelia was wearing an alarmingly bright dress, huge yellow daisies with blue centers, an ugly island design my mother used to wear on Saturday nights. Henry, in a chair next to her, wasn't eating that day, she told me. First fasting, then a sunset and an enema before bed.

"Like scrubbing the ring off a bathtub," Blaze said. He looked sicker, but also strangely expectant for someone who couldn't expect much of anything anymore. "Has to be done every once in a while so the water's clean. Give it to him, Cece."

"What's this?" I asked, and took the piece of paper Cecelia held out to me. There were fifteen names on the list, all Indian from what I could tell.

"I've invited my friends, just like I told you I would," Blaze said. "You got a few empty rooms at the moment, am I right?"

"A few," I said, weakly. I needed to sit down but leaned heavily against the patio railing, my back to the water.

"Some of them won't be able to come on such short notice, of course," Cecelia said, energized by her sudden usefulness to her husband, even in this deranged task. I couldn't bring myself to look at her, to see what she might or might not understand.

"They're Henry's friends, really. You know he was up late last night trying to arrange this over the phone."

"Not easy," Blaze said. "But believe me, I've arranged much more complicated deals than this one. It didn't take much convincing; I offered something for nothing. Most people are pigs." Cecelia laughed at this, and looked a little surprised at her gaiety. Blaze gave her a puzzled look.

"All these people are coming here," I said to Blaze. "Do I have that right?"

"You didn't think I was serious, did you. I can see it in your face," he said. "But a deal is a deal."

Cecelia ignored her husband, as I'd seen her do so many times before. "He's decided he wants them to be here when he dies. They love him." She slapped her hand over her mouth. The way the lowering sun caught in her eyes, I didn't know if she was horrified, thrilled, or both.

Blaze delivered on his promise, and over the next few days fourteen of his friends came to my island. Each arrival was another weight for me, more evidence of a debt I was expected to pay back. As a group, though, these people brought with them an attractive, buoyant life I'd never seen before, a new hymn that I sometimes found myself swaying to. They enthusiastically loved the place and wandered noisily into the dining room at the last minute and stayed for hours, swam at night, slept most of the morning, talked endlessly to me about the island, the birds, and Blaze.

Sanjiv Bhargava, a large and slickly confident man, was Blaze's closest friend among the group, and often sought me out with earnest questions of natural history and my childhood on the island. Three of the guests brought wives who rubbed oil on their dark skin for hours and melted into each other around the pool. Cecelia looked uncomfortable around them at first, so stiff with her mouth mimicking the curve of her arching hairline. She startled at their hands resting on her arms, her knees, the way they included her.

Blaze sat king-like in the middle, but shut out the sudden activity that now swirled around him. Watching him from the window in the main house that overlooked the pool, I was the only one who noticed that he was in deeper trouble now, that his face contorted with spasms, and he fell asleep with his mouth open. In the space of only a few days, his chest had collapsed so that a hollow preceded him, sat on his lap, sucked up his words. These friends of his—fully paid-for and loving their mid-winter luck— swam and teased, but they never turned their heads to check on him, as though he should be my responsibility now.

One morning Blaze's friends had left him while they went down to the beach. Squinting uncomfortably, Blaze sat in the direct early heat but appeared not to have the strength to move himself. Finally, when I could no longer stand to see him purpling and swelling in the sun, I came out of the main house and moved his chair into the shade. I was quick to hurry away.

"No, don't go yet," Blaze said, and caught my arm. "Tell me, Thierry, how does my future look these days?" The strength of his voice still surprised me.

"I don't know about your future," I stalled. I saw Cecelia and Blaze's friends circling around a pair of sailboats on the beach, considering their next activity. "What do your doctors say?"

Blaze laughed. "You want to know about my doctors? All right," he said. "They are institutionally optimistic. They should all be forced to wear buttons that say, 'Be hopeful,' and at night they should have to lay the buttons down next to their alarm clocks so it will be the first thing they see when they wake up, even before they take a leak. But enough already with the optimism, don't you think? It doesn't do me any good." He nodded toward the beach, his wife and friends, and his eyes teared. "Anyway, I've arranged everything. My friends will be back next year with their big brown families and business partners and silent, glaring grandmas who don't speak English—all on my nickel. So you'll be okay, Thierry, don't worry. Now put me back in the sun."

My mother called a little later. Cold as hell in New York, she said hoarsely, as though clots of snow were lodged in her throat. She'd just walked back from the museum and was thinking of buying a pair of snow pants like the ones all the kids had. Since my mother had left this island—ambivalent, but more than ready—she gorged herself on choice.

"I hear you're running a leper colony down there, you've got people throwing up in the dining room," she said. Her friend at Columbus Travel (sister of the reservationist who'd booked the Jensen family) had called to report. Several others had apparently done the same.

"Yes, a leper colony. We got body parts all over the place, but we can fit fifteen people in one bed." I wondered what she would make of Blaze, still alone and in the sun, if she would recognize him through his disease as someone from another time in her life.

"You can joke if you want," my mother said. "But if *I've* heard it, imagine how many other people have too. Word of mouth can kill your business in a second, Kip. I'm absolutely serious, it doesn't take much."

"I know."

My mother sighed. "This man, Jensen, claims he's going to report you—to whom and for what, who knows, but he's telling everyone. At the very least, he's looking for a full refund. There's an asshole in every crowd, remember that—you have to give him the Asshole Special, even if that means crawling to do it to save the business." My mother stopped short. Giving me advice made her uncomfortable when she'd never gotten or asked for any herself. I knew she'd moved over to the window and was thinking, with enormous, familiar regret, how slowly the traffic below her was moving. "Are you in trouble, Kip?"

From my window, I saw one of Tom's young nephews creep past Blaze's chair and slip into the pool. My staff and their kids hissed at him excitedly to get out of the pool which was off limits, but he dunked and came up sputtering, his eyes completely round as he rubbed his hands across his nipples, electrifying himself. Blaze stirred in his chair and smiled. Some muted chaos had taken over.

"I am," I told my mother just before we hung up.

Blaze threw something into the pool then, a shell he'd had in his curled hand as though he'd been waiting for this, and the children dove for it. The commotion and splashes which landed on his hot face pleased him, but his body seized with pain in retaliation. I thought he might die then, he was so close even if he lived for weeks or months. Would it be so bad to simply help along the inevitable now? I wondered for the briefest moment how it might happen. I could slip him an overdose in a glass of papaya juice which he would eagerly accept. In the privacy of his cabana, I could cover his face with a damp towel and look away. But I'd heard the body struggled violently on its own at the end—a thought that made me sick to my stomach—and who was I to hold this man down?

As I drove Sanjiv into town one morning he told me that he owned a chain of twelve shoe stores in New Jersey and had at least one relative working in every shop. Earlier, he had asked if he could use the kitchen that night—a meal for Henry was what he had in mind—and if I'd show him where he could buy some of the ingredients he needed.

"Full compliance with your requirements and schedule," he had said formally, meaning this was to take place after the regular dinner for the few other guests, and that he would pay for everything. He'd toured the kitchen, walking regally among the staff with their tilted stares and white aprons, found it missing what he needed, hiked up his perfectly pressed black linen shorts, and had given me a broad smile.

I parked the car off the main street, pointed out a few places he might try—though the town was a tourist rip-off and I didn't think he'd have much luck—and told him I'd meet him in the bar across from the post office. I hadn't been in Sportsman's in months, since before the season began. The place was empty and I sat at the bar. I made conversation with Louis, the owner, whom I'd known for years—a guy who came to the island after college and never left. Occasionally, he'd show up for dinner at my place with one of his girlfriends and drive home drunk, his hand probably already between her legs.

"Hey, I hear you have some weird shit happening over at your place," Louis said, in a conspiratorial whisper, though nothing on the island was secret. "Business sucks and you got all these Indians, for one thing. And a guy died?"

"Not that I know of," I said.

"That's not what I heard." Louis looked up at the planked ceiling, fingered a faded shell necklace around his neck. His face was wrinkled and a little vexed. I wondered if all of us island boys seemed alike, boyish and stunted. We were single and childless and might always be. "He died in the pool or something, right?"

Sanjiv walked in just then and put his heavy plastic bags down by the door as if they contained the most fragile flowers. He removed a thin, honey-colored wallet from his back pocket, placed it on the bar, and sat down next to me. It was unusually hot in town that day, and Sanjiv drank his beer in several gulps. He ordered another one, which he rested between his large hands, tapping the glass with his rings.

"Much better," Sanjiv said. "Now we can talk, Mr. Thierry."

"Find what you were looking for?" I asked.

"Surprisingly, yes. Completely successful." He named a few

stores. "And I poked around the video shop here as well, to see what's what in a place like this. Large porno selection, one might be surprised to know."

"It can get pretty quiet around here," I said, and Louis smirked. "Long, hot winters. Long, hot summers, long hot in-betweens."

Sanjiv considered this, sipped his beer slowly, and smiled condescendingly at Louis, who got the hint and backed away. "I will have to tell Henry he is well represented. It will give him great pleasure to know that he has reached even such a place as this."

"Blaze is into porno?"

"Well, he imports it, of course. You have to these days to make any money. It is a small part of his business, in fact, but a most lucrative one. He doesn't approve of the stuff."

"Art films, he told me, epics, that sort of thing," I said. "Blockbusters. *The Eighth Moon.*"

"You know that one? Ah, Henry. He's a dealmaker, an orchestrator. I am aware of all his business dealings." Sanjiv laughed. His accent was subtle and covered his words in silk. "You wouldn't think Mrs. Blaze would approve either, would you? And she doesn't, of course." He turned to face me and winked. "She pretends not to know—that and other things. It is a complicated thing, very sad, all of this, AIDS now. We have been lovers, Henry and I, for many years."

We turned back to our beers for a minute, and I felt an enormous pressure to say something, my own confession. "He wants me to help him die. He said he'd bring you here in return."

"Yes, I know that. Henry keeps a promise." Sanjiv nodded, his eyes tearing. "We're all here now to say good-bye. He doesn't look good, I agree, and I imagine he will die on this island." He took a sip of his beer. "Henry has told me about you, Mr. Thierry, that he has known you since you were a little boy, and now he will save your island for you. You're a fine businessman, a proprietor, and this is a wonderful place. You'll make a good decision about things," he said, knowingly.

"Jesus, killing a man is not a business deal," I said, angrily.

Sanjiv shook his head. "No, of course it isn't. It was never meant to be. I love him very much, and I will be sad to see him go, but sometimes this is right. You know, I will be sadder to have him dead in the end."

That evening, I was drawn to watch Sanjiv at work in the kitchen. Easily frustrated, he was also surprisingly awkward as he cooked, bending from the hips as though his back hurt him. The blade of the knife bit into his skin too often, he squinted unhappily at the chaos of chopped onions. His white shirt was stained, and the heft of the pans turned his wrists. When he rolled up his sleeves, I noticed that he wore a black bracelet like Blaze's that circled tightly against his bone.

I was not used to the thick aromas and yellow scents that rose from the pots, nor were the greengaw birds loitering around the open back door, who stopped their night singing as if another hurricane were whistling toward them. Steam pulsed from the food Sanjiv and I brought out to the dining room where Blaze, his wife, and friends were seated around several tables pushed together. They had lit a dozen candles. The few other guests watched from their tables where they were drinking and bored. The windows fogged up, and someone jumped to turn on the ceiling fan. A tape player stashed under the table hummed softly unfamiliar music.

I hadn't been invited to eat, and I had no appetite, but I saw that a place had been left at the table; they waited for me to sit down. The food was startling, and women piled it on my plate. Sweat collected under my eyes. Blaze forced small forkfuls into his mouth and chewed slowly. Every few minutes a toast would be made to him, stories of his generosity, affection, and humor. He stared at me as these testaments linked us closer together with expectation. A heavy silence fell over this farewell dinner. Some of my staff, usually long gone by that hour, smoked cig-

arettes on the patio and watched me. Something has happened
to Kip Thierry, who sat down to eat with these lighter-dark people, they would report. I was under an island spell that had left
me confused and could not be good. Nothing would ever be the
same after this.

"Now we should thank our host," Blaze said, speaking for the
first time that night and turning to Sanjiv.

"We appreciate your finest hospitality, Mr. Thierry." Sanjiv
raised his can of Coke. "And we have made Henry the promise
that we will be back next year. We will bring our families, if you
will have us."

"What do you think, Sanjiv?" Blaze said. He stared at me, not
unkindly. "Is a man in his position going to say no to a deal like
that?"

A shadow moved behind Blaze in the darkest part of the room.
My throat slammed shut, and the shadow passed behind me like
a pressing heat across my shoulders. Blaze extracted something
from his mouth. Sanjiv wiped his forehead and watched him
with a leftward slide of his eyes. Two women whispered like rustling leaves. Cecelia's eyes darted. They were waiting for me to
speak, but I couldn't. I thought I might fall over then, my head
cleave like a melon on the table.

"Ah, it's all right," Blaze said sweetly, and raised a thin arm
over the table. "Are you looking for someone?"

I thought he might help *me* now, when I could barely breathe.
But he was talking to a little boy who had wandered into the
room looking for his father and stood frozen, terrified by the
sight of Blaze in the candlelight.

I was up earlier than anyone else the next morning, and wandered my island, drawn finally to the path that led to the Blazes'.
At the turn of the bluff, I looked up at their cabana, which had
taken a particularly hard beating in the hurricane. I'd rebuilt
the pointed roof overhang myself out of aged purple heartwood,

which now gleamed with its oily veins. But some angles, I realized that morning, would never be fully realigned, and hints of splinter and tarnish were visible everywhere. Up on the stone terrace, I looked into the cabana and saw the single sleeping, sheeted form of Cecelia, her blond hair fanned youthfully across the pillow. At my back, the wind had picked up slightly and blew the smell of salt and the sound of Sanjiv's liquid voice up the island.

When I looked down to the pool that eddied between the two fist-shaped rock outcroppings, even more perfectly visible from this height, the shaded light was green at that hour. The water was clear down to the sand, the slow moving parrot fish, and Sanjiv, who held Blaze in his arms like a baby just above the surface. Sanjiv said something just before he leaned down. I knew that he would drown Blaze then—and wasn't that right for these lovers?—and I would be spared. I wouldn't stop it. Sanjiv kissed Blaze on the mouth and I waited. The currents rocked them, but still Sanjiv wouldn't let Blaze go. I knew at that moment he couldn't do it; he was waiting for me.

By the time I made it down to the eddying pool, I had no idea how long Blaze had been in the water. His skin was a puckered grayish white, and he looked as bad as a person can look and still be alive. There would be no startling transformation when he died, just the relief of pain and the boredom of this. To end it now would be a mercy. Sanjiv placed Blaze, chilled and practically weightless, in my arms. Blaze didn't open his eyes, and there was no struggle as I lowered him and pulled away my hands. His body darkened the water below the surface and warmed it.

Later I watched the island police prepare to take Blaze's body away. Sanjiv had his arm around Cecelia, who told him she had felt a pinch behind her ear earlier when she was in bed. She wanted to know if he thought it had occurred at the same moment Henry died. Sanjiv said yes, it seemed they were connected that way.

Tell me what happened, an island authority said to me.

What had I seen? Two men swimming in a dangerous spot, so I'd gone to help them. I told the authority, whom I'd known since childhood, that Blaze was sick and weak. Sanjiv watched me as though I understood everything now; I had offered my island, and an act of love is no crime. So I said that Henry had drowned, and he seemed to understand the power of the currents when I showed him the exact spot where it had happened.

# Inside Dope

GAIL GALLOWAY ADAMS

From *The Purchase of Order* (1988)

This is a story about being in love with a man named Billy Lee Boaz, only he's called Bisher, don't ask me why. You need to know what he looks like because Bisher is a type, if men don't recognize, at least the women will.

First, a Boaz is not big. Five foot six is about as tall as they get, and they are dark with black hair and eyes, real tanned skin, and bodies just as trim and tight as their lips are wet and loose. They have bandits' faces, with bright shiny eyes that gleam in a dashboard's light, white teeth that do the same, and they are as good in bed as they are at working on the engine of a Pontiac. They don't do sports, except sometimes if the high school is small enough you'll see them on the football line digging in like baby buffalo; stamina and spite keep them there against all odds. They usually aim their every action to rewards, and the mean variety end up in the service yelling at shaved-head recruits and being fussy over lockers. The civilian ones are good-natured boys, then men, who smile a lot. They are the kind who, when they come down to breakfast in clean white T-shirts and starched khaki pants, freshly showered and shaved, come smiling into the kitchen. Their hair is always cut the same, "some off the back and sides, just barely trim the top," and around each ear is pared an arch the color of their palms, their soles, and underneath their underwear.

They're jittery men too, jiggling change as they stand, walking forward lightly on their toes, slumping back hard into their heels, and somehow you are always aware of them from the navel down. Although they do nothing with their hands and arms to indicate their lower parts, still, the itch of lust is in the air. When they love you they are given to coming up and getting push-up placed with you against the wall; then they lean down to lick your throat. Before you gasp they unroll a pack of Luckies tucked like a second bicep in their shirt, and light one in a dramatic way: scratching the match against their thigh, snapping it in two with a nail, or deliberately letting the flame burn into their fingerpads. They are also the kind of men who groan when it feels good, and Bisher, who was my brother-in-law, had all these qualities.

But of course, finally, Bisher is different and that's why I'm telling about him. Bisher was, and is, a genius. Everyone attests to that, even the principal who threw him out of school. Bisher works (where he has for years) at the Standard Shell station and wears a blue blouse with his name embroidered on his chest, an oval with a red satin stitch of *Boaz, Bill* right over his heart. He's the one who taught me to call a work shirt a blouse. "More uniform," he grinned, explaining that in the Army they call them blouses instead of shirts and "no one ever called dogfaces feminine." Then he folded in the sides of cloth like wrappings on a gift and tucked them in his pants. That was the summer I was fifteen, and I sat on the shag rug listening to, watching, and admiring Bisher.

My sister Ellen married Bisher at the end of her junior year in high school, and there's no need to go into what that did to our family. First, everyone almost died; then they cried from March to June, and finally, when my parents realized those two would not give up, they were wed under my father's guiding prayers, and we all gave thanks that one of the two—probably Bisher— had the sense to hold off babies for a while. In towns like ours, as soon as a marriage was announced, countdown began. People bought layettes the same day they bought a plate for the bride's table setting.

After a return from a honeymoon in "Gay Mehico," Ellen and Bisher made our third floor home. The room had been ours— mine and Ellen's, I mean—and was really two rooms with a long hall in between, a sink curtained off at one end and a toilet in a closet near the stair. "Deluxe," Bisher said the day he moved in. "I'll add this to my list of ten best spots to stay from here to Amarillo." Ellen blushed to see him standing there amidst our pink stuffed bears and faded rag rugs. I moved reluctantly down to a room which was used once or twice a year for visiting missionaries, more often for making costumes for the church's plays. With Bisher upstairs, our lives took on new rhythms and new ways.

My dad did not, of course, like Bisher, but being a Christian thought he should, and tried to talk to his new son-in-law each day. "Well, young man . . ." Dad would clear his throat. "Well, Billy Lee."

"Call me Bisher, sir," said Bisher. So Daddy would nod and ask, "Have a good day?"

"Yes, sir," Bisher'd reply as snappy as an ensign in starched pants. Then he'd wink at me and purse his lips at Ellen, which made me giggle and her blush, then both snicker.

My mother always caught these three-way exchanges, saw us, her daughters, as traitors, and would draw her lips together and pale. She absolutely hated, detested, despised Billy Lee. She refused to call him Bisher, forbade our father to, cursed "that Boaz," his family, his pets, and malign chance that put him here in this town when he should have been in Houston getting mugged. "Just trash," she'd mutter, "nothing but trash. I never thought I'd raise my Ellen to marry trash."

I would sit on a high stool in the kitchen waiting for Mamma to finish washing the dishes I was to dry, and listen to her tirades against Bisher, and wonder why he made her feel that way. "It's lust, nothing but lust," she'd said once, then flushed, slapped me on the arm right where I was picking a scab off a mosquito bite, and yelled at me to get upstairs to my room and stop hanging around minding everybody's business, which I thought wasn't fair. But as I moped my way to the room beneath the bed where Ellen and Bisher slept, I knew then, as now, that no matter what my mother said, I was on my sister's side, and Bisher's. And I also knew that I would love that short dark boy until the day I died.

Bisher was able, finally and always, to get around my mother as he got around everyone. He won her over in the end, for all the time she was dying the one person she ever wanted to see was him. "Where is that scamp?" she'd ask. "He worries me to death." She'd pull at the collar of her bed jacket, push at her limp hair, and say, "I wouldn't care to see him again." The door'd creep open and Bisher's face would appear, dark and shiny as mischief. "Got a minute, madame?" he'd whisper, letting his eyes look shyly everywhere except at her until she'd say, "Come on in, you're letting air out to the hall." Then Bisher'd slip into the room so quick if you didn't know better you'd think he made his living as a second-story man, or maybe was a meter man gone bad and gone to bed with the lady of the house.

But like everybody else he touched, he touched our mother, made her do things she'd never dreamed of. He taught her to smoke on her deathbed. We could hear her gasp for breath and laugh between puffs and coughs. "Oh, Lord," she'd say, or pray, with stammering breath, "This is so wrong," and then peer closely at the end of her Camel to see if it would contradict. "Look here," Bisher'd command, and she'd watch him fill the room with smoky rings. She learned that too. It was disconcerting to creak open the door to check and see if she was resting well and catch her lying there, propped up on ruffled pillows, head tilted back to the ceiling, her mouth a perfect "O" as it puffed out those rings until they circled her like Saturn's do. Now I understand that that was one of Bisher's secrets. He's the kind of man who'll take you to a raunchy honky-tonk if you want to go, and all night while you are sipping 3.2 beer his feet will be tapping yours under the table and he'll be winking at you or nudging you as if to say, "Why aren't you bad?" He let you play it fast, but safe, and you were grateful to him for it.

I wouldn't say that Bisher's what they call a good old boy. He's not. At least, I don't think he is. For although he works on cars and engines and loves them, he doesn't care for guns. He has one, everybody does, but his hangs behind the door, forgotten as a worn-out coat. "I never liked hunting much," he said one night in the kitchen when we were helping Mamma skin rabbits a church elder had brought. Dumped out of a gunny sack onto the floor, the rabbits filled the room with their blood-splotched fur. Ellen, pregnant with her first, ran to throw up; Mamma murmured, "Oh, Lord," and even Daddy, who preached of death as a new beginning, looked distressed.

"Let's make them look like meat," Bisher said, "then they won't trouble us as much." He heaped them in a plastic tub where they hung limp as coronation trim to be sewed on, then took them to the porch. After they were skinned and all the leavings but their lucky feet buried, they bubbled pale and shimmering in a black iron pot.

"No, I never cared for hunting," Bisher said thoughtfully when all that had been done. "Because I always thought just before I shot . . ." He paused, looked apologetically at my father. "What if it's true we're born again, and in another body, say, like a deer? Why, I couldn't shoot a deer to save my life, cause every time I'd remember Lewis Moon and how he liked to run before he died. Why, what if Lewis was that deer? Excuse me, sir."

My daddy muttered, "Quite all right," and hurried out to write up a lesson for the Senior Sunday School with two main themes—Number 1: Do we need to hunt our animal friends? and

Number 2: Beliefs on coming back to life that Christians should put right on out of their heads.

But what made Bisher unique was that he was a genius, and how he got to be one is legend in our town. Others have tried his trick since, just to end up laughingstocks when they have failed. There has been only one other acknowledged genius in this whole county, and George Shapland was never any fun like Bisher. He was always tucked up in a book, which Bisher said proved he wasn't a natural genius. "Not that there is a thing wrong with books. It's just that they don't have no place." George graduated from high school at age fifteen after having proved the geometry teacher wrong and having put the history teacher down (both were coaches, so shouldn't be blamed for being soft in hard subjects), and then he went to State Tech where he took a double load of everything and made friends with others like himself who cluttered up cafeteria tables with maps and measuring instruments. Later it was rumored he became a monk. But Bisher's genius wasn't like George's ordinary kind, for Bisher's brain was pure, and how he brought it to the attention of the authorities was genius enough.

A new teacher came to teach English and the Romance tongues, and one week into French, Bisher's genius was revealed. Called on to read a page of Lesson II, he balked at his desk, slumped into his heels, and said in French he'd rather not. The rest of the students didn't know what he said, thought it was filth and that that was why the teacher gasped and said, "You read it, you canard." When Bisher quacked and waddled to the front, the others didn't know what was going on. They now thought Bisher was making bathroom gestures, sounds. He jumped on the teacher's desk; then, barely looking at the text, he read Lesson II, skipped on to IV, ending up with number XII, and he answered all the questions too. The other students still thought he was Danny Kaye-ing them, making Frenchy sounds, making fun of French, so they were laughing at his ooo la la's, but meanwhile the teacher had caught on to Bisher's brain and stood there listening to him reel off syllables like de Gaulle.

When Bisher finished a rundown of the hardest, longest words in the index, translating all of them, a silence fell upon the room. "Is he right?" whispered a semibright boy, and the teacher numbly nodded her head. When she did, Bisher, who was still standing on the desk, now holding the book across his chest in a Napoleon stance, suddenly, without a sideways glance, hurled that text out the window, splintering the glass. At the crash, he jumped to flee the room, the teacher in pursuit, screaming "My boy, my boy, my dear dear boy" in French.

Bisher got kicked out of school about ten minutes later, even though the teacher intervened, claiming (it was the first time) Bisher's genius. The principal would hear none of this. "Don't let me hear of this boy's genius. I call it fits myself. There's at least ten idiots in the institute can reel off dates and times better than this Billy Lee 'Bisher' Boaz boy. And as for this last—this French episode—why, I don't know." He shook his hands from the wrist as if that limpness signified Paris and all its decadence. Then he threw Bisher out, saying the reasons were breaking windows and the backs of books and disrespect for a foreign land.

Once expelled, Bisher was stripped not only of the lessons he already knew, but of all the offices he held, which, though many, were not various. He was the sergeant at arms for every club from Future Nurses to the Lindbergh Boys. He had more pictures in the *Cattle Call* annual than anybody but the Snowball Queen, but that year he was officially excised, and every organization picture had an oblong blank that once was Billy Lee. He signed those anyway with Greek signs.

The second reason he was a genius was inside dope. What that means is that Bisher knew something about everything—he really did. Like all smart men, he claimed to have read the dictionary from *A* to *Z*, and was always threatening to start in on the *Britannica*. In every conversation Bisher had things to add, and always they were interesting. He was like those columns in the newspaper called "Ask Mr. Tweedles" where people write in to ask "What are warts made of?" and "Why are tulips bulbs?" That is what Bisher Boaz could do too—not only explain warts in scientific terms, he could tell you about all the different kinds of warts, from plantars on your feet to venereal on your you-know-where. But, unlike a Tweedles, who had to stop at column's end, Bisher didn't. If you showed the slightest bit of interest, as I did, since my hands were always covered with warts-seed pearls of them ringing my fingers, grits of them on my fingertips-he'd tell you how to make them go away. Every night press half an onion and some lemon juice on your palms, then put your hands in gloves so the acid would start to eat away those knobs. Salt and hot water rags might work, but not as well, and he'd heard from a sailor that in Madagascar the natives called warts "woolies" and smeared them with cornmeal and lard and exposed them to the sun. "Are you sure, Billy Lee," my mamma questioned, "he didn't get that mixed up with cooking techniques?"

"No, ma'am," said Bisher, "no siree. And Old Man Allison—he spits on pennies, then ties them to your hands." I shivered to think of wet copper staining my hands green, melting my flesh.

But warts were just one of the things that Bisher knew, could do. For instance, he knew names, real names of movie stars—Bernie Schwartz for Tony Curtis, Judy Garland/Frances Gumm. "Archie Leach, now that's a laugh," he'd say. "Imagine. Cary Grant!" He knew the made-up names of every level down to grip, and watching a movie with Bisher could be a chore. "Bobby Raymond's his real name," he'd whisper when the villain appeared; "Hers is Susie Moore," when the girlish victim smiled at death. "Oh boy," he'd crow, then clap his hands. "Old Lyman Harkney's playing that soda jerk." And even when the story was spoiled by these outbursts, you didn't mind, but wanted to see old Harkney make a comeback shake. You wanted to know Norma Jean Baker by her real name, even when Bisher would argue against that change. "Now why?" he'd say. "Norma Baker is a good star's name. Norma Talmadge made it. Baker sounds so clean, so why'd she change? Brought her nothing but bad luck, poor kid. Did you know she had a round white bed?" He knew political nicknames too, and was the first person I ever knew to call FDR "Frankie Dee." Bisher said, "His own family did that in the confines of their room. The missus, that's Eleanor, I've heard she called him F. Dee Dee."

And Bisher knew the names of things like knots. He never tied a shoelace, his or his kids', without telling you just what it was: half-splice, granny circle, mariner's wheel, whichever one he'd chosen for that day. Once he macrameed his oldest boy's laces halfway down, naming each loop and twist as he taught the child to tie. It was the same with ties. "Windsor, Crown, Full-Dress, or Brummel Bunch," he'd say, and later, when my dad was old and unable to sort out the ends of his own, Bisher was always there on Sunday mornings "to arrange cravats." "A Fanchon Loop?" he'd ask. My dad would nod, then watch in the mirror as Bisher, shorter, hidden behind him, deftly moved the material into wings.

Names of tools, nails, brads, a half-lug screw, a soft-headed angle iron—all these are in my memory, along with others I never try to find in hardware stores. All are inside dope and fun to know. You can see why children always loved him, wanted to go with him to the Dairy Queen to hear him order "Dope and Dodos two by two" or "Adam and Eve on a raft with a side of down." My daughter loves her hamburgers "dragged through the garden," and she'll eat almost anything if Uncle Bisher says it is "a meal with a story behind it."

I am married to a man who is as different from a Bisher Boaz as any man can be. My Mel is tall, lean, pale, wears wire-rimmed glasses, and is a chemist with hair thinning at the crown. He was appalled at tales of Bisher until he met him, then fell under his spell as hard as anyone. When those two are together I love my

Mel more as he tries to slouch his frame down half a foot and bounce tough in Bisher's stride. It can't be done, but I love him for the trying.

Bisher knows what he's about with Mel, teasing, making frogs on my husband's arm, and laughing, scuffling out a foot to kick Mel in the rear. "Break your behind, my old Max. You ain't nothing but a hoked-up cook." He nicknamed Mel "Max" the second day they met. Because, he said, Mel had "the look of Maximilian Schell, or the Emperor of Mexico." My husband, immensely pleased, laughed, betrayed himself with a blush. He's wanted a nickname all his life, not just Mel; a shortened version of your name is not enough. Years ago, at a summer camp, he'd tried to start a nickname of his own. Tall and awkward at first base, he'd chatted up his teammates, addressed himself as "Stumpy," encouraged the others to do the same, but Stumpy didn't stick. Until Bisher's baptism, my Mel remained just what he was, a two-syllable Jewish boy good at math and "chemicals." As "Max" he expands in blue jeans that fit rather than cling oddly to his waist, and the whole of him is revved up by Bisher. He's sparked. He starts making lists and listing things as "Number 1."

Oh, Bisher's lists . . . he has one for everything: ten famous redheads, five deadly Arizona snakes. When my daughter squeals, tumbles backwards on the grass, hurling her legs over her head to show cotton bloomers with a ruffled hem, I know if Bisher were here he'd have her on a list. "Want to hear a list of five famous women who showed their private pants in public places? Number 1: Marilyn Monroe on a hot-air grate in New York City, 1956." And the names remain, for Bisher nicknamed everyone. Ellen had a dozen or more, but "Mistress Mellow" was the one she liked the best. I was "Grits" because "You love 'em, you're full of 'em, and your warts feel like 'em." Far from being insulted, I loved that name, signed "Grits" to papers until I was married. My mother was "Miz Matty Mustard," my dad was "Mr. Chaps." Every friend that Bisher had was changed, renamed.

Frail Danny Sells became "Dan, the Panic Man" who tried feats like hanging from a window ledge at noon, while C. C. Collins, a druggist in his daddy's store, was called "Chuckles Capistrano, that fine chap," and he grew to specialize in oily giggling. Bisher had nicknames for every pet he met. "Here, Wolf," he'd coax and our old collie Fred would try to growl, and then he'd croon, "Hey, Big Rufus Red," as he stroked our orange striped tomcat Sam.

But what I always loved the best was to listen to Bisher talk about all the places that he'd like to have been. He knew those nicknames too, and the way that the natives said them, like Newpert News and San Antone. I loved the ones that ended in a liquid *a*: Miama, Cincinnata, Missoura, or when he'd give you a choice of pronunciation, say between Nawlans and New Orleans. My favorites always were the "Sans": Peedro, San Jo, Frisco, San Berdoo.

I have often wondered what it would be like to make love to Bisher, or one of his type, and even, on occasion, have worked myself into a frenzy over this. In those early days I watched Ellen with a discerning eye that only sisters have, to see if what she and Bisher did "showed." On her it did. She was and is a woman who is lush, not fat but full, and her skin glows. A man would have to want those deep wide breasts, those soft round thighs that show you she's a natural blonde. Sometimes I wonder who it was I envied most: Bisher, sinking into her to be subsumed, or Ellen, having him with all life's energy.

But for all my dreaming I am aware that Ellen's not had an easy time of it with Bisher being like he is. It's a funny thing that there are men who zero in on a woman they want, as the only thing in life they'll ever want, and once they've gotten her, they start to roam. My husband sees Bisher's episodes as excess energy or misdirected compassion—Bisher's attempts to help some poor girl out. Beginning with advice, he always ends up in bed.

Ellen realizes that these lapses don't mean anything, that she is secure in her position of Number 1. The problem is that it still hurts. She cries her eyes out over each new blonde, and each year I settle down to write a letter telling her that once again all will be well, that Bisher will behave, realize the error of his ways, not to pack her bags and move out here to us, not to storm the honky-tonk, not, whatever else she does, to go to the hussy's house to fight it out with her. Above all, I write, just be calm, you've been through this before. Take up guitar, I urge. You've always had a pretty voice, you like to sing. Bisher likes to hear you sing (not that that matters, I say with an exclamation mark), and that will turn your thoughts away from what is going on at Ruby's Watering Hole. Just get through it, Ellen, one more time. You know you are his everything. And all my love. Then, because I know Bisher would be hurt—and, oddly enough, so would Ellen if I left it out—I add, P.S. Give our love to Bisher but hold off giving it to him for a while.

It always seemed to me that the love story of my sister and Bisher should have high drama in it: a shooting outside The Broken Spoke with Boaz slumping down, wounded in a limb, to be lifted into the back of a pickup truck and jolted into town to have the lead removed. I've pictured that scene a thousand times: Ellen in a cotton dress, shivering in the air-conditioned corridor, waiting for a word about her man, and, at the other end of that linoleumed aisle, a swinging door behind which sits the hussy who has caused it all. She's a brassy blonde wearing stretch pants and patent go-go boots, but close up, to complicate things, her eyes are tired and vulnerable. It would be her ex-husband, released from Huntsville on a 2–10, who shot Bisher down, and that man's now cuffed and crying in the city jail.

But even as good a character as Boaz was, he couldn't make his fate a better story, and I always find the ending sad, the way it petered out. Finally, it was just what you'd expect of anyone— not a Bisher Boaz genius with all his sweet teenaged love. It was one blonde too many, and too trashy, and then it wasn't bearable any more. Ellen couldn't laugh, as she'd once done, at the tales of woe they'd tell Bisher and he'd repeat to her as to why he'd got involved. Although he'd hardly aged, had stayed almost as trim as his boyhood self, he was older now and should know better. He should think of the kids, be more considerate of her. By now Ellen was wider, heavier, her tolerance covered over by both knowledge and flesh. So they were divorced, like one out of every four, and within the year my sister married a widower, a vet who wore pastel polyester leisure suits and had chains dangling on his exposed chest (he is another type who deserves a story of his own). But he seems to love Ellen about as much as he does Samoyeds, and she seems quite content. As for Bisher, within a month he'd married his latest blonde craze, who promptly hung up her dancing pumps, let her hair go brown, and started in making meringue pies with too much tartar in the gelatin.

On our first visit home since the divorce, Mel said he wanted to go see Bisher and I could come if I thought Ellen wouldn't mind, but he meant to go anyway. At breakfast Ellen said she didn't mind, that she saw Bisher almost every day or so to discuss the kids, or just to talk. Pouring coffee for us, she flushed, glanced at the empty place where the vet would sit except he had to attend the birth of puppies, and said, "You know that Bisher. He's always got the inside dope on everyone."

We drove out to see Bisher at his station, and I stayed in the car because it was so hot out there on the concrete where Mel and my ex-brother-in-law were sparring, making plans to go fishing on the coming Saturday. Then, suddenly, Bisher was walking over to the car. Smiling, he leaned into the window frame and said, "Give me a kiss, sweet Grits," and offered me his sweet wet lips. I inhaled that old smell of him: sweat and nicotine and gasoline and the lotion of Old Spice and Lava soap, and began to cry. "Oh Bish," I blubbered, and he said, "Now, Grits, don't cry." As he massaged my shoulder blade, I heard him say, "Got a brand-new list of five dark men who married blondes and then went wrong. Number 1: Joe DiMaggio." Then we three laughed. That night in bed beside Mel, knowing Ellen and her new man, whose hands smell of Lysol and dog hair, are down the hall, I wondered again of sex and love and Bisher. How can she bear it? I thought. To know somewhere not far away he is in bed, in love with someone else who listens to his whispering of names like Frisco, Nawlins, San Berdoo?

Leaving town, we swung by the station to beep good-bye to Bisher. As we honked, drove off, and left him standing on the platform next to the pumps, I saw he didn't wave.

"The Arapahoe Indians invented waving bye—did it backwards to their own faces" was the first piece of inside dope he'd ever told me. And so Bisher never waved good-bye. Instead he bobbed his head. Now, this morning, he nodded us away, as if to say it was his energy that moved the engines of our lives.

# Simplifying

CHRISTOPHER MCILROY

From *All My Relations* (1994)

Easter morning Julia was dressed for church, watering her plants, when the air left her, as if her chest, while straining to expand, had flattened. From her knees she dialed 911.

The oxygen mask was a fuzzy lump in her field of vision. White-jacketed EMT's circled her. At Emergency her gurney flew down the corridor.

Her son Tim stood over the bed, hair awry, shirttail untucked. He squeezed her hand.

After visiting hours the busy noises ceased, replaced by the wheezing of therapeutic machinery, the bellows-like breaths of hospital maintenance systems, punctuated by rhythmic groans of a patient across the hall. Uniform gray light left objects distinct but without relation to each other. Certain her breath would stop if she slept, Julia remained vigilant.

Since the moment was unendurable, she chose another— Tim's first apprehension of her, not as food or warmth, but a person, age four months. She had been swinging him in his canvas pouch. With his every downward swoop she reared back, hands upraised, in open-mouthed astonishment. Tim's laughing shriek squinted his eyes and showed his pink gums. But then he simply stared at her, I know you, you wonderful being. For two or three passes they beamed at each other.

The gray set around her again, like gelatin.

"All this brouhaha for someone who's dying," she said to the nurses and technicians who monitored and tested her the next morning.

No, the doctor insisted. Although bronchitis had degenerated into emphysema, her most acute symptoms were anxiety and fatigue. "You will never lose this disease, and it will shorten your life, but we're talking years," he said. Unless she continued to smoke. "Then you might as well hop under a bus."

"Stay with me tonight," she told Tim.

He fussed. "Against hospital regulations. I'm not a whatchamacallit, garlic around the neck for vampires, a talisman."

"Make an effort," Julia said.

Tim arranged a bed of chairs beside her, and she slept. Within a week prednisone had stabilized respiration and she was discharged.

When Julia stepped into her townhouse, even the gaudy Persian carpet was stale with her confinement. She had been ill for months before hospitalization. Nothing had changed except she wasn't coughing. She would watch PBS and attend theater and symphony with her reliable friends. Tim would appear at metronomically paced intervals. The current agreement was once every three weeks.

Julia tried to organize a routine. Retired two years, she was a zoo docent, but the connection had lapsed. Phoning booked her three days in the zoo's information booth.

Paying for groceries at the supermarket checkout, she yearned for a cigarette, that perfect moment when the body relaxed, the smoke jetted through mouth and throat to the lungs, out the nose, a continuity, complete. At even the crinkle of a package in her hand she was swollen with fondness like an escaped balloon. She bought Carltons.

Lighting the cigarette she hyperventilated and it burned halfway before she could inhale. She sipped experimentally, drew more deeply. After fifty-three years of a carton a week, she must retrain herself to smoke.

Sunday, when the Unitarian congregation volunteered personal announcements, a man named Philip said, "I love to cook, but there's no one but myself to enjoy it." He wanted to exchange dinners. A newcomer, he was six and a half feet tall, with a beard like fleece to his chest. He wore a gold earring.

To Julia the moment presented itself as a question: Am I acting for my life or against it? She felt she existed only through what she did. She stood. "I'd like that, too," she said. They agreed on the following Saturday.

Since her husband's death six years before, Julia hadn't dated, not from deference—they had been divorced sixteen years—but simply believing that whole business was over. Saturday she chose a heavy cotton smock, jungle green threaded with scarlet and yellow. She even brushed on makeup.

Philip's second-floor apartment was one room with bath and kitchenette, walls bare. Though he had lived there two years, stacked books occupied the floor, crowding desk and futon into a corner.

Philip's meal consisted of thin-sliced abalone stir-fried with vegetables, and fat black mushrooms like those unspeakable sea-bottom creatures that one tried to accept as equal living things. The whole was drenched in chili oil.

Cross-legged on a mat, they ate from bowls. The food scalded Julia's mouth and flushed her skin. Their eyes teared, faces dripping sweat. Rocking, they laughed at the ridiculous agony.

"I'll never eat anything like this again," Julia said. "Whoops, no, give me the recipe and I'll cook it for my son. Just kidding."

"He lives with you?"

Julia explained the schedule, one visit every three weeks, that Tim had dictated.

"Grotesque," Philip said. "A crueler deprivation than absence altogether."

"No. At least I have him this much."

Philip was childless. "For my wife and me, making a baby would have implied too much optimism about our future," he said.

Tim was an only. "Opportunities for conception in my marriage were rare," Julia said lightly, but again her face burned. She had decided to hold back nothing from Philip. "If we're going to be friends, I don't want to offer myself under false pretenses. I've been through a difficult episode."

"Oh?"

Since childhood Julia's sicknesses inexorably progressed to bronchitis. "I can't sleep with your barking all night," her father had told her. Every winter, for two or three weeks, a month, coughing from a chest cold interrupted conversation, eating, and her job as a home visitor for D.E.S. She canceled outings with friends.

The past November a tickle in her throat descended to her lungs. For five months the cough flapped her like a rag. Sleepless at night, Julia fell into afternoon naps on the couch. Without appetite, she drank soup. By Easter catches occurred in her breathing, when the ribcage would lift, diaphragm push—finally, whistling, a shallow expansion of the lungs.

Bent, hacking, Julia felt inescapably herself. Her shame at the noise, helpless jerking, sputum balled in Kleenex, was linked to the profounder embarrassments: her husband locked in the study with vodka and the Sons of the Pioneers. Tim accusing her, "You give me a *Peanuts* cartoon book, and when I don't laugh you say I've lost my sense of humor. *Your* sense of humor. When I'm with you I have to make a mental checklist of who I am."

Embarrassment alone could make her cough, knocking the air out of her.

Julia had begun smoking in boarding school, where the girls called their cigs "little man," as in "I have a rendezvous on the balcony with little man." Beyond this delicious intimacy, Julia's cigarette was a complete if momentary satisfaction, a devotion to wholeness in things, the opposite of embarrassment. Of course it aggravated the cough.

As she concluded with her release from the hospital, Philip wrapped her in his arms. "Poor Julia."

"That's not what I meant," she said, but his broad hands cradled her back, and she settled into his embrace as if it received her exhaustion, not only from the recitation, but the months themselves. Philip straightened his legs to give her a lap. Smelling him through the faintly soapy denim shirt, Julia lay without speaking until, nearly asleep, she said, "I've got to go."

Philip was unavailable the next weekend, so they set Thursday before, at her place.

When he arrived, Julia suggested a turn around the zoo. The coq au vin she had stewed the previous night; it needed only reheating. The park was so near her townhouse that nights she heard whooping, roaring, and trumpeting. May was still spring, temperature 85, and evening shaded the paths. Philip strode leisurely, hands in pockets, head swiveling with curiosity. In the aviary his eyes, intent, enlarged comically, tracking parrots' arrows of color.

"Why don't I do this?" he said. "The air is marvelous. I never go out."

Julia chirped to the elephant. Swaying toward them, it greeted her with raised trunk.

"Julia, Dame of the Beasts," Philip said.

"This is Philip," Julia said. "Let's see, we toured the cat enclosures, and the lions were asleep, but the tiger was swimming, which I've never seen before." His flanks had dripped, the sheen of his coat red-gold.

The elephant slapped its trunk side to side, head down, in cadence with Julia's voice.

"That great head with its ludicrous tweak of hair. The animal is so unselfconscious," Philip said. "What separates them from us," he muttered. "But not you. You don't seem to formulate yourself for the world."

Quickly Julia skirted the sun bears, who, still awaiting their promised habitat, paced the cage, thrusting reproachful noses.

"For all that I love the tiger," she said, "and the elephant—and the otters—and the polar bears—and the birds"—she laughed—"I keep coming back to the monkeys." The macaques showed their gums and launched into a dizzying orbit of stump, trapeze, and bars.

Leaping for an overhanging mesquite branch, Philip swung one-armed, grinning. His teeth were weathered like piano keys. The plummet of feeling about him, not yet for him, filled Julia with dread.

Though landing softly, Philip winced.

"You're quiet," Julia said presently.

"My feet." His gait became delicate. "According to the doctor, heaving around my bulk all these years has jumbled the bones. Like a paleontological dig, fossils heaped up. I like to think that the burden has left the bones sad, disoriented. Anomie has set in."

"That's the most highly developed thought about anyone's feet that I've heard."

He laughed. "Curse of my life."

Sunset ignited the haze of dust over the veldt herds. In the fullness of the moment Julia opened her purse for a cigarette—

she'd kept a half-pack daily limit—but imagined Philip's exclamation, "Emphysema?" Idiotic, she agreed, abashed as if he'd actually spoken, and withdrew her hand.

At the dinner table Julia fork-separated the tender chicken, but Philip ate with his fingers, gray sauce running into his beard, bones protruding like catfish barbels beyond his face.

"You look like an amiable sea monster," she said.

"Mmm." He seized her hand and nibbled up her arm. She scrunched back in her chair.

Rising, stooping over her, Philip lifted Julia in his arms until she stood tight against him. His heartbeat accelerated by her ear.

Julia's hands pushed against his chest. "Not yet."

But when?

Julia poised on the deck of the community pool. Since her hospitalization the mere thought of swimming, the labored breaths, had constricted her chest. Now she craved the churning of arms and legs, the euphoric fatigue.

Julia had not made love as an old body. To conceal loosening skin she wore garments to her wrists and ankles. For occasional dips, always at night, she'd hiked panty hose under her suit. But this shyness would not lessen with waiting. Refusing Philip now, she understood, would be final.

Floodlights fanned a seething blue across the pool's surface. Beneath, the water was black, leaves circling. Julia would be diving into her own shadow, a thought she found unnerving and recklessly pleasurable. She splashed in, stroking easily.

When she and Philip undressed, Julia was compelled to imagine herself through his hands—skin sagging from the bone, flesh shrunken—and she could not respond.

Driving home in lemony brightness, Mother's Day, she resigned herself to not seeing Philip again. The affair already was a gift, more than she'd expected from her life. She memorized, for the future, Philip's trunk of a body at the window, arms spread, sunlight playing over chest and belly hair.

Awaiting her guests, Julia felt acute but out of control, like a clear-headed drunk whose body consistently lurches into furniture. She drilled the vacuum cleaner into a spot of ground dirt by the entranceway.

Two weeks before as an amendment to Julia's celebration, Tim had requested including his new girlfriend, Linda.

"Come yourself on Saturday then, for lunch," Julia had said.

Recognizing the ploy, an extra visit, Tim hesitated.

"Mother's Day is a freebie," Julia said.

Tim blushed. "Sure."

"I've had two dinner dates."

"Wow. Congratulations." The burden of her affections visibly slid from his shoulders.

"He's a poet but looks like a pirate. Gilbert and Sullivan, pirate and pilot."

"Apprentice to a pi-rate," Tim had sung, surprisingly. *Penzance* was a childhood enthusiasm.

Julia had sung a verse. "I'll put it on," she said, starting for the records.

"No, that's O.K.," Tim had said.

Julia stuffed the vacuum in the closet just as Tim arrived with steaks and Linda, a woman with flat, functional hands and a stupendous bust restrained by a snug flowered jump suit.

"What a relief," Linda said, admiring the lace-embroidered bodice of Julia's blouse. "I was afraid I'd overdressed." She and Tim were dancing later, she explained.

"Tim might not remember, but he's always been a dancer," Julia said. The blunder loomed, yet she couldn't fend off the words. "Until he was seven or eight we would dance naked together, Shostakovitch, running up and down with scarves."

"Great." Tim flipped his hands. "Now tell her how I breast-fed until I was twenty."

But Tim, who honored holidays, righted himself, telling amusing work stories. He was Target's store manager.

Through dinner Julia's stomach still clenched from his anger. "Katherine," she said, "could you pour me more wine while you're up?" Katherine was Linda's predecessor, and Julia's favorite, in Tim's succession of women.

"Mom!"

"I'm sorry. Linda. It's habit."

"I understand." Linda smiled as if to gobble the world's unhappiness, bite by bite. "Your vinaigrette was delicious." She complimented each course in detail, wielding praise like an iron over a wrinkled shirt.

The pie was heated. Linda chatted through hers, Julia dawdled, Tim ate silently and quickly. Utensils clicked on the plates. The scraped-clean surfaces gleamed as if the evening had disappeared into them. Pressure built in Julia's chest. She gasped and swallowed air.

"I bought Kahlua," she said.

No, they said, the club already would be crowded.

At the doorway Linda kissed Julia thanks, twined her arm around Tim's waist. Solitary, Julia felt conspicuous, as if the others were ignoring a comical deformity, hands sewn on the wrong wrists maybe. "Tim, I almost forgot," she said. "I've organized my papers in a filing cabinet, insurance, the will, investments, taxes. Alphabetized. It'll only take a minute. You must know, in case anything happens to me. Much as we want to avoid the fact, I am ill."

"Mom, good God, not on Mother's Day."

By 10:30 Julia had smoked her daily quota. The pact with herself was inviolable. Instead she watched a Cary Grant double feature. Cary waltzed and feinted through the heroine's amorous lunges as if greased. At midnight Julia lit #1 for the following day.

She awoke with what she thought was a severe hangover, though she had drunk moderately. After phoning in sick to the zoo she returned to bed with the blinds drawn, a shirt over her eyes. She saw Philip turning from the window, approaching, nothing between them but the sheet drawn to her chin. Cigarettes tasted like smoldering chemicals and made her head throb. She wasn't aware when night fell. The next day was no better, so, she decided, there was no reason not to work.

"I have something for you," Philip called to say. Julia said fine but didn't fix her hair or change clothes, drawstring pants and a jersey.

He arrived empty-handed. "It's a massage. No protests." He covered her mouth. She was clairvoyant, he said; the outfit was perfect. He was unrolling a pad, popping a Bach harpsichord concerto on the stereo. She was face down on the floor.

"Petrified wood," he laughed, fingertips playing over the base of her skull, her neck, back, legs. Indeed Julia felt all hard grain, indissoluble knots. As his fingers probed she yelped and started to rise.

"Patience. Bear with me," Philip said.

Flowing blood did tingle in unexpected far parts of her body. Philip cautiously gave weight to his hands, then lifted her from beneath, let fall. Julia had the image of a board, clapped to her back, being pried loose. Now Philip could knead her flesh. The circling strokes of his palms were erasing her form. Even the pressure released her further.

"I don't feel anything," she mumbled into the cotton. "I mean, I do"—she laughed—"but I'm disembodied." The music advanced and receded, lacy waves breaking on the beach. She was a bubble, zigzagging from spume into the pure air.

Julia became absorbed in the carpet before her eyes, its thickness, geometry, flagrant colors. She tumbled through the weave, the pile separating, closing over her. "It yields like water," Philip panted, "and the colors stain your skin." Their merging of thought Julia accepted as natural.

Philip rolled her over, kissing. Their stripping altered nothing. She might always have been naked. At Philip's touch nerves opened until she was entirely this fresh, ageless openness. Caresses were partaking and giving in the same movement.

"These are *your* hands," she exulted.

Julia was swimming powerfully from shore, cutting a straight line through the water. When they finished she floated in a million miles of ocean, one with the currents.

"Now we truly are bonded," Philip said.

Energy begets energy—Julia's credo. Editing the zoo newsletter, she also drafted press releases and mailings to fund the stalled sun bear enclosure. Days off she and Philip might decamp for an Anasazi ruin, Mexico, the Santa Fe Opera.

Swimming sixty laps a day had firmed her muscle—and toughened the cardiopulmonary system, the doctor commended, examining her. She had virtually quit smoking. In Philip's presence she wasn't tempted. Exercise suppressed the desire in four-hour blocks, one before, one during, two after. The surviving indulgences, over tea and at bedtime, didn't satisfy as before, the inhalation pinched, and often Julia skipped even these.

A slow, hot July morning, she daydreamed in the zoo's information kiosk. Until he was upon her she didn't recognize him—Philip, in floppy beach shirt patterned with exploding firecrackers, cantaloupe-sized knees protruding beneath green bermuda shorts.

She laughed uncontrollably. "Alaska. Gigantic vegetables that grow in two weeks." She clipped the price tag from his belt loop.

Together they cast fish food from a keeper's bucket, a privilege of the veteran docents.

"Nice motion," Philip said of their arms' lazy sweeping. Cattails nodded in a breeze skimming cool off the water. Clouds puffed by.

"I'm happy," Julia said.

Linda, who missed the large family left behind with a past marriage, adopted Julia. Accompanied by Linda, Tim dropped by as often as twice a week. Without complaint he replaced a leaky faucet washer and soldered a loose connection in the stereo. "Need anything from Target?" he said. "I'm right there." A haunter of swap meets, Linda brought ceramic owl salt-and-pepper shakers, a touching, unusable gift.

"What do you do," Julia asked Philip, "on those weekends when I don't see you?"

"My survivalist cadre holds its potlucks."

"O.K." Julia held up her hands. "No questions."

"You know what would be lovely?" Julia said. A joint dinner for Philip, Tim, and Linda.

Philip was noncommittal.

After a few days Julia mentioned the idea again.

"My interest is in you," Philip said.

"But they are me, Tim is."

"That's an overpopulated armful for me." Philip smiled.

"Don't put me in a position where I have to have all these little drawers, 'Tim,' 'Philip' . . . Please."

"I like my drawer."

Though she hadn't disbelieved him, the tangible evidence of Philip's literary accomplishments stunned Julia. She turned over in her hands the hard-paper quarterlies with their austere cover designs, to read his name on the contributors' lists. The most recent was ten years old.

She borrowed them. Rhymed but metrically unpredictable, his poems, even the youngest, were predominantly elegaic. One conjured a circus from its abandoned grounds, overgrown with thorns. In another two friends discoursed ironically on love amid the fleshpile of a public beach.

Always a reader, Julia now studied literature systematically, analyzing texts in a notebook, to prepare for talks with Philip. For his birthday she composed a poem.

"Poetry isn't your forte," he said, adding hurriedly, "but you are definitely in this poem. The sentiment is quite affecting."

When a rancher friend presented her with veal steaks, Julia again proposed the family dinner.

"Our balance is delicate," Philip said. "Let's not tip it."

"I wasn't aware," she said. "I thought we were quite robust. Tim and Linda keep asking to meet you."

Philip was adamant. "You haven't made Tim sound like the greatest company."

"How can you care for me and not want to know him?" Tightening vocal chords made Julia's voice strident. "You can't squirm away from them indefinitely. It's absurd."

"Why not? I'll credit them with going cheerfully about their business, content without stalking me."

Citing a need for "heart gossip," Linda brought lunch. So eager was she that Julia confessed, yes, she and Philip were "intimate."

"All right!" Linda pumped her fist.

Frankly, Julia said, the intervals between dinners were lengthening. Weekends, especially, were canceled. "A person doesn't need sex. For nine years I did without. I didn't join a nunnery or the Communist Party. I wasn't bulemic. Flying penises didn't flock the skies."

Linda rolled onto her back, feet kicking. "You didn't grow a beard. You didn't put ice cubes in your undies."

"How come I feel like I'm going nuts?" She'd awaken fighting to breathe, as if steel bound her chest. The cough, when it came, was a relief.

"I never know when Tim's going to show up either, two days, a week, three in the morning."

"How do you stand it?"

"Here's me," Linda said, semicrouching. "I can go this way, that." She pivoted left, right. "I never see Tim again, I'm sad, I'll live. Meanwhile I have a helluva lot of fun. Take it day by day. Tim zips me off to a ballgame, or picnicking in the mountains. One night we made masks and grass skirts from newspaper and called the house 'Hawaiian Zone.' And then . . ." Linda whistled, drumming her fingers.

"Good for you. I don't see that side of Tim."

"I should hope not." Linda laughed.

"My idea of heaven," Julia said, "is two people giving recklessly to each other, world without end. Amen."

"Why do I always initiate our lovemaking now?" Julia asked Philip.

"You're the one who holds back sometimes. So I let you choose."

"Don't you think maybe I'd like to be compelled by you, for that to make my choice?"

"I'm not much for coercion."

"It's persuasion I'm asking for," Julia said. "I don't want it to be all the same to you whether I say yes or no."

Philip prepared an evening of tantra, "a true yoga, serenity in motionless sexual union." He positioned himself on the mat, the half lotus. Setting Julia on his lap, hooking her feet around his back, he entered her. Within minutes his breathing had subsided to a dilation of the nostrils, sigh. His eyes shut, the blue-veined lids unclenching. The forehead smoothed.

Julia's skin burst with excitement and frustration. When finally he stirred, she choked her limbs around him, mauled his chest with her teeth. Quick-quick-quick she moved, bouncing her rear on his ankles, beating against him.

"I have to beg off tonight," Philip said over the phone. "My feet won't get me down the stairs." He'd been complaining.

Julia covered the hot dishes in foil and drove them over. "This place may have had its day," she said. "If you were closer at hand, I'd be more available."

"Is that a suggestion that I move in?"

"I suppose it is. The shambles is charming"—she gestured around the apartment—"but why not live graciously for a change?"

"Can you imagine us rattling around each other twenty-four hours a day?"

"It's not so outlandish," Julia said. She'd keep the top floor, he'd have the bottom, more territory than he was used to.

"Julia, your forays tire me."

"Me, too, Philip, I couldn't agree with you more. Please do me the one favor. Meet Tim."

A day later Philip said, "A concession on my part is called for. I'll come."

Philip was due at six. Tim and Linda arrived an hour early to help set up. Linda, diminutively voluptuous in a tight sheath, hair coiled, arranged the snack tray. Acting out family stories, she revealed a flair for mimicry. Tim had prepped for the evening to the extent of dredging up college lit notes. He discoursed on symbolism in *The Mill on the Floss*. Dusting the London broil with garlic, he quoted verbatim passages from *Anna Karenina* in the dog's point of view.

"Sweetheart," Julia said. "I'm really moved by this support." Tim kissed her.

A glass of sherry, intended to calm, made them giddier. Picking at the hors d'oeuvres, they had nearly emptied the tray when, at six sharp, the phone rang.

"I'm sorry, it's wrong. I feel coerced. We need to talk," Philip said.

Julia turned to Linda and Tim. "You guessed it."

"*Shit*," Tim said. The explosive "t" made the word particularly ugly.

Julia and Philip stood at his kitchen counter half an hour, as if sitting hadn't occurred to them. They conversed with a distracted fluency, statements already thought through that they now borrowed from themselves. Neither referred to a purpose for the meeting.

Julia asked why Philip no longer wrote.

He did, but rarely, nothing to keep. "I won't write depressed," he said. "That's ego, not poetry. I have no affinity with the vogue of inflicting one's every hidden recess upon 80 million readers."

Why so depressed? "Your feet," she joked.

"Yes." He laughed. "And my wife."

"Your ex-wife."

"I've resumed with her."

Julia rejected the attempt to believe she had mis-heard.

Vera was fifty, Philip said, still beautiful, copper hair and cream skin.

"Where do you go?" Julia asked numbly, as if interviewing.

"Here in town. Unfortunately, she's hopelessly unstable." After leaving him, Vera had jumped off a bandshell roof during a rock concert. "I moved her back in the house, and I left. I knew she'd be more at peace there."

Driving home Julia awaited the inevitable cough. Like the braying of an onager, it came, accompanied by runny nose. She screamed in the closet, muffled by coats.

By phone she broke off with Philip. "I can't think of words to despise you enough," she said.

To expand the newsletter Julia recruited correspondents. The sun bear drive cracked its goal, and construction began. Member of a YWCA with indoor pool since fall set in, she slogged through laps when the cough allowed. Sunglasses hid the dark circles around her eyes.

The following weeks Tim was so peevish and erratic—most often Julia entertained Linda alone—that Julia considered imposing a once-a-month quota on *him*. Despite the persistent cough she again bought cigarettes. Linda berated her.

"At a certain age, character becomes simplified," she told Linda. "Julia plus Philip equals Tim minus smoking. Julia minus Philip equals smoking minus Tim."

Bundled in a quilt against the damp chill, feet to the electric heater, Julia thought of Easter, herself in the ambulance, a gray stick, tassel of brownish hair, the oxygen mask a malignant flower covering her face. The cough boomed.

Napping, Julia dreamed of Philip in the form of a joke. The prototype she'd actually heard, a series of exchanges, increasingly damning accusations culminating in a punch line that was, as usual, all she could remember. In the dream the words were enormous stone monuments, unreadable from her perspective. Among the letters Philip scurried, a gnome with hairy rump and tail, mischievously peeking. Some of the joke's lines, rather than words, were film clips of him—striding naked, leaning back from the table wiping his beard, among trees, tinted green from their leaves.

At the punch line—"Well, nobody's perfect"—Julia awoke laughing.

Through the church grapevine Julia learned that foot surgery had confined Philip to his apartment, his wheelchair unable to navigate the stairs. She assembled a CARE package of deli items, fresh fruit, and a bottle of Dry Sack, along with mundane necessities.

Grinning, Philip held out his arms. Even seated he was huge.

"I've missed you so much," Julia said.

"Moscarpone! Smoked oysters!" He twisted the sherry cork and poured two glasses.

Lit only by a gap in the Venetian blinds, the disheveled room showed no sign of outside intervention—a wife's, for instance.

Philip's bandages were cloddy white blocks. "The idea of someone cutting," he said. The wince bared his teeth. "I keep imagining them stepping into an egg slicer." For another two months he mustn't walk.

Julia did some picking up. "Today's man on wheels needs room to roll," she said, shoving books against the walls.

Philip beamed, sipping. "You are dear," he said. "Now we have a dance floor." He put on Vivaldi. Grasping Julia's hands, he lilted her to and fro. From behind, she lumbered him through figure eights. A hub caught books, loosing an avalanche. Deliberately Philip rammed another tower, toppling books and a broom, spilling the wastebasket. Flouncing her onto his lap with a thick arm, he said, "Have you ever made boom-boom with a mechanical centaur?"

"Philip," she said, "I love you, but that aspect of our relationship is past."

"My regret." Stretching for their glasses, he clinked. "And deepest apology."

Leaving, Julia demanded a key, and they argued. "What if you called for help and couldn't get to the door?" she said.

"All right." He slapped the key on the counter. "Not because I need it, but because you deserve it."

"Thank you thank you." Julia curtseyed. "I shall wear it like a diadem on my forehead."

"I'm an ass," Philip said. "Please take the key."

The morning of Christmas Eve, a dressed goose under her arm, Julia unlocked Philip's apartment and stepped into a glow like played-out neon, candles in red glass chimneys. "Boo," said the black hulk in the corner. "Happy Halloween."

Julia set the bird in the refrigerator and poured herself wine. "I apologize," Philip said. "I'm undergoing a seizure of reminiscence."

"You can talk about Vera," Julia said.

As if continuing an interrupted monologue, Philip said, "We were trekking in Nepal, our honeymoon. The sun fell toward the peaks"—his head dropped to one side and his voice thinned—"which went molten orange, as if just pulled from the fire by the glazier's tongs. Then we were rising, forced apart, until we found ourselves on separate peaks. The burnished ice fell away in all directions. We regarded each other across great distance, yet in perfect awareness and sympathy."

Philip's hands pressed together. "I steered our lives by that vision for years. So what if we were miserably incompatible. I willed us a couple, and now she can't live without me."

"I married my husband for his sadness," Julia said. "A mistake I undid. You're not bound to this lunatic!" she exclaimed.

"I become loquacious," Philip said, toneless. "I'm imposing on you."

"No, Philip. Wrong. This is what people do. They talk to each other." Her arm wrapped around his head, fingers in his beard.

Philip jerked back. "Ah, yes, the orgy of 'sharing':

'I have cancer of the bowels, and your breath stinks.'
'Thank you for sharing that with me.'"

"Call me when you are yourself," Julia said and ran out the door.

From a pay phone she retracted "lunatic." Until ambulatory, Philip said, he was unfit for company. They should limit contact to the telephone.

Obsessively Julia pictured Vera, red hair billowing, filmy dress clinging to her white limbs, bouncing on the pavement. Appalled at herself, she researched outings for Vera—chamber music, gallery openings, the botanical gardens, a bird sanctuary an hour's drive away. Reporting these to Philip, she added recommendations for therapeutic books and magazine articles.

"How is Vera today?" she asked him.

"Buzzing off the wall."

In this proxy existence, through Vera, Julia felt disconnected, as if there were no footing beneath her.

"Julia," Philip said, "our material is stale. My topics are few." He would be responsible for calls, which stabilized at two a week. Tacitly the phone arrangement remained in force even after his first gingerly steps, on crutches.

Linda commiserated over the passing of Julia's sex life.

"It's not even the sex," Julia said. "When he calls, I feel the same as when we used to make love. When he doesn't, it's just as maddening. Suffocating." In fact, she was resorting to a Bronch-Aid inhaler frequently for shortness of breath. Coughing fits had ended the swims. Mornings, swinging her legs out of bed, she'd fall back, dizzy. Her limbs always were cold, her legs felt leaden, two minutes' walk tired them.

The inability to smoke enraged Julia. To outwit her lungs she puffed while limp in a hot bath, or nearly asleep, over bourbon or steaming tea. Her lungs convulsed.

"I'm glad to see you and Linda working out," Julia said.

"I'm in a holding pattern," Tim said. "Eventually we'll break up."

"You were a sweet boy, Tim. There, I'm Generic Mom. But it's true. I have every card you hand-made for me, birthday, Mother's Day, Christmas, Easter, Valentine's, for twelve years. Our first visit to the Grand Canyon," she said, "we stepped to the edge, and the ground was broken in pieces as far as we could see. We grabbed hands, clasping so tight I think we both believed we could have floated down together. "And you know what? That boy still exists, as much as you do."

"You mean in your head. These guys are thirty-one." Tim wiggled his fingers.

She'd depended on him for a sense of future, Julia thought, not happy, simply tangible. But he defeated her like a TV after sign-off, a gray static buzz.

Philip sent a letter. "Our phone calls have outlived their usefulness. Increasingly they are an obligation."

Julia laughed out loud at herself, pacing the floor until she gained the equanimity to sit and type:

> You will be happy to read that this letter relieves you of your duties. Please don't call. Don't write. The books I've lent you, you may keep. Their meaning to me henceforth would be deformed.
>
> You probably consider withholding yourself as manly, a guarding of old virtues. It is not. It is monstrous selfishness. Caring people share themselves. I feel sorry for you. The loss is to us both.
>
> For the record, those burdensome phone calls, as our entire association, were delightfully stimulating to me.

Philip wore a loose gray shirt outside his pants, loafers sans socks. "Come in." He beckoned like a hotelier. The room was unchanged, though brighter, blinds open.

Julia handed him the envelope, which he laid on the counter. "Don't put it aside. Read it."

"Not under this scrutiny."

Julia slit the envelope with her fingernail and read the letter aloud.

Philip rubbed his face. "Quite fair," he said. "Points well taken." Off to the house, he said, for a packet of old manuscripts. Come with? He hadn't invited Julia to his home before.

"Will she be there?"

"No. At the shrink."

Driving, Philip was expansive, head dipping toward her, hand flashing. In fantasy Julia had made this journey repeatedly—rescuing Vera from another suicide attempt, supporting Philip across the threshold after her death, tipsily dousing him with champagne after Vera's divorce. That she was actually rounding Philip's corner she attributed to two factors. One, without a more satisfying resolution, which she would not get, she could not give up this final moment. Two, in Philip's view she no longer existed.

Tidiness shielded the interior of the solid brick house. Amazed at her detached curiosity, Julia searched for clues, nothing so obvious as a photo presenting itself. A pleasant scent, spicy, lingered. Philip rummaged in another room, drawers slamming. By the open French doors a curtain stirred.

Julia stepped into a profusion of snapdragons, tiger lilies, gladiolus, trillium, red poppies, crocus, plants she hadn't seen growing in the Southwest. Rustling trees filtered the sunlight. Cool, broad leaves slapped her thighs as each tread crunched, releasing a musky vegetable smell.

"I haven't trimmed the fruit trees. They're looking shaggy," Philip said. "I've wanted to introduce dogwood—those starburst blossoms are a vivid growing-up memory—but I suspect the climate would be too much of a shock." He lowered himself, knees swaying, to pull a weed. "Planting the rose bushes was hell on my hands. My gloves weren't thick enough. Beyond punctures. Lacerations."

He looked up at Julia. "I retreated here from our love affair. This suits me. Vera and I scarcely meet. She's content to know I'm puttering nearby."

Julia saw the scene as a paperweight, an exquisitely-wrought foliation of colors, encased in glass. In the midst stood Philip, feet transfixed by long pins topped with red hair. Placidly he stooped with the watering can. It was set in Julia's mind, the vision of what he'd chosen over her.

Although lying still in bed, curled on one side, Julia felt as if she were bounding. Flinging out her limbs brought no relief. She wrenched from side to side.

She dreamed she was floating on a sea of burning oil, the ship's prow silhouetted, sinking. Fire crawled over her skin. Thirst cracked her mouth. Flaming vapor wriggled skyward, sucking oxygen, as the hot air collapsed, closed like a fist. Inhaling, her lungs seared. Gasping, the sheets drenched, she yanked the chain to the bedside lamp. The room's white and greens harmonized tranquilly to the point of eeriness; the scene looked stilted. Julia read.

A canopy of flame crinkled overhead, following her. Julia would sit, hand to her chest, laboring for air. After a few yards' walk her knees buckled.

Without loving Philip, Julia thought, she had sickened. Loving him, she had sickened worse, more quickly. How could it have become so simple?

Rising from the typewriter, the newsletter complete, she lost her balance. She could not control her legs, which skidded from under her. The second fall she waited until sensation returned, rubbing her calves. Crawling, she backed downstairs to the phone.

Within minutes Tim was carrying her to the car. "Oh, no," he said, shutting the door, but the sound, broken as the latch clicked, had no origin. It could have been spoken by the dash-board.

Tim whizzed through red lights, emergency flashers blink-ing, horn beeping. His face was serene with purpose. Traffic in the left-turn lane slowed them. Alongside, in the center median, a cloud of butterflies bobbed across shrubs, an entity not quite whole, not quite dispersed. They reminded Julia of a meadow she'd once hiked years before, as a teenager. Breaking from the woods, she'd happened on a field strewn with deliriously yellow flowers. The air was so clear she'd felt no barrier between herself and the sky, earth, the fluttering petals. Running, with cleans-ing, full-chested pants, she leaped into their midst.

# Maggie and Louis, 1914

LINDA LEGARDE GROVER

From *The Dance Boots* (2010)

The first time Maggie saw Louis she was sitting at the work table in the laundry building, next to the window for the light, mending stockings. She sat erect on the wooden chair, her body held inches away from the back in order to demonstrate proper posture to the group of girls learning how to set the darning egg into the curves of toes and heels.

"Watch how I do this, first," she said, demonstrating to the silent row that sat across from her at the table. "Use the darning needle to pick up the ends of knitted weave not torn or frayed, like this, do you see? Then cross it back and forth to the other side of the hole or the worn-out spot, do you see? And then do the same on the other two sides, but this time weave the needle over and under the threads you cross over. Don't bunch up the threads, and don't pull too tight; we want to leave a darn with edges smooth and even so that when the stocking is worn it doesn't rub against the foot or the shoe—that makes the hole come back bigger, and you will have wasted your time." She mended over a frayed heel and held up the stocking. "Do you see?" The girls nodded.

"You may thread your needles and begin." The girls' matron, who would stay with the sewing class until she was sure that

Maggie was capable of keeping the group in order, directed the girls in her deep and ringing voice. Maggie distributed a wooden darning egg and several black machine-knitted cotton stockings to each girl. They silently wetted and pinched the ends of threads between their lips, squinted to thread their needles, dropped darning eggs into their stockings, and sat straight as Maggie, their backs inches from the backs of the chairs as they began to mend.

So quiet they were. All she could hear was breathing. One girl snuffled and swallowed; the matron glared. The girl said, "Pardon me, Miss," dragging out the *a* and dropping the *r* in an accent from north of Miskwaa Rapids.

Next to Maggie a heavyset girl with thick, coarse black hair braced her mending against her bosom, her nearsighted eyes wide open and nearly meeting at the bridge of her nose with the effort of trying to see black thread against black stocking. She looked up at Maggie; her pupils slowly uncrossed, focusing. Her smile was dazzling, her mouth a crescent of perfect white teeth, her round face dark-skinned and smooth. "She looks like she must be from Fleur de Pomme," Maggie thought. The matron rapped on the table with her knuckles. "Eyes on your work," she said sternly. The nearsighted girl ducked her head.

Breathing. Some girls breathed lightly, some heavily, through their mouths, concentrating both to obey the matron and to please the new helper, an Indian girl dressed like a white lady, like a teacher. After a while, warm breath, curling ribbons of air, gently waved and wound through the room, twining air tendrils around the girls, around Maggie and the matron, around the work table and chairs, the baskets of mending, the ironing table, the gaslight that hung from the center from the ceiling on a heavy chain. The room became dreamlike, the seamstresses sleepy. Someone's nose whistled softly and plaintively, reminding Maggie of the cries of ducklings swimming behind their mothers at the shore of Lost Lake in late summer, paddling strenuously with infant webbed feet, straining to keep up. "Don't leave me behind, don't leave me behind," their tiny weeping coos begged pitifully. Warm late-summer air wound and curled over the lake, twining damp tendrils around the ducklings and their mother, around Maggie and the rushes that grew higher than her shoulders, around the pale green frieze of ripening wild rice near Muk-kwe-mud Landing, across the lake. Maggie leaned into a crescent of air that supported her as she bent forward from the waist to scoop up and cradle in her hands the last duckling, the smallest and slowest, the one forgotten by its mother and left behind, the duckling that was really a darning egg inside a crumpled long black stocking, and stroked its downy back. "Shh, shh, she'll back soon," she soothed the baby, her lips against its soft feathers.

An adenoidal gasp and snort from the girl with the accent from north of Miskwaa Rapids broke the rhythm of the room; the ribbons of air roiled and snapped, and Maggie jumped, sticking the duckling with the darning needle.

"Pardon me."

"Elizabeth, do you need a drink of water?"

"Thank you, Miss, no," she said, pronouncing the *a* as an *e*.

"Well then, for goodness' sake stop that, or you will have to leave the room."

As the rhythm resumed, Maggie lost her concentration, distracted by Elizabeth's desperate efforts to breathe quietly through her mouth. To cover the distressing stifled gasps, she hummed, stopped, caught the matron's eye. "Can they sing while they work?"

"Yes, that would be fun, wouldn't it? Let's sing. But, before we do, don't forget to sit up straight." The matron clapped her hands twice, for emphasis. The sleepy girls roused.

"Do you know 'Jeanie with the Light Brown Hair'? That's a pretty song I like." Maggie began to sing. The matron followed in her ringing voice, waving to direct the girls to do the same.

They sang the song over several times, until the girls followed most of the words and the melody. The mood in the room again became dreamlike as Maggie, the matron, and the row of young girls sang wistfully about the lovely and beloved Jeanie, "borne like a vapor on the soft summer air," singing wild notes that were then warbled by blithe birds. Jeanie with the light brown hair, happy as dancing daisies. Their hands and wrists mended stockings gently and gracefully in time to the melody; the needles and black stockings might have been silent violins. Maggie led the girls again to the end of the song, holding, in her voice like a silver flute, "bo-orne li-i-i-ike. . . ."

The matron's voice cracked slightly, and she cleared her throat. Embarrassed, she smoothed the false fringe hairpiece pinned over the top of her head, where the hair had thinned, and adjusted her spectacles, peering and squinting at the girls. "Let's hum it this time," she suggested.

As the silent and industrious violins accompanied the song without words, the old matron swayed and smiled pensively. What was she thinking about? Maggie wondered. A lost love, or a longed-for love? A memory, or a dream? Matron was young, Maggie imagined—her blue eyes were round as a kitten's, her light brown hair a silken puff of pompadour above her smooth white forehead. A duke's daughter, she danced gracefully in the arms of a tall young man—a soldier, perhaps, thought Maggie, who had read and reread every novel in the St. Veronique Mission School library—a commoner, whose feet, in shiny black boots, twirled deft scallops around her ruffled and sweeping skirt. Their love was the more beautiful because it was doomed, denied. Alone and bereft, Matron would live out her life teaching Indian girls to sit up straight, to make their beds with sheets pulled and mitered tightly at the corners, to emulate the bleak motions of her existence. Maggie sighed at the poignancy of Matron's life; the humming girls sighed with her at the poignancy of Stephen Foster's dream of Jeanie with the light brown hair.

With a light tap against the window, a shadow flew across the black wool oval held in the palm of Maggie's left hand, so quickly that she thought a bird must have become confused by the glass and dashed against the window, thinking it was part of the sky. She looked up for the swoop of a wing; instead, a brown gingham shirt appeared to dance momentarily in midair—the sleeves fluttered and waved, the tails lifted, then the shirt half spun and sped away. Black broadcloth, a man's coat, moved into the space and stopped, flapping its sleeves. "McGoun! Robineau! Stop that boy!" The black broadcloth coat moved away from the window and down the stairs toward the yard and the barn. Scarecrowlike in his baggy pants, which rippled in the seat beneath where the wind lifted the pleats of his jacket, the upper-school teacher, Mr. Greeney, continued to shout. "McGoun, where are you? Robineau! Stop that boy!"

The brown plaid grew smaller and smaller as the boy ran toward the brush at the edge of the school grounds, blurring into the dull dusty brown of dried leaves. Except for the color of his hair he might have become lost to the sight of Mr. Greeney and the young Indian man who ran out the barn door in pursuit. The color was his betrayal, a near-black copper that the intensity of the oblique late-day sun lit to a red beacon.

"It's Louis!" one girl whispered.

"Lisette's brother!"

"Is he going run again?"

"He'll get caught, him!"

The matron clapped her hands. "Silence! Young ladies, eyes on your work. We are mending stockings here."

The girls quieted; then the sound of the cook ringing the triangle that hung outside the dining hall created a rustle of dresses and heads turning and whispers, the sound of doves in wind.

The matron clapped twice. "Put your things away." The girls gathered thimbles, needles, thread, and scissors into small cardboard sewing boxes that they placed on a shelf. "Line up." They formed a queue, shortest to tallest, by the door. "March." The smallest girl opened the door and held it as the girls filed out. Each said, "Thank you, Miss" as she left. Then the small girl closed the door and joined the line.

"You did very well, Marguerite. They were following your directions, I think." The matron held several stockings up into the light from the window. "There will always be mending for them to do, of course, but some of the girls, if they show a knack for sewing and get something done, can start cutting out summer-weight dresses for the little ones soon."

"Have they learned to follow a pattern, Matron?"

"Some have; the others will have to learn. Please call me Julia—among the female staff we use first names. With the men we don't, of course."

"Of course."

She would have to call Andre "Mr. Robineau."

"Shall we walk to the dining hall? We use the cook's lavatory to wash before meals." She looked curious. "Is Harrod anything like the Catholic mission school?" she asked, wondering if it was true that the young woman, newly hired to help sew and care for the younger children, had been taught by the religious sisters to speak French and make lace.

"It was smaller, and there were only girls, no boys. And the teachers were Sisters." Sister Cecile might at that very moment be grasping a little girl's arm and leading her to the front doors of the classroom building to kneel on the wooden stairs, on a white navy bean. She might be scolding the little girl, as she had Maggie, lisping through a fine spray of spit, "This is what happens to girls who talk like savages. Next time you'll remember English." Her fingers and thumb might leave light blue-gray prints on the little girl's upper arm, four small circles on the underside, one larger on the outside, that the little girl might press with an index finger as she examined them before putting on her nightgown, just before prayers, feeling and controlling the faint ghost of pain and remembering the grasp of Sister Cecile's strong and holy fingers.

"Did you enjoy your studies?"

"Yes, I did, but I enjoyed sewing the most." Her sister, Henen, had been the better student, and the Sisters' favorite; if she had been white, she might have become a Sister herself. Henen stood up straight, kept her fingernails clean, and enunciated carefully, copying Sister Jean Baptiste—"Mar-geh-reet. Hell-en. Par-don me. Good mor-ning." She read aloud without stumbling. Her mathematics problems were solved correctly and written neatly. Her lacemaking was exquisite. Her handwriting samples, disciplined Palmer Method arabesques and curlicues that matched the lace she made, were exhibited on the wall for the Indian agent to see when he visited the school. So delicate and refined was her touch that she was excused from kitchen work to assist Sister Therese with the preparation of the communion hosts before they were consecrated. At morning Mass she knelt without fidgeting while she prayed; at the altar railing she concentrated on the gift of the Eucharist with beseeching eyes, which closed in prayer as the priest placed the host on her tongue.

"Why can't you be more like Helen?" Sister Cecile asked the girls, nearly every day. The girls looked away from the paragon in sympathy; it was mortifying to Henen, of course.

They were, actually, more like Henen than Sister Cecile knew; or, Henen was more like them than Sister Cecile knew: before being sent to the mission school, Henen had, more than Maggie, absorbed all that had been taught at home by a baptized mother and old-fashioned, traditional grandmother—to be thrifty, industrious, helpful to others, modest, reserved and soft-spoken—virtues that she practiced so overtly that the nuns didn't feel the need to watch her closely and never heard that she talked in Ojibwe language to the younger girls while she braided their hair in the morning or helped them to keep their clothing neat and their shoes clean and their sums and letters lined up in rows as neat as the two columns the girls made to march from the dormitory to morning Mass. The girls could see that Henen had been raised properly at home: she had been kind and generous, respectful and humble, concerned with the other girls' well-being. Left at home, she might have become knowledgeable about healing and herbs or about the old sacred stories that grandparents told during the dark winter months. She might have learned the old ways by heart and might have chosen and taught others to do the same when she became an old woman, the venerable grandmother of a large clan family. Instead, Sister Cecile thought that Henen would make a fine mother's helper, perhaps for a wealthy family in Duluth or Minneapolis, when she finished school.

It was quite a shock to everyone, but especially the Sisters, when Henen was sent home from the mission school in disgrace.

"I hope that you will enjoy working at Harrod," said the matron. "There is a great deal to be done here, and as you have probably guessed, some of the students, the boys in particular but some of the girls, too, are quite wayward. Not completely their fault, of course; their families are so backward. So unfortunate. It is our task to correct what we can."

The walkway between the classroom building and dining hall was wide enough for only two people, and so the three males who approached from the opposite direction stepped off of the concrete to allow the ladies to pass. One man removed his hat; the other looked quickly at Maggie, then at the sky. Each held an upper arm of the boy in the brown gingham shirt, which was open and missing its buttons. The skin of one shoulder showed at the seam, where a sleeve had been torn nearly off.

The larger man nodded courteously at the women. "Miss Hall. Miss LaForce. We got him. He didn't get very far this time."

The matron shook her head. "Tsk tsk. What a shame. What a lot of trouble it is to have to spend time on this, Mr. McGoun."

"It is. We are on our way to the laundry. It will be solitary tonight for this boy. Once again."

"Miss LaForce," the matron asked, "have you met Mr. Andre Robineau? He works in the barn and helps with handyman duties, but as you can see all of the staff must take care of other situations as they arise."

"Yes, we have met." The matron must not have realized that they were both from Mozhay Point, Maggie thought. Of course, everyone from Mozhay knew Andre Robineau. He was the handsomest man on the entire reservation, the handsomest man she had ever seen.

Andre tipped his cap and looked Maggie directly in the eye, like a white man; she felt flustered. "Good evening, Miss LaForce." He had gone to Harrod since he was six years old and stayed to work after he finished the fifth grade, at seventeen. He knew the proper way to address a young woman who worked for the school, Indian or white.

During the exchange, the captive boy in the brown gingham shirt waited courteously, as if he were on a stroll with two friends, as though the men beside him weren't each gripping one of his arms. As though his hair weren't a sweat-stiffened mass of dark-red flames. As though his shirt weren't torn, his breathing weren't exhausted and ragged, as though there weren't welts rising on his exposed shoulder. His eyes were clear and calm; above all, they were patient. "Don't feel sorry for me," they said to Maggie. "It doesn't hurt at all. It's nothing to me at all. I don't even notice. There is more to life than this."

She didn't see Andre in the dining hall. Maggie helped the matron oversee the children's table manners; he stayed in the kitchen to do the cook's lifting and carrying. The children ate quickly and neatly—not a drop of milk or single baked bean or potato lump or slice of carrot or crumb of bread was left on the tables. Each child waited silently for the others to finish, hands folded neatly on the edge of the table, then when the matron clapped her hands, two children from each table of twelve collected the plates, spoons, and mugs and brought them to the kitchen. When she clapped again, the children stood and pushed the long benches under the tables. When she clapped for the third time, they marched out the door in line, table by table. After the children left, the matron and Maggie filled plates and carried them into the small teachers' dining room off the kitchen. They sat at the cold end of the table, near the drafty outside door, below the teachers, who had finished their own dinners and were drinking coffee.

Andre backed through the swinging door from the kitchen with a tin plate in one hand and a tin cup in the other. He placed them on the table. "For the solitary room."

"When you have quite finished, Maggie, will you take Louis Gallette his dinner?" The matron had removed her shoes and was cooling and resting her feet on the wooden chair across the table. In the chair next to them, Maggie tried to ignore, while she ate, the fetid raisin-and-onion scent that rose from them and mingled unpleasantly with the aroma of the beans and potatoes on her plate. Inhaling through her mouth and exhaling through her nose she had nearly bolted the food, which pressed in an unpleasant lump just below the base of her throat.

"Yes, I can do that now, Miss."

"Julia," said the matron, wiggling her freed and airing toes.

Maggie listened to the matron's instructions courteously, keeping the expression on her face smooth and pleasant. She had seen similar instructions carried out when the "recalcitrants"— disobedient girls at the mission school—were disciplined.

Outside the laundry building, she opened the slanting cellar doors to the basement and swung them as far as they would go on their hinges, leaving them resting wide open to light the stairway, which was dark and smelled of lye soap and mildew. The wooden steps felt cold and soft through the thin leather of her soles. When she opened the door at the bottom of the stairs, the carbolic mustiness that had been growing and expanding within the heat and confines of the basement hit her face like a damp rag thrust over her nose and mouth. "Huh," she breathed to expel the smell, and was answered by a gasp and huff from the dark and empty hallway. Fighting the impulse to run, she asked, "Is someone there?" The hallway huffed again. Her eyes adjusted to the near dark, and she saw the coal-fired water heater at the end of the hall, sucking in wet lye and mildew air, which it expelled with a huff into the rusty cylinder below the cistern of heating water. The gaslight in the middle of the hallway, turned low, provided just enough light for her to see the two doors that Julia had told her to look for. The one to the coal bin was solid; a square had been cut into the top half of the other, the door into the solitary room, and was covered by wood strips nailed to the outside that created a latticed grill, rougher than but similar to the window into a confessional. "Bless me, Father, for I have sinned," Maggie thought.

A boy's unchanged voice, mild and sweet, answered from behind the grill, "Yes, Miss."

Louis stood with his face pressed to the grate when he heard the cellar doors being swung open and leaned against their hinges. Supper, he thought. He had been there before and so knew that it would come after the other children and the teachers had eaten, brought by Mr. McGoun, Mr. Robineau, or the matron on a tin plate, and that there would be smaller portions of food, not enough to fill his stomach, as part of his punishment.

The second time that he saw Maggie was through the wooden

grate of the solitary room door, and every time he remembered it he pictured the shaded outline of a young woman against the twilight let into the cellar of the laundry building by an opened doorway. The shadow bent to pick up a tin plate and cup from the ground that she had set them on and walked cautiously down the cellar steps. At the bottom of the stairs she placed the cup into the crook of her other elbow and opened the door with her freed hand.

He heard steps, light on the basement stairs, then the door-knob turning. The steps into the basement were hesitant, brushing the concrete with a soft, gritty-sounding scrape. It's not Mr. Robineau, he thought. Not McGoun.

She walked from the dark end of the basement into half-light, a motion of cotton shirtwaist that captured yellow stripes against brown from the gaslight in the middle of the basement ceiling. Through the grate he saw her, then, in partial images that appeared, disappeared, and reappeared rapidly through squares of wooden strips. Woman, he saw, carrying a tray of food. She turned toward the door. Dark hair in a knot on the back of her neck. That Indian woman, the one he'd seen walking with the matron. Strong-looking, tall as Mr. Robineau. She was looking around, trying to peer into the corners. She sighed, hummed under her breath. She ducked nervously to look under the slate tub. She cleared her throat, swallowed. "Is someone there?" she asked. Her voice was soft, a near whisper.

"Yes, Miss," he answered from behind the grill.

Punishment. The first time he ran away was the day after he arrived at Harrod from Grand Bois. He waited until bedtime, when the boys were undressing and putting on their nightshirts. The night before, he had laughed at the sight of boys' heads above those long white dresses that looked like women's underwear.

"Mindemooye," he had said to the boy in the next bed. "Old woman, gonna put on your nightgown?"

"Nightshirt. It's a shirt."

"Gawiin, it's a dress! You look like a mindemooye!"

"Mindemooye, giin!" the other boy laughed and pushed Louis in the chest. "Old lady, yourself!"

Louis balled up his nightshirt and tossed it at the other boy. "Here! Bring it home to your grandma!"

The prefect had tapped them both on the head with the doubled leather strap he carried. "No horsing around. Talk English. Get undressed and get into bed."

The boys slept on their backs with hands at their sides above the blankets. "We look like a bunch of dead people laid out," thought Louis. "I ain't staying here."

The second night he approached the prefect while the boys were undressing. "I have to go outside," he said.

"Nobody goes outside. Get ready for bed."

"Have to." He walked toward the door.

The prefect grabbed him by the back of the shirt. "What do you think you're doing?"

The boy from the bed next to Louis's explained. "Where he comes from, they mean the toilet. He don't really mean outside, he means the toilet."

"Is he stupid? He knows the toilet is down the hall."

"He just means the toilet; he's mixed up because they always say 'outside' when they mean they have to do their business at Grand Bois, and that's where he comes from."

"Do you mean the toilet?" the prefect asked.

Louis nodded.

"Well, from now on, say so."

Louis had walked out of the dormitory room and down the hall toward the toilet, moving more quickly and quietly as he passed the door, and then sprinted down the stairway and out the front door, where he was caught by Mr. McGoun, who wrapped one heavy arm around Louis's skinny waist and the other around his skinny neck and half-carried the boy, who struggled like a cat, to the solitary room in the basement of the laundry building, where he spent only one night, because it was his first offense.

His mother's family, the Eberts, were known for their patience; his father's, the Gallettes, for their ability to endure discomfort, even hardship, without complaining. Louis bore each confinement, beating, and deprivation of food with calm, dry eyes and watched and waited for the next opportunity to escape.

"Are you hungry? I have brought your supper." He watched Maggie, through a series of strips and squares, set the plate and cup on the floor. "How does the door open?"

He told her where the key to the padlock was kept, how it needed to be pushed deeply into the keyhole and forced to the right.

She tried it several times, thinking, "What if the laundry building caught fire? The boy would die." On the fourth try, the side of her index finger caught on the padlock as it clicked open. She wound her handkerchief quickly over the bleeding finger and opened the door. The boy blinked in the half-light.

"You must sit on the bed." Orders from the matron. "I will put your food on the chair."

"I can carry it in for you. Did you hurt your hand?"

Louis stepped outside the cell, which was strictly forbidden, Maggie knew; she stepped inside. She saw a cot with a dirty mattress and a moth-eaten, linty blanket, a wooden kitchen chair, and in the corner a chipped and rusting chamber pot. It was so dark, the smell so foul. She turned back to the doorway, to the boy whose dirty, dark-red hair gleamed like feathers under the gaslight. "Just a moment, I will tidy this." Would he run? "Wiisinin," she said, to comfort him. "Eat your supper."

He had intended, once he maneuvered her into the cell, to push past her and run up the stairs and out of the building. It was nearly dark; she didn't know where McGoun would be. She did not look as though she would want to scream. She would have to try to find McGoun, to find help. This would take time; he would have a good start. By morning he could be nearly halfway to Duluth; by night he could be in a boxcar, on his way home to Grand Bois.

"Gii bakade, ina?" she asked. "Are you hungry?" In English, her soft voice had a slight accent; in Ojibwe, an inflection of home. "Namadabin. Wiisinin."

He didn't run. He sat on the floor and ate, watched her bend to pick up the chamber pot and carry it to the slate tub next to the furnace, where she poured out the urine and then rinsed the pot with water from the cistern. She carried it back into the cell and came out with the blanket, which she brought up the cellar stairs. Seated on the basement floor, outside the cell door, he heard the dull flap of the blanket being shaken in the night air, of a woman's hand swatting dust out of woven wool. He watched her walk back down the stairs. Her feet, he saw, were small; her shoes were ladies' boots, like a teacher's, with high heels, laced severely at slender ankles.

"Will you help me turn the mattress?"

The cell was so small that the young woman and boy had to carry the mattress out into the basement in order to turn it. Under gaslight, the stains took on brilliant incandescent colors: blood was maroon and pink, urine sepia and mustard. He turned his head, ashamed, wanting to lie, to tell her that he had not caused this, to spare them both the embarrassment.

The other side of the mattress was as stained, but in duller hues, and she thought it felt dryer.

"This will be more comfortable, I think."

He nodded. Should he run? In the near darkness of the cell, her white shirtwaist absorbed most of the yellow gaslight. She looked so clean, he thought, to be in that bad place, to be touching the filthy mattress. He had looked at her fingernails, which were short and immaculate, had accidentally brushed her hand, which felt so smooth and dry against the gritty sweatiness of his own.

"I will take the plate and cup. Will you be going to sleep, now?" She was standing beside him, under the gaslight. A strand of hair had come loose from the knot with the work of carrying and turning the mattress and hung at the side of her face, curving in an S shape around her cheekbone and down to her jaw. She bent her head to that side, pulled a hairpin from the knot, and held it between her teeth while she tucked the strand back into the knot. Her teeth looked as clean as her shirtwaist, he thought; her mouth, which she closed as she pulled the hairpin from between her teeth, gentle and kindly.

"Thank you, Miss." Louis answered. "Mino pagwad. The food was good." He re-entered the cell and lay on the mattress. She covered him with the blanket and closed the door.

He saw her again, through the grate, in a series of strips and squares under the gaslight. "When you shut the padlock, you need to push it together hard, or it won't stay locked," he told her. "Don't cut yourself again."

The mattress and blanket smelled of night air, almost like sleeping outside, he told himself. He closed his eyes and imagined stars, a half-moon, and, just as he fell asleep, the northern lights arcing and bowing in waves of green, blue, and purple. One of them became Miss LaForce, who gracefully bent into the crescent of air that supported her to place a plate and cup on a cloud, then shook a damp wool blanket into the cold night sky, loosening bits of lint that crystallized into a spray of ice that fell to the earth, green and purple and blue crystals blowing and drifting outside the cellar door, filling in the footprints that Miss LaForce's shoes had made in the freezing mud. In his sleep, Louis heard the sound of ice falling on ice. He rose and floated through the grate, in strips and squares that became his whole and solid self standing on the basement floor. He walked up the stairs and touched the slanting cellar doors, which opened like a pair of wings. Above his head the northern lights grew larger and stomped mightily in the sky around Miss LaForce, whose pointed lady shoes kneaded a cloud, toes-heels, toes-heels, Miss LaForce, who pivoted slowly in the sky, her brilliant shawl rising and falling over her broad shoulders and bent elbows, like the wings of a dragonfly.

"Ambe niimiwin, come and dance," came the invitation from the sky. "Ambe nagamon, come and sing."

"Waas noodin, shining wind," he acknowledged, inhaling cold, icy air, which cleared his lungs and opened his eyes. Humming, with his eyes on the lights, he danced into Maggie's footprints.

# The Pale of Settlement

MARGOT SINGER

From *The Pale of Settlement* (2007)

Her mother told her bedtime stories. The stories were about her mother's childhood and they were always sad. Her mother would sit on the edge of the bed and smooth her hand along the quilt. Once upon a time, she would begin, as if the stories might be made-up tales, the girl someone other than herself.

Tell the one about your grandfather, Susan said. Tell how he was a horse thief and got sent to Siberia. The furrow between her mother's eyes grew deep. He was a Jew from a village near Lwów. Someone told a story that he stole a horse. It makes no difference if it was true or not. They sent him to the gulag anyway.

The places her mother talked about had vanished into a pink blotch that spread across the top of the map that pulled down over the blackboard in Susan's classroom like a window shade. Vilna, Lwów, Bessarabia, Belarus. The Pale of Settlement. You couldn't go to those parts of the world any longer. They were gone.

My grandfather came to live with us after the war, her mother said. Of all the relatives my parents left behind in Poland when they ran away, only he survived. He told stories in Yiddish and held me on his knee. We were each other's only friend. Her mother sighed, a sharp exhalation, as if a weight were pressing on her chest. He died when I was eight.

There was one photograph of Susan's great-grandfather, a passport square distorted by the embossment of an official stamp. His face was gray and grizzled, with hollow cheeks and sunken eyes. His jaw thrust forward, his mouth pressed into a line. Susan imagined him just freed from the work camps, standing like a character in a Cervantes tale beside his loyal stolen horse.

Susan's mother stood, straightened out her shirt. They said his wife never forgave him. For what? Susan said. For abandoning them the way he did, when he was sent away. But it wasn't his fault! Susan's mother pulled up the quilt and tucked it in. Well, no. Now go to sleep.

Susan remembers the touch of her mother's cheek, her accent, her powdery perfumed smell.

*Layla tov*, she'd say. Good night.

Here is what I see, James said. They were in bed together and it was late. Back in the early nineties, when he was still living in New York but wasn't married yet, James slept on a futon on the floor, overhung with netting like a Bedouin's tent. The walls were painted terra-cotta red, the windows bare and open to the sky. Telling stories was his idea. You had to close your eyes and describe the first thing that came into your head.

He lay back and folded his arms behind his neck. I see a sailboat floating on the sea, he said. A sleek racing boat with polished wood, shiny trim. Only the sails are slack. The sailboat is you. You're bobbing on the ocean swell, waiting for the wind to catch your sails.

What a line, Susan thinks now. Only becalmed was exactly how she'd felt.

She ran her hand along his arm, wrapped her fingers around his wrist. He was a big man and her thumb and middle finger didn't reach all the way around. The back of his hands and arms shone with reddish hair, like a golden idol. Because of this, or maybe because he spoke with an Australian accent, she endowed him with the power of prophesy.

She remembers the orange glow of the night sky, the rumpled sheets, the haze of netting overhead. Your turn, he said. She closed her eyes but what she saw was only darkness, pulsating like space.

Tell me a story, Susan said. Her mother's stories gave her a hollow feeling behind her ribs, as if there was a trapdoor inside her that dropped open to her mother's pain. But she asked to hear them anyway. The stories kept her mother there with her, put off going to sleep.

When I was a little girl, I never got so many stories at bedtime, her mother said. She scrunched her lips together, fixed her gaze beyond the darkened window frame. My own mother was always busy. Always tired. Although sometimes I remember she would sit in an alcove outside my bedroom and crochet. I liked to be able to see her from where I lay in bed.

There were photographs of Susan's maternal grandmother, doomed and gone long before Susan was even born. She had high cheekbones, pale gray eyes. Cossack blood, her mother said. It was many years before Susan understood that *Cossack blood* meant that someone had been raped.

Susan's mother drew in her breath and let it out, a heavy sigh. My mother married a man from the old world, do you understand? She did not have an easy time. A wife was expected to behave a certain way. My father demanded that she wait on him. She had to have his breakfast ready the moment he was dressed. We had to listen for the shower turning off, the creak of the bedroom door. If she didn't time his eggs exactly right, he would explode. He tormented her, belittled her with words. She was an educated woman, not from the shtetl like him. She was a lovely person, everybody said. But in our house she was no better than a slave.

Susan's mother stood up, smoothed the sheets, tucked them in. Now go to sleep, she said. It's late. Susan took a breath, dug her nails into her palm. But what was it like? When she died? In the doorway, her mother stopped and turned. Honey, she said, I don't think that's something you need to know. Backlit by the hallway light, her features disappeared.

But Susan did need to know, the way she covered her eyes during the scary parts of movies but peeked between her fingers anyway. She heard her mother shift her weight. There was a smell of sickness in the flat, she said at last. Something you'll never know—a terrible smell of camphor. They kept all the windows closed. At night I could hear her crying out in pain. Later, I saw the scratch marks in the plaster from her nails. I shut myself away inside my room and read. Romantic novels. Mysteries. Anything I could find. What could I do? I was just thirteen. No one explained anything to me. One day a neighbor woman came to my room and told me she was dead. She took me by the hand. As we passed my mother's room, I saw that the bed was empty. They had already taken her away.

Now Susan reads so she can fall asleep. She folds two pillows behind her head, props her book against her knees. The bed is broad and billowy with down. Steam rises in the radiators, swirls up from the subway grates on the street below. The alarm clock ticks.

In the novel she is reading: Tel Aviv in the first fall rain. Wet leaves littering the pavement, a low-slung sky, the scudding sea. She's been to Israel many times, but never in the fall. In the story, a young woman flirts with her boyfriend's father. The father is an accountant who can't sleep. The boyfriend, whose mother has recently died, is off trekking in Tibet. The young woman sleeps with his best friend instead. The narrator shows up in his own story, gives his characters advice. Everyone is sad.

Out her bedroom window, Susan can see into the top-floor apartment of a brownstone two blocks away. Every once in a while, late at night, the man who lives there will open the blinds and shine a floodlight on himself. She can't see well so far away, but his movements are clear enough. He unbuttons his shirt, steps out of his pants, takes his penis in his hand. He casts an elongated shadow against the wall. Sometimes she forgets that if her lights are on, he can see her, too.

It's not long before he hunches forward, hurries from the room. She squints, makes out a bookcase, an armchair, a potted palm or fern. An orange poster on the wall. She wonders if she would recognize the exhibitionist if she passed him on the street. It's not unlikely that they've brushed shoulders many times. Then the light across the way snaps off and everything is dark.

It was James's stories that seduced her, the way he made her feel as though he could see beyond the limits of the tangible, straight into her heart. That first night, when he brought her back to his apartment and undressed her and made her come but wouldn't yet have sex, he told her about the Aborigines. They were sitting next to each other on the couch, still behaving as if talking were something other than a precursor to making love.

There was a time, James said, before the world was fully awake, when the ancestors emerged from their underground sleep and began to sing their way across the land. They crossed the continent with song lines, inscribing stories on the landscape, on the rocks and creek beds, rainforests and hills. *Alcheringa*, he said, with his long flat vowels and intense gaze that made her believe everything he said. *Dreamtime*. It still exists, he said, just below the surface of consciousness. He picked up a coffee table book of Aboriginal art, flipped through the pages, reading out the names. Emu Woman. Dreaming Wallaby Man. Susan pictured the ancestors, vaporous as djinns, their bodies cracking through the earth. James pointed to a picture of a hide traced with constellations of tiny dots, red and green and blue and gray. This is the Lizard Ancestor, he said. See, there's his tail. The story goes like this: Once upon a time, the Fringed Lizard and his beautiful young wife walked all the way from northern Australia to the Southern Sea. There a southerner stole the wife and sent him home with a substitute instead.

Susan didn't know then that the book was, in fact, Nicole's. Nicole who imported Aboriginal art for a SoHo gallery. Nicole whose naked body was right there, in black and white, in the photograph hanging on James's bathroom wall.

In those days, James spoke in the singular: *I, my, mine.* Because he didn't talk about Nicole, she didn't yet exist.

We lived in the quarter of Sanhedria when I was a little girl, Susan's mother said. It wasn't a religious neighborhood back then. Behind the house was a garden with some olive trees. My brothers used to climb the trees, pretend that they were spies. All you could really see, though, was into the bedroom window of the house next door. If you were lucky, you might catch a glimpse of the fat Hungarian lady who lived there taking off her clothes.

Susan tried to imagine this part of Jerusalem where she had never been. There were no photographs of her mother's childhood home, so she had to make it up. The bald hilltops, cracked concrete, chalky stones. Dusty plots littered with bits of scrap iron and curls of rusty wire. The wail of a muezzin in a minaret. The smells of cooking cabbage, garbage, diesel fumes. Quilts flapping over terrace rails. The piercing desert light.

The roof of our building was flat, her mother said, painted white against the heat. From there you could see the yeshiva at the corner, the tin-roofed *makolet* where we bought our milk and bread, the old Arab house across the street. The house was made of stone, with a red-tiled roof and windows covered with iron grilles. The family who lived there ran away to Egypt in '48. Al-Rashidi—that was their name. They had a daughter around my age. After they left, the house stood empty for many years. Sometimes my brothers said you could see a strange flickering in the windows, late at night, as if someone were moving around upstairs. Later, they put an army barracks there.

Her mother reached forward, pulled her close. Susan pressed her face against the softness of her breasts. *Layla tov.* The shadows deepened in the corners of the room. Passing traffic cast rectangles of light along the wall.

Once, years later, Susan asked her mother if what she'd said about the old Arab house across the street was true. What did I say? her mother said, wiping her hands on a dishtowel. How it was haunted, Susan said. How you sometimes saw a light. Her mother made a face, pushed back her hair. Don't be ridiculous, she said. I never said anything of the kind.

Once Susan invited James to her parents' place in Riverdale for dinner on a Friday night. It was still the early days when they weren't really sleeping together yet. She was excited to show him the place she came from, a part of the city he'd never been to before, a place you couldn't get to easily by subway or on foot. She drove and he sat beside her, slightly hunched in the front seat of the Honda, eager as a boy. She took a detour along the Hudson, stopping at Wave Hill. They parked and walked across the sloping lawn and flowerbeds to look out across the river at the view—the flaring red and orange of the autumn leaves along the Palisades; to the south, the George Washington Bridge, strung with lights. A wedding was going on inside the mansion. The bride stepped out onto the stone terrace, surrounded by her bridesmaids, their hair and dresses fluttering like birds. Toscanini lived here, Susan told James, during the war. The wind riffled the hair back from his forehead. In the sharp light, with his wind-reddened cheeks and faint spray of freckles across his skin, he reminded her of her cousin Gavi. A Scotch-Irish version, with reddish hair instead of black, blue eyes instead of brown. God I love this place, James said, shielding his eyes from the setting sun with one hand.

But bringing James to meet her parents had been a mistake. How alien he'd looked, standing there in the doorway with its brass mezuzah, the print of Chagall's green lovers floating on the facing wall. She could feel her parents taking in his ruddy solidity, his height. James O'Reilly? her father repeated as he shook his hand, and Susan felt ashamed. He might as well have had a crucifix around his neck. They followed her parents into the living room and sat stiffly on the couch as if they were foreign guests. You know I spent a month in Israel, James told her parents, when I was seventeen, on an exchange program organized by the Australian government. *Ani medaber k'tzat ivrit,* he said proudly, in an accent that made Susan cringe, but her father exclaimed *yoffi!* and her mother touched his shoulder and said she'd teach him more Hebrew any time he liked. It's a deal, James said as if he meant it, unaware of how they condescended to him, an Israel-loving goy. Susan remembered looking down at the familiar pattern of the Persian carpet distorted by the coffee table glass, trying to decide if her parents thought James was her boyfriend. (They were being so very friendly; surely not.) She remembers noticing James's shoes, flimsy leather slip-ons no American guy would dream of putting on.

After dinner, her parents accompanied them down to the street. They stood with their arms folded across their chests against the wind and kissed Susan on both cheeks and shook James's hand. *Layla tov,* they said. *Az yalla.* Bye. And then Susan and James were back in the Honda, driving south along the Harlem River Drive, back in Manhattan, heading home. She felt, as she always did, a guilty sense of relief at her escape. She glanced over at James, at the line of his forehead and jaw silhouetted in the glare of the oncoming lights, and suddenly it was her parents, not he, who seemed foreign and awkward and out of place. You're lucky, he said. Your parents are great. She remembers the way he reached out across the gearshift then and took her hand.

The suicide bombing in Haifa on October 4, 2003, is the first to strike a place Susan actually knows well. The Maxim restaurant is down by the beach, adjacent to a Delek station—not a fancy place, but with good falafel and a nice view of the sea. She's been there many times. It's a popular spot, owned jointly by an Arab and a Jew.

The bomber is a twenty-nine-year-old woman, an unmarried lawyer from Jenin. She walks up to the security guard in the glass-walled foyer of the restaurant and detonates her explosive belt. Twenty-one people are killed, including four Arab workers, three children, and a baby girl. Two families lose five members each.

Susan rushes to call her relatives in Haifa when she hears the news to make sure they're all okay. She has to repeat her name three times over the static of the cell phone before her aunt understands who it is. Ah Suzi, she says. She shifts to English. Thank God, everybody's fine. Only the son of upstairs neighbors, a boy Susan and her cousins used to play with when they were young, was there at the restaurant with his wife and kids. They were thrown out of the windows by the blast, but, thank God, survived. If the parents had been there, too, as they'd planned, before the mother got a migraine and decided to stay home, they would surely have been sitting at one of the larger tables near the front. Then they'd all be dead.

After every terrorist attack, cell phones begin to ring. On the charred and bloody ground, in the bags and pockets of the dead, they ring and ring, bleeps and jingles and bits of broken song.

———

My brother Avi and I didn't get along so well when we were young, her mother said. Turn over, I'll rub your back. Susan rolled onto her stomach, pulled up her pajama top, waited for the touch of her mother's fingers, the reassuring pressure of her palms. My parents favored him and Zalman, her mother said, because they were the boys.

Avraham was an uncle Susan did not know very well. She pictured him as a stolid child with curly hair and hands clenched into fists. She didn't have much to go on, so she superimposed the image of her own brother Jonathan instead.

Her mother ran her nails along Susan's skin, sending a tingle along her spine. Go on, Susan said. Her mother sighed. He ripped up my precious paper dolls. But what did my parents do? Nothing. What did you leave them lying about for? they yelled. Now you'll learn to put your things away.

The curly-haired boy tears the doll, severing head from limbs. He throws the crumpled paper to the floor, stamps it beneath the tire-tread sandals on his feet. He stands defiant, legs apart, fists against his waist.

Her mother withdrew her hand, pulled the covers up over Susan's back. Okay Suzi, now it's late, it's time to sleep. Again that heavy sigh. That weight upon her chest. My brothers didn't have it so easy either, her mother said. My father beat them with a belt, the old-fashioned way. My mother cried, but like everything she did, it had no effect.

The boy's bare bottom is lifted over his father's knee. His pants are puddled at his ankles, his shirt pulled up to expose a sharp white ridge of spine. Thwack! The boy cries out. The father's jaw is set. In the shadows, the mother presses her fingers to her mouth.

It was their mutual friend Patrick who said, You know James really has a thing for you. James? she said. Me? That euphemism:

*a thing*—as if something that could not be named could not be completely real. It said something, she thinks now, that Patrick had to say it out loud before she knew. Were there signs she hadn't seen? She knew James from parties, various press events; he was on the business side of the Murdoch empire, a rising star. It wasn't true that she hadn't noticed his eagerness, the way he locked his eyes on hers. He was all forward motion, like a laser beam. She'd just assumed he wasn't aimed at her.

But not long after her exchange with Patrick, James called. Even though she was going out with someone else, she let him take her out for dinner and back to his Hell's Kitchen penthouse. She let him tell her stories about the Aborigines. She waited on the couch, flipping through the glossy pages of the book, while he went and ran a bath. He lit candles along the edges of the sink and dimmed the lights. She let him undress her like a child, lead her by the hand. The bathtub wasn't really big enough for two. He leaned forward in the water, wrapped his legs around her waist, and pulled her close. You are very powerful, he whispered, his lips against her ear. It was an odd thing to say—she didn't think of herself as powerful at all. He leaned back and slid slowly down until his head was underwater, his bent knees lifted high. Bubbles streamed from his mouth and nose. When he sat up, he hit his forehead on the spout, and drops of blood rolled down his face like tears.

It was only later that she took a close look at the photograph hanging on the bathroom wall. There was Nicole, naked as a virgin, lying on her back on windblown sand. Her eyes closed as if she were asleep, or dead. Her hair fanned out along the ridges of the dunes, sea grass arched across her legs. Her skin almost translucent, pale as sun-bleached bone.

Everything looks different in the snow. The city feels muffled, as if it were holding its breath. Susan's own breath condenses before her face. In the park, the paths and rocks and branches are shades of white and gray, the light luminous and blue. It is days like this that remind Susan that Manhattan is an island, a space carved out by rivers opening to the sea. Her boots squeak along the snow-packed path. Her bag, slung like a messenger's over one shoulder and across her chest, swings against her hip with every stride. There are no runners out today. Along the borders of the park, cars are completely buried beneath the banks thrown up by the plows. Funny how on days like these, she feels most at home. Usually she has the feeling that she could live anywhere in the world, even though New York is the place she's always been. When she first started working as a reporter, she'd assumed that she would be living somewhere else by now, a foreign correspondent in some exotic place. She'd be willing to move yet, she thinks, if she only had a reason—even to a place as far away as Australia, though she has only the vaguest idea of what it is like. Dusty ranches and crocodile-wrestling men and strange animals like wombats or bandicoots. And probably not too many Jews, although there did seem to be Jews in the most unlikely places, like Utah or Shanghai.

The Sheep Meadow is a billowy sea of snow. She'd walked with James along this very path, one drizzly afternoon in fall, not long after they first met. Wet leaves littered the pavement; the low-slung sky was gray with scudding clouds. He told her about his father, whom he hadn't seen in years. His father was always making money on some harebrained scheme and losing it all. He'd show up without warning, and then abandon them again. The last time he turned up, James said, he wanted me to invest in some real estate venture up in the north. This one's for real, his father said. James loaned him five thousand dollars, which, of course, he never saw again. He told Susan the story without a trace of anger or resentment in his voice. That's the way he is, he said. He can make you believe that anything he says is true.

Later, Susan made a comment about how his childhood had been tough. Tough? James said. What gave you that idea?

My father, Susan's mother said, was a terrible man.

This isn't the same story Susan has heard from other relatives. They talked about how he saved his family from the Holocaust. How as a physician, he was adored.

He was abusive, Susan's mother said, to everyone except his patients, who worshipped him as if he were a god. He lacerated us with words.

Her mother showed her photographs, flipping through the pages of her grandmother's album. Its black pages were interleaved with translucent onionskin stamped in a pattern of a spider's web. It contained photographs of Susan's grandfather from his medical school days in Germany, in the twenties, leaning like a dandy against a tree, one leg crossed before the other, a cigarette tipped between the fingers of one hand. He had wedge-shaped eyebrows, narrow eyes, a square forehead and jaw. A few of the photographs had holes cut in them: an absence like a silhouette, a body marked by empty space.

My mother did that, I think, Susan's mother said. It must have been the girlfriend he had before he married her.

So she must have loved him, Susan thinks now. In the beginning anyway. Enough to sit there with a scissors in her hand and cut the woman she had replaced out of every photograph. Enough to change the story, excise memory. Susan pictures sewing scissors, the kind with a silver swan's head wrapped around the finger holes. Or was jealousy different than love?

My father kept a row of glass jars in his surgery, Susan's mother said, filled with colored pills. They were sugar pills, although, of course, the patients didn't know that. Placebos. In those days, of course, there wasn't much you could do for people's pain. He measured the pills out carefully, placed them into folded newspaper cones. People took them and were cured.

But how, if they didn't really work? Susan asked.

Her mother's mouth twisted into a smile. Does it matter? People believed they did.

A few months after the Maxim restaurant attack, another woman blows herself up. This time it's a twenty-two-year-old mother of a three-year-old boy and baby girl. She tells the guards at the Gaza checkpoint that the metal detector went off because of an implant from surgery to repair her broken leg. As they approach, she sets off her bomb.

Susan scrolls through clips from the videotape released after the blast. The woman is wearing combat fatigues and a headscarf, a green Hamas sash draped like a beauty pageant banner across her chest. *I wanted to be a* shahid *from the time I was thirteen*, she is saying on the tape. *It was always my wish to turn my body into deadly shrapnel against the Zionists, to knock on the doors of heaven with their skulls*. The rhetoric throws Susan off. Is this a tale the woman was forced to tell, or what she actually believed? Susan studies an image of a crowd of men thronging the streets of Gaza City, their fists raised in the air. It looks almost like an outdoor concert, until you notice the green headbands covered in Arabic script, the placards with the blown-up photograph of the martyr's face. A mother carries a toddler dressed as a suicide bomber, a fake explosive belt strapped around his waist, a toy Kalashnikov clutched in his pudgy hand.

The Koran, Susan knows, says that when you become a *shahid*, you go to paradise, where seventy-two sloe-eyed virgins in long white gowns await. A popular music video on Palestine TV shows a young man joining his virgins after being shot in the back by Israeli troops. The maidens dance in flowing water. They are nearly translucent, white and pure. They wear their black hair long and loose. According to a recent poll, more than a quarter of the children in Gaza aspire to *shahada*, to die for the jihad. Even the girls. Susan wonders what the appeal of the seventy-two virgins would be for a little girl. She should write a story about that. Maybe, she thinks, if all you have to look forward to is becoming a Muslim wife, an afterlife among the virgins wouldn't seem so bad.

James believed in soul mates and telepathy, psychic emanations and powerful flows of energy that you couldn't rationally understand. He used words like *intention* and *bliss*. They sounded odd coming from such a big man, plumped and filled with promise by his Australian vowels. Susan didn't generally put much stock in New Age philosophies, but with James she found herself going along, trying to convince herself that the things he said were true. She lay back and closed her eyes as he recited aphorisms from Rumi, platitudes by Richard Bach. He kept a paperback copy of the *Tao Te Ching* in his briefcase, among the pads of graph paper and manila files. *The tao that can be told*, he read aloud, *is not the eternal Tao.* Coming from him, even the flakiest things seemed wise.

Eventually, he told her about Nicole. He'd met her on a flight from New York to Sydney; at the last minute, he switched seats and wound up sitting next to her. He didn't believe in coincidence; there was no such thing as a lucky stroke of chance. You choose what happens to you in life, he said, knowingly or not. Nicole had dazzled him by telling him things he didn't even know about himself that turned out to be true. Like the Aboriginal women who knew how to tap the power of the Dreaming Track, she had the uncanny ability to read the language of desire. Our souls go back a long, long way together, James explained. We need each other, though we can't stand being with each other half the time.

So what about me? Susan wanted to say. What about me?

But like Scheherezade, she was just a visitor to his Bedouin's tent. She knew he meant it when he said he'd soon be going back to Oz. She gathered up her clothes and left in the flat gray light of dawn.

Her mother sat on the edge of her bed. Tell me a story, Susan said. It's late, her mother said. You need to get your sleep. Susan touched the veins that ran blue as map lines along the back of her mother's hands. Strips of yellow light moved along the bedroom walls. Just a short one, Susan said. Tell about the time when you got sick.

Her mother let out a breath and pushed back her hair. When I was five years old, she said, I got an ear infection. This was before penicillin, the wonder drug. They had to operate to scrape the infection off the mastoid bone. I remember the awful smell of ether, the salty taste of the huge red sulfa pills they ground up in a spoon. They said I nearly died. I was in the hospital for seven weeks. My parents left me there alone. My father—the doctor— was busy working, and my mother was occupied with taking care of him and the boys. I don't remember them visiting me at all, although I suppose that can't be true.

Feel, her mother said, taking Susan's fingers and placing them behind her ear. The ridge of bone felt thin and flat, the skin a little puckered, although Susan couldn't make out a scar. The whole time that I was in the hospital, her mother said, no one ever combed or washed my hair. When I got out, my hair was so snarled and matted that my mother had to cut it off. My father screamed at her that I was ugly now. It was a long time before my hair grew back.

Susan leaned forward, stretched her arms out for a hug. She pressed her face against her mother's chest. She wanted to hug the little girl buried inside her mother now. She wanted to say, Don't leave.

*Layla tov*, my sweet, her mother said. Go to sleep.

———

If James hadn't gotten sick, Susan thinks now, probably she never would have seen him again. She lies back against her pillows and stares into the dark. She has finished her book but still can't fall asleep. She's sorry the story is over; she had wanted to read slowly, but found herself rushing, in spite of her intention, to the end. The blinds are open to the glow of the night sky. Her own reflection wavers, like a phantom, in the glass.

It was in 1995, a couple of years after James and Nicole had moved back to Australia, that she ran into Patrick at the airport, getting off the shuttle from D.C. Haven't you heard? he said. They stopped along the ramp by the racks of free magazines. Travelers hurried past as he shouted over the noise of the flight announcements crackling overhead. James had been diagnosed several months before. Some form of cancer; Patrick didn't know the details. The doctors had given him a 40 percent chance to live. He was in chemotherapy now. Yes, he was only thirty-three.

When she got back to the newsroom, she sat down right away and wrote James a note. How could she not have gotten back in touch? He was dying, for all she knew.

Two blocks away, the top-floor brownstone light snaps on. Susan squints, but the exhibitionist is nowhere to be seen. There is just the empty armchair, the bookshelf, the potted palm or fern. A yellow rectangle floating in the dark.

They all had lunch together a few months later, Susan and James and Nicole. He was in New York on business; Nicole was tagging along. It was the first and only time she met Nicole face-to-face. Up close, she was not as beautiful as Susan had supposed, although her eyes were a clearer blue and more intelligent than she'd wanted to believe. She had the kind of changeable face that could be made up to look elegant as a model's or scrubbed until all you noticed were the bare rims of her eyes, pink as a rabbit's. Good bones, Susan's mother would have said. Nicole was sitting at a table by herself, wearing an azure coat. James was late. She greeted Susan warmly and they clinked glasses of wine. She had the confident air, Susan thought, of a woman who had got her man. Despite the circumstances, she radiated calm.

Susan had readied herself for the worst, but James hadn't changed at all. He still had his energy and even all his hair. The latest test results were very good. The tumors were completely gone. If you had to get cancer, he joked, this was the one to get. Nicole smiled and reached out to take his hand. James kept his eyes on Susan as she did. But as usual, she misread the signs.

The light in the brownstone is still on, but the exhibitionist has not appeared. Could this be a signal of some kind? Susan reaches to turn off the bedside lamp, then changes her mind and dims it instead. She pulls off her own nightgown, leans back, slides her hand between her thighs.

It was a day or two after that lunch that she ran into James in the lobby of her building, as if by chance. That night he took her to a restaurant downtown. Over a bottle of wine, he told her the whole story of his illness—the meditation techniques he'd used to harness the healing energy of his mind; how, on what he'd imagined was his deathbed, a vision of her had suddenly appeared.

Me? Susan said.

Tears slid down his cheeks as he leaned forward across the table to take her hands. He clutched them so tightly she could feel her bones shift against his. Yes you, he said. His eyes were bright and blue. I had to see you again, he said, to let you know the way I felt. I couldn't believe that you might never know how much you meant to me. When I got your letter, I knew it was a sign.

My mother was only thirty-seven when she died, Susan's mother said. My father tried to save her. It drove him crazy that when it mattered most, he failed.

Susan has a disjointed memory of her own mother standing at a window, circling a hand over her breast. Sunlight shone through the thin cotton of her nightgown, revealing the outline of her belly and thighs. I am already older than she was when she died, her mother said. Susan's father said, Come on, Leah! You're strong as an ox! Her mother made a face, but it was obvious she felt relieved.

Susan never knows quite what to put on those doctor's forms that ask for your family history. *Cancer, check.* By the time they operated on Susan's grandmother, it was already too late. It had metastasized, spread everywhere. *Melanoma? Breast?* Back then no one knew how to read the warning signs.

Now Susan follows doctor's orders, inspects her skin for changes, taps her fingertips in concentric circles around her breasts. She, too, is already older than her grandmother was then.

Susan's father calls her on her cell phone. Her cousin Gavi, he says, was four cars behind the bus that blew up in Jerusalem today. He'd gone there for work and was heading back to Haifa when it happened, right in front of him. Too close, her father says, this time.

Susan thinks about calling Gavi but can't decide what she would say. She sends him an e-mail instead, but he does not reply. At a distance, it's hard to tell what's going on. Perhaps the language barrier is too great. Or perhaps he simply doesn't want to correspond.

She hasn't seen much of Gavi in the years since his breakdown and divorce, since Sharona got the flat and custody of their kid. He was living with his parents again, she'd heard. He'd been in and out of work and couldn't afford an apartment of his own. He'd left the "group," her father said, but now he said he had no friends.

Susan has a fantasy in which she rescues Gavi from what she

thinks of as his house arrest, restores him to his life. She flies to Israel, sets him up in a new flat, restores him to happiness with her love. He's perfectly fine! she declares.

But what does she really know?

Here is what I see, James said. They were in bed together and it was late. They met at Susan's apartment in those last days, on James's periodic business trips to New York, or in out-of-town hotels. We're at your parents' place, out on the balcony. It's a lovely summer night, very dark and still. We're looking out at the Hudson, just like that time when you took me to—what was that place called?—the place where Toscanini lived. Yes. Wave Hill. So we're looking out at the Hudson in the dark and then I turn and lift you up and we start making love. Yes, right there. Of course you could! I lift up your skirt and you wrap your legs around my waist. Like that. Very slow. Only what you can't see, because you're turned the other way, is that your parents have come home. No, just listen. They see us but they don't turn on the light. They just stand there in the dark, watching us. It's not disgusting! They're happy. They're happy for your happiness. Why can't you accept that? Well, maybe that's what you want to believe. Maybe *you're* the one who can't let go of being their little girl.

He rescued me, Susan's mother said. She turned and smiled down at Susan, her hair swinging forward around her face. She was sitting on the edge of the bed, the mattress tilting slightly beneath her weight. Susan pressed her toes against her mother's back. By the time I married your father my parents were both dead. The first time we met, he stared at me and said, You are the girl I'm going to marry. What a line! I fell for it anyway.

Susan loved this story of her parents falling in love at first sight. It was the only happy one her mother told.

Even so, her mother went on, I kept hearing my father's voice inside my head. Does he come from a good family? Is there a history of mental illness or disease? My father had crazy, old-world ideas. They're not like us, I heard him say. Those assimilated German Jews are practically goys. I hadn't met your father's parents yet—in those days one didn't just zip around the world like we do now. How did I know he was really who he claimed to be? my roommate warned. He could be making it all up.

Susan's mother sighed and looked away, out of the bedroom, toward the hallway light. But he wasn't making it up, Susan said. No, her mother said. I don't know what I would have done if I hadn't met him. He saved my life.

Still, Susan wasn't sure her parents ever really got along. You wouldn't have called them soul mates, anyway. All her life, Susan worried that one of them would leave, but, for whatever reason, neither one of them ever did.

I always knew I wouldn't die, James said. It was early in the morning and they had just finished having sex. The smell of their bodies rose from the rumpled sheets. James liked to start making love to her while she was still asleep. She would wake to his lips against her ear, his hands circling her breasts, his insistent hard-on against her thighs. Nicole won't let me touch her like that, James said resentfully. She has everything she wants. The kids, the house in Paddington, backrubs every night.

Through the window, Susan could see that the exhibitionist's blinds were drawn. His apartment seemed farther away in daylight than lit up in the dark. Susan thought of that photograph of Nicole lying prone on windblown sand. The ridgeline of her pelvic bones, the round curve of her breasts. Now Nicole had an unfaithful husband, two small kids. Susan thought she understood that withholding was a form of power, too. She wouldn't trade places with Nicole. No.

James reached for the alarm clock, then swung his feet out of bed and ran his fingers through his hair. I have to go, he said, it's late. She looked up at the spray of freckles across his shoulders, the broad line of his back. He wasn't really her type at all. Probably that was what made them so well matched. Because she didn't try to keep him, he kept coming back.

She listened to the sound of the shower turning on. She waited for James to come back to the bedroom, freshly showered, his hair still wet, dressed in his suit and tie, for him to bend and kiss her on the forehead like a child while she pretended to have fallen back to sleep. You are very loved, he'd whisper, his lips against her ear, as if love were something that could envelop you like air, as if the one who loved her might be someone other than himself. She reached to the night table for her book, but she wasn't in the mood to read. She thought about how Hebrew had no word for *fiction*. A novel was simply a *sippur*, a story. A form of narrative. The closest term for *fiction* was *bidayon*, from the word *b'daya*, a falsehood or a lie. You never could tell which parts of stories people had made up, Susan knew. People told you what they needed to believe.

# CONTRIBUTORS

GAIL GALLOWAY ADAMS is professor emeritus at West Virginia University, where she taught creative writing for over twenty years. Adams served as fiction editor for *Arts and Letters: A Literary Journal* and for the *Potomac Review*. She has been a reader/judge for several short fiction awards series. She has recently taught at Kenyon College, West Virginia Wesleyan College, and the Wild Acres Writers Workshop. She also works privately as a short story and novel editorial consultant and lives on a small family ranch in central Texas.

TONY ARDIZZONE is the author of seven books of fiction, most recently *The Arab's Ox: Stories of Morocco*, an updated edition of his previously published collection, *Larabi's Ox*. His novels include *The Whale Chaser*, *In the Garden of Papa Santuzzu*, *Heart of the Order*, and *In the Name of the Father*. His work has received the Milkweed Editions National Fiction Prize, the Chicago Foundation for Literature Award for Fiction, the Virginia Prize for Fiction, the Pushcart Prize, and two NEA fellowships, among other honors. A native of Chicago, he currently lives in Portland, Oregon.

WENDY BRENNER is the author of two books of short fiction, *Large Animals in Everyday Life*, which won the Flannery O'Connor Award, and *Phone Calls From the Dead*. Her stories and essays have appeared in *Best American Essays*, *Best American Magazine Writing*, *New Stories From the South*, *Oxford American*, *The Sun*, *Allure*, *Travel & Leisure*, *Seventeen*, *Guernica*, and elsewhere. She is the recipient of a National Endowment for the Arts Fellowship and teaches writing at the University of North Carolina, Wilmington.

DANIEL CURLEY was one of the editors of *Accent* and founded and edited its offspring *Ascent* from 1974 until his death in 1988. In addition to three novels and several collections of short stories, he wrote criticism, poetry, plays, and three books for children. A posthumous collection, *The Curandero*, was published in 1991.

LINDA LEGARDE GROVER is a member of the Bois Band of Ojibwe and a professor of American Indian studies at the University of Minnesota, Duluth. Her novels, stories and poetry have received the Wordcraft Circle of Native Writers & Storytellers Fiction Award, the Minnesota Book Award, and the Red Mountain Press Editor's Award. Her memoir, *Onigamiising: Seasons of an Ojibwe Year*, continues in essay form her research and writing on Ojibwe families and their connections to land, history, and tribal communities. LeGarde Grover lives in Duluth, Minnesota, near Lake Superior, with her husband and near her children, grandchildren, and large extended family.

DENNIS HATHAWAY grew up on an Iowa farm and now lives with his wife in Venice, California. He has been a journalist, building contractor, and, most recently, head of the Los Angeles–based Coalition to Ban Billboard Blight. He was the founding editor of *Crania*, an online literary magazine, and taught fiction writing at UCLA. His latest book is *The Taste of Flesh*, a collection of poetry.

HESTER KAPLAN is the author of the novels *The Tell* and *Kinship Theory* and of the short story collections *Unravished* and *The Edge of Marriage*. Her short fiction and nonfiction has been widely published and anthologized, including in *The Best American Short Stories* series. She is a recipient of an NEA fellowship, several state arts council grants, the McGinnis-Ritchie Award for Nonfiction, and the Salamander Fiction Prize, among others awards. She is cofounder of Goat Hill Writers and is on the faculty of Lesley University's MFA Program in Creative Writing. She lives in Rhode Island.

CHRISTOPHER (KIT) MCILROY lives in Tucson, Arizona, where he is an author-in-residence for the Tucson Unified School District. His story collection *All My Relations* won the Flannery O'Connor Award in 1992. Between 1987 and 2010 he developed and implemented writing programs for the non-profit ArtsReach, which served Native American communities in southern Arizona. Some of those experiences were distilled into the non-fiction *Here I Am a Writer*, which was published in 2011.

DEBRA MONROE is the author of two story collections, *The Source of Trouble* and *A Wild, Cold State*; two novels, *Newfangled* and *Shambles*; and two memoirs, *On the Outskirts of Normal* and *My Unsentimental Education*. She is a "fierce" writer who presents "ever-hopeful lost souls with engaging humor and sympathy" (*Kirkus Reviews*), in prose that's "rangy, thoughtful, ambitious, and widely, wildly knowledgeable" (*The Washington Post*), always "fine and funky, marbled with warmth and confusion, but not a hint of sentimentality" (*The Boston Globe*). She lives in Austin, Texas, and teaches in the MFA program at Texas State University.

ANNE PANNING, Flannery O'Connor Award winner in 2006 for *Super America*, is also the author of a previous short story collection and a novel. Her memoir *Dragonfly Notes: On Distance and Loss* is forthcoming from Stillhouse Press. She teaches creative writing at SUNY–Brockport, where she lives with her family.

BILL ROORBACH's newest book, *The Girl of the Lake*, is a collection of stories that was longlisted for the 2017 Story Prize and finalist for the Maine Literary Award in Fiction, 2017. Also from Roorbach are the novels *The Remedy for Love*, a finalist for the 2015 *Kirkus* Prize, and the best-selling *Life among Giants*, which won a Maine Literary Award in 2012. Nonfiction books include *Temple Stream, Summers with Juliet*, and *Into Woods*. "Big Bend" is from his first collection, *Big Bend*, and first appeared in the *Atlantic* and won an O. Henry Prize. Roorbach was a 2018 Civitella Ranieri Foundation Fellow in Umbria. He lives in western Maine.

MARGOT SINGER, Flannery O'Connor Award winner in 2007 for *The Pale of Settlement*, is also the author of a novel, *Underground Fugue* (2017). She is also the coeditor, with Nicole Walker, of *Bending Genre: Essays on Creative Nonfiction* (2013). She teaches creative writing at Denison University in Granville, Ohio.

SANDRA THOMPSON has published a novel, *Wild Bananas*. She was a columnist, writer, and editor at the *St. Petersburg Times*, where she directed and edited a series that won the Pulitzer Prize. She lives in Tampa, Florida, and New York.

SIAMAK VOSSOUGHI is an Iranian-American writer whose collection *Better Than War* came out in 2015. The collection was shortlisted for the William Saroyan International Prize for Writing. He has received a fiction fellowship from the Bread Loaf Writers' Conference. He lives in San Francisco.

THE FLANNERY O'CONNOR AWARD
FOR SHORT FICTION

DAVID WALTON, *Evening Out*

LEIGH ALLISON WILSON, *From the Bottom Up*

SANDRA THOMPSON, *Close-Ups*

SUSAN NEVILLE, *The Invention of Flight*

MARY HOOD, *How Far She Went*

FRANÇOIS CAMOIN, *Why Men Are Afraid of Women*

MOLLY GILES, *Rough Translations*

DANIEL CURLEY, *Living with Snakes*

PETER MEINKE, *The Piano Tuner*

TONY ARDIZZONE, *The Evening News*

SALVATORE LA PUMA, *The Boys of Bensonhurst*

MELISSA PRITCHARD, *Spirit Seizures*

PHILIP F. DEAVER, *Silent Retreats*

GAIL GALLOWAY ADAMS, *The Purchase of Order*

CAROLE L. GLICKFELD, *Useful Gifts*

ANTONYA NELSON, *The Expendables*

NANCY ZAFRIS, *The People I Know*

ROBERT ABEL, *Ghost Traps*

T. M. MCNALLY, *Low Flying Aircraft*

ALFRED DEPEW, *The Melancholy of Departure*

DENNIS HATHAWAY, *The Consequences of Desire*

RITA CIRESI, *Mother Rocket*

DIANNE NELSON OBERHANSLY, *A Brief History of Male Nudes in America*

CHRISTOPHER MCILROY, *All My Relations*

CAROL LEE LORENZO, *Nervous Dancer*

C. M. MAYO, *Sky over El Nido*

WENDY BRENNER, *Large Animals in Everyday Life*

PAUL RAWLINS, *No Lie Like Love*

HARVEY GROSSINGER, *The Quarry*

HA JIN, *Under the Red Flag*

ANDY PLATTNER, *Winter Money*

FRANK SOOS, *Unified Field Theory*

MARY CLYDE, *Survival Rates*

HESTER KAPLAN, *The Edge of Marriage*

CPSIA information can be obtained
at www.ICGtesting.com
Printed in the USA
LVHW091745110419
613835LV00003B/348/P